The Power of Three

Dear Bessie and Angus
Happy Reading ☺
Love
Lynda

L. L. Wiggins

DEDICATION

To C, J and B
My very own power of three.

CONTENTS

CHAPTER 1

IT ALL STARTED WITH A TERRIBLE NOISE

George and Eddy drank their tea in silence in the sitting room. George was tired and grumpy after yet another failed experiment had resulted in nothing more than a large scorch mark. Eddy was tired and grubby. The gardener was still missing so Eddy had spent the morning frantically repotting hundreds of grumbling and impatient seedlings before they withered and died.

The sitting room walls had been recently repainted – one orange, one purple and the rest green. George was sitting in a favourite armchair, having been delighted to find it back in its old position next to the fireplace after a brief absence. Eddy was reclining next to the armchair on a brand new red sofa, stroking an extraordinarily large black cat. The cat was sitting with its back facing pointedly at George, its singed tail still smoking slightly as it flicked back and forth.

Suddenly, a shrill ringing sound pierced the quiet morning air.

'WAH!' George screeched, leaping six inches into the air, knocking a pile of papers flying and, more importantly, a hot cup of tea all over Eddy.

'Ah!' Eddy yelped in pain.

Both quietened as the strange ringing sounded again. They looked at each other, confused and a little alarmed.

'What's that terrible noise?' George whispered finally, sitting up straight and clutching a cushion anxiously.

'I don't know.' Eddy looked around bewildered, trying to figure out where the sound was coming from whilst also endeavouring to mop up the spilled tea.

'Well make it stop, would you,' pleaded George.

'I just said I don't know what it is so how can I make it stop?' Eddy snapped. 'Listen. I think it's coming from the hall, let's investigate.'

'Do be careful, Eddy, it could be anything.' George rose slowly from the chair and timidly followed after Eddy.

'I'm sure there's nothing to be afraid of,' Eddy declared with false bravado.

Clutching each other's hands, they inched forward, easing open the sitting room door. The noise instantly became louder.

They shuffled hesitantly into the hallway, George cowering behind Eddy's taller frame.

'I think it's coming from underneath the stairs.' Eddy pointed.

'How did the noise get under the stairs?' George squeaked in alarm.

'I don't know,' Eddy replied slowly through gritted teeth, trying to remain calm while George was clearly making no such attempt. 'Look! There's a small door beneath the stairs, I think it's coming from inside.'

'Where did that door come from?' George exclaimed. 'It wasn't there before.'

'I don't know that either, George, but we have to make the noise stop.' Eddy was by now more irritated with George than troubled by the noise. 'Go on, open the door.'

'Why do I have to open it?' George asked fretfully.

Eddy sighed. 'Fine, I'll open it. Stand back.'

George didn't need to be told twice and hurriedly retreated, trembling slightly while Eddy cautiously turned the handle and slowly opened the door. The terrible noise immediately became even louder.

'What is that thing?' George gasped, peering over Eddy's shoulder.

Eddy exhaled in relief and laughed. 'That "thing" is a telephone.'

'What's a telephone doing in a cupboard underneath our stairs?'

'Never mind that now,' said Eddy, 'answer it.'

'How can I answer it?' George asked confused. 'It hasn't asked a question'.

'Oh for pity sake!' Pointing to the phone for emphasis, Eddy explained, 'Pick up that handle-like bit, put that part to your ear and speak into the other end.'

'Why do I have to answer it?' George now looked less alarmed but wasn't making any attempt to move closer.

'Because I opened the door,' replied Eddy, 'and besides, you're the oldest. It's about time you started acting your age.'

'Fine.' Grudgingly, George picked up the headset as instructed.

'Speak!' George commanded into the mouthpiece.

'Oh thank goodness, someone is there; I was just about to hang up. Is that Georgina?'

'It is,' declared George in surprise.

'Thank heavens! Georgina, it's Arthur Spratt speaking. I know it's been a long time but I need your help. It's about your niece.'

George's knees gave out beneath her and she slowly sank to the floor, cradling the phone to her ear.

George sat like that for a while. She said "oh" a lot and occasionally nodded her head up and down or side to side. Eddy felt it best not to point out that whoever George was talking to couldn't actually see her head nodding. After a few minutes of nodding and more "ohs", George stood up, pushed her shoulders back and said 'Of course we'll do it, Arthur, that's what family is for. See you soon.'

George delicately replaced the telephone receiver as if it was a most prized possession and softly closed the door, deep in thought. She no longer seemed bothered about the mysterious appearance of a telephone in a never-seen-before-cupboard underneath the stairs.

'Well?' Eddy was practically hopping from foot to foot with impatience. 'What was that about?'

George turned slowly to face her younger sister. 'That was Arthur. You know, the young lad that Sam married. It turns out we have a niece. Sam had a baby just before... um, well before she... um... well, you know. Arthur has been raising the child on his own all this time.' George struggled to control the emotion in her voice.

'And we're only finding this out now? More than ten years after Sam, um... well, you know?'

'That's not what's important right now.' George was strangely calm. 'What's important is that our niece is coming to stay with us. Arthur has to go away. He's asked us to take care of her for a few weeks, perhaps longer. Come, we need to prepare.' In this moment George was no longer the timid and scatter-brain sister Eddy was used to.

As Eddy absorbed the news, a tremor ran through the house like a tiny seismic shockwave that started beneath their feet in the hall and rippled up and out throughout the building. It was as if the house had a gigantic, involuntary shiver. It was over in an instant and the house immediately stilled.

Eddy grabbed George's hand.

'Did you feel that George?' It had started and ended so suddenly that Eddy wondered if she'd imagined it.

'I did', said George, 'I definitely did. Things are about to change, Eddy, things are definitely about to change. I can feel it.'

* * *

Over a hundred miles away, in a tiny rundown one bedroom flat above Mrs Kahn's Kebab shop in the dodgy end of London, Lucy Spratt was also feeling that things were about to change and was not happy about it.

'It isn't fair!' she cried, hands balled at her side, stamping her foot. 'Why do I have to go and stay with smelly old aunts I've never heard of? Why can't I go with you or stay here with Mrs Kahn?'

Arthur Spratt, who was hurriedly packing all he could think Lucy might need into a battered old suitcase, paused. He ran his fingers through his fine sandy hair which was already sticking up in at least three different directions, knocking his glasses off centre as he did so. He sighed and sat down heavily onto the bed, upending the neat piles of clothes he had carefully constructed only moments before.

Arthur was feeling guilty. He was also feeling excited and this made him feel even more guilty. Earlier that day he had received a phone call from Professor Potts. Arthur had been flabbergasted to hear from him, not the least because he had dropped out of the professor's Marine Biology class. How Professor Potts even remembered Arthur after more than ten years, let alone managed to track him down, was a complete mystery but one Arthur was happy to ignore for now. Because, you see, Professor Potts had offered Arthur the chance to fulfil his lifelong dream. He had asked Arthur to join his team leaving for the Arctic to study a rare deep sea fish. The very fish Arthur had been planning to write his final report on. If he helped with the research, Professor Potts said he would give Arthur the remaining credits needed to finish his degree. A university degree meant new opportunities for Arthur and Lucy. It meant Arthur could finally get a full time job in the field he loved – fish!

Arthur had been beside himself with excitement. This type of luck never happened to him. It was only after he had eagerly agreed to meet Professor Potts at the harbour to set off on the expedition in two days' time that he'd come back to reality with a bump. What an idiot. Of course he couldn't go. What would he do with Lucy? In all the years of her existence, he had never once been apart from her, not even for a single day and now here he was facing weeks away, possibly longer.

Just as Arthur was cursing the fact he hadn't any contact

details to call Professor Potts and sadly decline his offer, Mrs Kahn had come bustling into the flat. Being the landlady, she tended to come and go as she pleased, letting herself in at all times of the day or night. Mrs Kahn was a large lady, both in size and character. She wore long, brightly coloured, flowing kaftans and liked to talk with her hands, emphasising whatever she was saying with sweeping arm movements or rapid stabbing motions of her finger.

'What is the matter, Arthur? You look like you're going to your own funeral on Christmas day,' Mrs Kahn had exclaimed seeing Arthur's forlorn expression. Arthur had learned a long time ago that it was always better to tell Mrs Kahn exactly what she wanted to know otherwise she would nag relentlessly.

Once he had fully explained his situation, Mrs Kahn had looked at him sympathetically.

'Ah, I see Arthur, this is truly a dilemma. I wish I could help you but I have my hands full with the kebab shop, which is no place for a young girl to spend her summer anyway. Do you not have any family you can ask? What about your parents?'

Arthur had pulled a face, 'My parents are on yet another one of their cruises. They seem to plan their trips for the school holidays so there's always an excuse why they can't spend time with Lucy. They never approved of me marrying so young and they certainly didn't approve of me dropping out of university to look after Lucy when she was born. I think they actually blame her for the fact I haven't been able to "fulfil my potential", as they put it.'

'That is a terrible shame, Arthur, but what about Lucy's mother? Is there any family on her side you could ask?'

'Well,' Arthur had replied slowly, 'There are two sisters who I met before Lucy was born. In fact, Sam and I used to visit them regularly. But one night, Sam woke up screaming from a nightmare. She made me promise we would never see her sisters again and she wouldn't explain why. I tried to talk her around but she wouldn't budge. Then, when everything happened after Lucy's birth... well, I felt I had to keep my promise. Besides, I have no idea how to get in touch with them now.'

'Are you sure you don't have a way to contact them? A telephone number perhaps?'

'I'm quite sure. I haven't spoken to them since before Lucy's birth.'

'Why don't you go and check anyway. You never know what you might find,' Mrs Kahn had insisted. She had been wearing her determined face. Arthur had recognised that this was a face not to be argued with. So he had made a half-hearted attempt to look. He'd gone over to the only drawer in the tiny kitchenette where he shoved all his important documents. The drawer was overflowing with paper of varying colour and size. He'd picked a few pieces up and sifted through them, not really paying much attention. Suddenly he'd paused and retrieved a piece of paper he had just discarded.

'This can't be possible.' He had stared, unbelieving, at the scrap of paper that had George and Eddy's name on top with a phone number underneath in large red handwriting.

He was almost sure, but couldn't be certain, that he'd never seen that scrap of paper before.

So here he was, an hour later, trying to reason with his distraught daughter, who in turn, was trying to reason with him.

'Lucy, we've been through this already.' He reached out trying to catch her hand but she snatched it away and held it behind her back out of reach. Arthur let his hand fall back onto his lap.

'You know I wouldn't be doing this if there was any other way.' Arthur looked beseechingly at his daughter. 'This is the chance of my lifetime; the chance of *our* lifetime,' he pleaded, trying to look Lucy in the eyes but she was staring unblinking at the peeling linoleum floor. 'If this goes well we could have a better life. We could have a flat with a bedroom each. I wouldn't need to sleep on the sofa anymore, not that I mind. We may even be able to afford a small house with a little garden. Wouldn't that be nice?'

Lucy still refused to look at her father. She knew she was being childish but she just couldn't help it. Only yesterday she had finished school for the summer and now today, her father was sending her away, possibly for the whole holiday.

'But why can't I come with you?' she said, gripping Arthur's hands and falling to her knees in front of him. 'I'll be no trouble, I promise!'

'Lucy, a ship in the middle of the Arctic Ocean is no place for a young girl.'

Lucy quickly dropped her father's hands as if they were burning her. 'Fine, but I'm still not going to stay with smelly old aunts. I'm staying here with Mrs Kahn and Ali.'

Just then, Mrs Kahn flounced back up the narrow rickety stairs that connected the flat with her shop kitchen below. 'Now, now, my darlin' one, you know if it was just for a night or two, this would be no problem. But we simply don't know how long your father will be away and I am simply too busy in the shop to be able to take care of you properly.'

'I can help in the shop and Ali can look after me,' Lucy implored.

'Pah! My no-good good-for-nothing son can barely look after himself let alone a ten year old little girl,' Mrs Kahn replied, pursing her lips as if she'd just tasted something sour.

'I'm almost eleven.' Lucy stood up straight, trying to gain extra height. 'Besides, I have holiday plans with all my friends here in London,' she continued although this wasn't entirely true. In fact, none of it was true. As hard as she tried, Lucy couldn't seem to make friends. At school, they called her "Lucy Splat". Whenever she approached them, the other kids would pretend to swot a fly until one of them would clap their hands together loudly and say "Splat! Got you!". Then they would laugh and point while she pretended to ignore them.

They also accused Lucy of "creeping up" and "jumping out of nowhere". It was true that she tried to be as quiet as possible when walking up to a group of kids. She hoped if she could just join in the conversation at the right moment with the right witty comment, they might let her hang out with them and not swot her away. But she always made them jump when she eventually did speak. They never seemed to notice her until she was standing right behind them. They called her "freak" and "creep" and told her to "get lost" as they swotted her away.

Lucy told herself she didn't care anyway. She found girls her age silly. They liked pink sparkly things, painting their nails with glitter polish and other stuff like that.

Lucy hadn't got on with girls any better when she was younger either. Back then, they wanted to play make-believe about princesses and fairies and magic and other such rubbish. Lucy had no time for fantasy. Make-believe and magic was all nonsense as far as she was concerned. She was too busy for that. She had to look after the flat. She also had to look after her dad even though he thought he was the one looking after her. She made him beans on toast when he was too tired from juggling three jobs to make them anything decent to eat. Most evenings, she would gently remove his glasses and cover him with a blanket when he fell asleep on the sofa reading one of his many books about fish. Lucy worried about her dad. He worked so hard and was too thin for his clothes. And he was tired; all the time.

Lucy's only real friends were Mrs Kahn and Ali. Ali was often waiting to walk her home after school if her dad couldn't get away from work. The other kids never called her names when Ali was around. He looked so fierce with his leather jacket, sunglasses, gold jewellery and tattoos on his biceps that he made sure were covered up by the time they got home so Mrs Kahn wouldn't see. Ali talked to Lucy like she was a grown up and was always making her laugh, particularly when he was pulling faces behind Mrs Kahn's back. Lucy so much wanted to stay here with Mrs Khan and Ali. She would never admit it, but the thought of going away from the hot, stuffy, scruffy flat she had known all her life filled her with just as much dread as the thought of being separated from her dad, even if it was only for a few weeks.

Mrs Kahn put her hands on Lucy's shoulders and gently

turned her so she was looking directly into her eyes, 'I know this seems unfair right now, my darlin' one, but this really is the best thing for you at this very moment in your life, trust me.' She patted Lucy reassuringly. 'Now, where is that no-good good-for-nothing boy? He is supposed to be driving you both to the train station. ALI!' Mrs Kahn shrieked down the staircase.

Lucy sighed. This really was happening. She couldn't believe she was going to spend the summer in the middle of the country with two old women she had never met before and away from the only three people she knew and loved. Things were definitely changing and she didn't like the feel of it one bit.

CHAPTER 2

A PUFF OF GREEN SMOKE

The journey had been long and tiring. Ali, after a big telling off from Mrs Kahn, had dropped them off at Paddington Station. It had then taken Arthur and Lucy three separate trains and a long wait in between to get to their final stop. The journey's end was less of an actual train station and more like a bare platform sticking out of the ground with a faded sign that read "Little Wick Station".

The train pulled up slowly, almost warily, alongside the platform and came to a juddering stop. The conductor stuck his head out the window. He looked confused and scratched his head. In all his years working on this train line he was almost sure that he'd never seen this platform before and that no train, as far as he knew, had ever stopped here either. He double checked the route map as Arthur opened the carriage door and heaved Lucy's two big suitcases down onto the platform whilst Lucy hoisted her backpack more securely as she sluggishly followed behind.

'Crikey, Lucy, what have you got in these suitcases?' Arthur grunted as he strained to lift the second one.

'Well, I decided to add some essentials,' Lucy replied huffily. 'I've brought loads of books and Ali gave me some old CDs and DVDs. Although, even with all this, I know I'm still going to be totally bored out here in the middle of nowhere.'

The door slammed shut behind them, the conductor still scratching his head as the train began to pull away, picking up speed. He was wondering why he had never noticed this stop on his route map before. But there it was, printed in black and white, plain as the eye could see. Perhaps it was time to have a break and take that long awaited holiday he and the missus had been talking about. He must be tired. How else could he explain the platform that he was almost sure, but couldn't be certain, he had never seen before in his entire life?

As the train disappeared around the bend, Lucy heard the sound of an engine spluttering and coughing, coming towards them. She turned just in time to see an old car wobble up to the platform. As it came to a jerky stop, what looked like a small puff of green smoke escaped the exhaust. Lucy blinked and looked again but there was now no trace of smoke, green or any other colour.

The sun, which was starting to dip towards the horizon, shone brightly as one tall slim figure and one shorter, slightly rounder one stepped out of the car. Lucy blinked hard. Against the silhouette cast by the sun, the two figures formed dark outlines against the sky but each head appeared surrounded by a coloured halo – red for the taller figure and purple for the other. Lucy blinked again as the two figures stepped towards her, their halos disappearing in an instant. Must have been the sun shining in my eyes, Lucy thought.

She looked up at the two ladies who now stood staring down at her, smiles stretched wide across their faces. They weren't old at all. The taller of the two actually looked quite young. Her long black wavy hair fell down to almost her waist. Lucy was not very good at guessing the age of grown-ups. This lady was definitely older than her but was also certainly younger than her dad, who had started to wear a slightly weathered, slightly greying look about his face in the last few years.

The lady took a step towards Lucy and bent down so that they were eye to eye. Her green eyes twinkled brightly and she was dressed entirely in shades of red. Her tight burgundy trousers were fastened by a large silver buckle. She was wearing a loose red silk shirt and, over this, she wore a waistcoat of deep red velvet. Her high heeled maroon boots came up almost to her knees. She was extraordinarily pretty and Lucy thought she was quite the best thing she'd ever seen.

'Hi,' the lady said to Lucy in a breathy voice, 'I'm your Aunt Eddy but you can simply call me Eddy.' She took Lucy's hand in hers and pumped it up and down vigorously.

Lucy stared at her, open mouthed, for a moment. 'Eddy's an unusual name for a girl,' was all she could finally muster.

'My full name is Edwina but I only make people I don't like call me that. So you definitely need to call me Eddy.'

The older lady stepped forward. She was still smiling but Lucy noticed there was something a little sad about her eyes. She had blonde hair that tumbled past her shoulders but it was shot through here and there with streaks of grey, as if someone had woven silver thread through it. She wore a long flowing purple skirt and an embroidered violet jacket.

'So this is Lucy,' the older lady declared. 'What an unusual name, so untraditional.'

Lucy was stunned by this remark. She had thought a lot of things about her name over the years – "old fashioned" was one, "plain" was another but "unusual" and "untraditional" had certainly not come to mind when thinking about her boring old name. What an odd thing to say.

'My name is George,' the lady continued. 'My, don't you look the spitting image of your mother?'

Arthur cleared his throat, took George by the arm and quickly led her out of earshot. 'Like I said on the phone, Georgina,' he whispered urgently, 'there is to be no talk of Samantha while Lucy's here. I don't know why Sam was so adamant that Lucy was not to know anything about your side of the family, but the least we can do is try to respect some of her wishes, if not all of them.'

'I am sorry, Arthur, of course, I won't mention it again. It's good to see you... both of you.'

Arthur nodded and turned to pick up the luggage.

'Let me help you.' Eddy bounded up to where the suitcases were piled. She was still smiling broadly and her eyes twinkled even brighter, if that was possible.

'Be careful, that suitcase is very heavy,' Arthur warned. Without breaking her stride, Eddy swooped up the case and started to swing it back and forwards as she walked towards the car, as if it was no heavier than a feather. With a flourish, she opened the car boot and, twirling the case around her finger, neatly placed it inside. Arthur followed more slowly, grunting with the effort of lifting Lucy's remaining suitcase into the boot.

Now that the unexpected excitement of meeting her aunts was over, Lucy let out a sigh of relief and started to smile. Just in time, she remembered she was supposed to be making her father feel guilty, so she quickly rearranged her features into an unattractive scowl and shuffled listlessly towards the car. She was still hoping Arthur would change his mind and let her go with him. The thought of being away from him, even for one day, was more than she could bear.

A gentle hand on her shoulder made her pause mid-shuffle.

'It's going to be okay,' George said quietly.

Without warning, Lucy's bottom lip began to quiver and she felt tears sting the back of her eyes but she managed to mutter "whatever" as sulkily as she could whilst shrugging her aunt's hand away. Tugging the iPod Ali had loaned her out of her pocket, she plugged the headphones in and turned up the volume. Pulling the hood of her sweater over her head, she hunched down so no one could see the tear that trickled down her cheek.

A strong wind gusted around the car as Lucy climbed into the back seat besides Eddy who clapped her hands together and grinned eagerly at her. She reminded Lucy of an excited puppy. Lucy pretended to ignore her and looked out the window as George steered the car away from the platform.

They travelled down a windy dirt track heading towards a small woodland. Turning her head, Lucy glanced back to look at the platform one more time, but it was gone. It seemed to have vanished into thin air. She couldn't see any sign of the train tracks either. She scanned back and forth along the road they had just travelled but saw nothing other than long grass swaying gently in the evening breeze. That couldn't be right. Maybe there was a dip in the field that she hadn't noticed and the platform was simply hidden from view. That had to be the answer. What else could it be?

After ten minutes of bumping along the meandering country road, with the woodland on one side and open fields on the other, the car turned a sharp corner and immediately drove through a set of imposing wrought iron gates. In front of her, Lucy saw the most astonishing house. It sprawled across the yard in a haphazard fashion and was constructed in a multitude of styles. There were stone bits, brick bits, cement bits, glass bits and painted bits. Thatched roofing gave way to lead tiles that, in turn, gave way to stone turrets. Some parts of the house were single storey, some double and some triple. There were at least two battlements that Lucy could make out. One was completely round and over six stories tall; the other was square and resembled something from a medieval castle. The only thing about the house that was the same was the climbing roses. Every wall was covered – red ones, yellow ones, pink ones, white ones, purple ones and other colours Lucy couldn't even begin to identify. Never had she seen such an extraordinarily peculiar, mishmash house but it was strangely beautiful. It was also oddly inviting. Lucy stepped out of the car and stared in awe, her mouth hanging slightly open. Eddy came up behind her and said softly, 'She's quite handsome, isn't she?'

Before Lucy could reply, a low groan came from the direction of the house and it seemed to give a little shudder. Lucy blinked. She looked at Eddy who was still smiling at her as if nothing had happened.

'Did you hear that?' Lucy croaked. 'It sounded like... like...the house is going to collapse!'

'Not at all,' Eddy smiled reassuringly, 'they're growing pains. She's just settling into her foundations. She's been a very busy girl these last few hours, bless her.' Eddy smiled fondly at the house.

Lucy stared at her aunt, her mouth hanging open again. First her eyes were playing tricks on her with the train platform disappearing, and now her ears were clearly acting up as well.

'Do you mean that the house is growing?' she asked incredulously.

'Not at the moment, silly. In fact, she hasn't grown in years but she has been doing quite a bit of remodelling lately.'

Lucy looked from her aunt to the house and back again several times. Her aunt was clearly quite mad. Why was her father leaving her with these strange, crazy women?

Lucy peeped over her shoulder at her dad for reassurance and was surprised to see that he was still sitting in the car, staring blankly ahead.

Eddy retrieved Lucy's suitcases from the boot and, swinging them easily back and forth, practically skipped along. 'Come, let me show you to your room. You're going to love it. House has been very busy.'

Lucy turned once more to see if her father was following her but he still hadn't budged. Noticing this, George opened the car door and climbed back into the driver's seat next to Arthur.

Ignoring Eddy, who had by now reached the front door, Lucy walked as quietly as she could back over to the car. She positioned herself just behind the passenger door, where she hoped she wouldn't be spotted, as she listened through the open window.

'I don't want to talk about it,' her dad was saying.

'But Arthur, why don't you let us try to help her, there may be something we can do. You shouldn't have waited this long.'

'I said I don't want to discuss it,' Arthur raised his voice slightly, running his fingers through his hair. Lucy had never heard her dad speak in such a sharp tone before.

'I knew this was a bad idea. I should never have brought Lucy here. I made a promise and now I'm breaking it. I've let Sam down.' Arthur's shoulders hunched over and he dropped his face into his hands.

'Now, now, Arthur, you did the right thing,' George replied soothingly. 'We will take excellent care of Lucy. She will be quite safe with us.'

'Well of course she'll be safe with you, why wouldn't she?' Arthur asked in alarm.

'No reason, Arthur, it's just an expression,' George quickly reassured. 'Let's get you into the house. You can freshen up before dinner.'

Arthur looked over to the sprawling house and his shoulders drooped further. 'I don't think I can,' he eventually said, his voice so quiet Lucy had to strain to hear him.

George put a comforting hand on top of his. 'Arthur, we all know how much you loved Sam and how hard you tried to take care of her. She wouldn't want to see you like this. Come in, please. Come in and remember the happier times. We used to all have such fun together.'

Arthur put his hand on the door handle as if to open it, and then dropped it again. 'I can't!' he cried, visibly shaking all over. 'I can't stay. I thought I could but I can't. I must go. Please fetch Lucy for me, I need to say goodbye to her and I need to go.'

George sat quietly for moment, her hand still lightly covering his. 'Yes,' she replied eventually, 'I feel this is probably for the best.'

Exiting the car quickly, George spotted Lucy before she had a chance to duck and hide. Lucy knew she would get told off now. People were forever telling her off for being where she shouldn't be, particularly when they wanted to have private conversations that no one was supposed to hear.

George looked at her curiously and then a faint smile touched her lips, although Lucy thought her eyes looked just a little bit sadder. 'I see you have a special gift,' she murmured quietly as she beckoned Lucy to follow her a few feet away from the car. Then she raised her voice and called out, 'Here she is, Arthur.'

Lucy was both relieved and surprised her aunt didn't scold her for eavesdropping.

Arthur climbed out of the car and reached for Lucy, drawing her into his arms. 'I'm afraid I'm returning to London straight away, darling. I can't stay the night after all.'

Lucy started to cry as the wind suddenly shook leaves free from the trees. 'No! Daddy, please don't go. Take me with you.' Lucy felt like her world was collapsing and she sobbed even louder. 'I promise I'll be good. I can help you with your research and I'll stay out of the way. You won't even know that I'm there.'

Arthur stroked the pale blonde fringe away from his daughter's distraught face. Could his heart really break twice in one lifetime? He steeled himself, mustered a smile and crouched down in front of her.

'We've been through this, sweetheart. This is for the best. I'm only going so I can make a better life for us. I'll return as soon as I can, I promise.'

'Don't leave me here, Daddy!' Lucy cried hysterically. 'I don't even know these people. I'm going to hate it here. How can you do this to me? I hate you!'

Arthur knew Lucy didn't mean it but her words hurt nevertheless.

'I love you,' he whispered in reply. Before he could change his mind, he pried Lucy's arms from around his waist and handed her over to Eddy who had appeared beside them. Eddy held onto Lucy as she sobbed into her side, refusing to look at her father one more time. Heaving a sigh, Arthur rested his hand on top of Lucy's head for a moment.

'Never forget how much I love you,' he murmured.

'I've called the train for you', George said as she climbed back into the driver's seat, 'it should be waiting when we get back to the platform.'

Arthur appeared not to have heard but Lucy looked at

George curiously through her tears. Surely you can't call a train? You can call a taxi but not a train. How odd. She must have misheard.

CHAPTER 3

THE HOUSE THAT MOVED

Lucy watched forlornly as the car drove out of sight. She waited for her father to turn around and wave but he didn't. He stared straight ahead, his shoulders shaking slightly. Just before the car turned the corner and drove out of sight, Lucy was almost sure, but couldn't be certain, that a small puff of green smoke escaped from the exhaust.

'Come on,' Eddy beckoned excitedly to Lucy, 'let me show you to your room now.'

Lucy reluctantly followed Eddy through the giant front door. The moment her foot crossed the threshold, the house shuddered once more but this time it was accompanied by a vibration that travelled along the ground and through the air, like an earthquake and an electric pulse at the same time, picking up speed and force as it went. Lucy felt the floor move beneath them an instant before they were knocked off their feet. The vibrations quickly moved on and Lucy turned her head just in time to see the wrought iron gates shake violently in their frame before they stilled abruptly as the tremor swiftly passed by.

Eddy scrambled to her feet and helped Lucy up.

'What was that?' Lucy's face was pale with fright.

'Oh, um, we have the occasional earth tremor in these parts, nothing to be alarmed at.' Eddy avoided eye contact as she picked up the suitcases that had scattered across the floor. 'Come on, follow me.'

As Lucy fell into step behind her aunt, she couldn't quite shake the feeling that Eddy had just lied to her.

They climbed up a majestic flight of stairs and came to a wide landing.

'Wow, what's that on the wall?' Lucy motioned to a large mural that went from the floor to the ceiling.

'That's our family tree.' Pointing to the painted picture, Eddy continued, 'House even added you on this morning. Look! There you are at the bottom.'

'Who's House? Is it someone else who lives here, like a butler or a housekeeper?'

'Look, there's me, George and your mum just above you. And that's our mother Jo and her sister, our aunt Harry.' Eddy continued explaining as she gestured at the mural, seemingly not having heard Lucy's questions.

Feeling certain she was bound to meet House soon, Lucy studied the picture and was instantly enthralled. 'How come there are only women on the tree?' she eventually asked.

Eddy stood perplexed for a moment, 'You know, I've never given that much thought. As far as I know, there's never been mention of any men in our family. Besides, all our names can be shortened to a boy's name anyway, except yours of course.'

Lucy studied the tree more closely and noted that, indeed, with the exception of her own, every woman in her family tree could shorten their name to that of a boy's. She noticed something else as well. 'Why are there names of places on the tree?'

'I know the answer to this one. That shows where someone has moved to. House can only keep track of people who stay here. Once they leave, we lose contact.'

'So why is there a question mark underneath Harriet's name?'

'That's because we don't know what happened to Aunt Harry. She just disappeared one day. She never told us where she was going, she just packed a bag and left without so much as a goodbye. We've not heard from her since.' The smile that Eddy had been wearing ever since Lucy had met her finally withered and slid down.

'But why –'.

'There'll be time for questions later,' Eddy interrupted gruffly. 'Let's get you to your bedroom. It's getting late.'

Eddy quickly moved on leaving Lucy with no option but to follow as she was led on a winding route through the house.

'This is the most direct route to your bedroom but there are many other ways you can get there,' Eddy explained as she practically skipped ahead, having clearly regained her earlier excitement. Lucy was already confused. They had climbed up stairs and down stairs, walked along dark passages, burst into big bright rooms overstuffed with armchairs and tables, and squeezed through a tiny room where Lucy could practically touch the walls on either side. They walked around bendy corners and opened and closed more doors than Lucy could keep count of. Finally, they ascended another grand staircase with a wraparound landing at the top. On the landing were four doors, one on each side.

'This is your room,' Eddy said, indicating the door closest to them. 'On the left is George's bedroom. Mine's that one on the right.'

Lucy looked around, each door was completely different. Her door was white with painted red roses weaving all over and a big round brass door knob. The door was almost entirely oval. George's was a tall grand double door affair. The wood gleamed darkly and had twin gold handles. A large ornately carved grandfather clock stood next to George's door like a sentry. Eddy's entrance was a stable door made out of battered weather-worn wood with a large traditional bolt holding the bottom half closed.

'Well, it's the family joke,' Eddy said noticing Lucy staring, 'I was born in a barn after all.' Eddy threw her head back and gave a barking laugh so sudden and loud, Lucy jumped an inch off the floor in fright.

Composing herself, she glanced over her shoulder at the door on the opposite side of the landing. It was a beautiful pale grey door with frosted glass panes running the length of it and an elegant bone door handle. There seemed to be a faint shimmer that radiated from the door. Lucy stood transfixed.

'That was your mother's room,' Eddy said softly. Lucy's breath caught. This was the closest she'd ever got to something of her mother's. Her father refused to talk about her, no matter how many times she asked. He told her that all she needed to know was that her mother had loved her very much. Only once had Lucy asked if he could take her to see where her mother was buried, but he had brusquely replied that it was impossible and had walked away, visibly shaking. Lucy hated seeing her father so upset and hadn't brought it up again.

But she was desperate to know more about her mother. Maybe this holiday with her aunts wasn't the end of the world after all. Perhaps she would be able to find out more while she's here, staying with her mother's family, in the same house where her mother grew up. Perhaps she might finally find out what happened to her mother.

'Right,' Eddy said clapping her hands in delight, bringing Lucy's focus back onto her oval bedroom door, 'it's time for the big reveal. House has been frantically redecorating ever since we got your dad's phone call.'

'That's very kind of House. Will I meet him or her soon?' Lucy inquired.

Turning the brass door knob, Eddy continued without answering, 'I do hope you like pink.'

'Ugh, I hate pink!' Lucy said without thinking.

As these words left her mouth, Lucy caught a glimpse of the bedroom beyond – there was pink everywhere; the floors, the walls, the bed, even the ceiling. No sooner had she spoken than the bedroom door slammed shut with such force that Eddy yelped, cradling the hand that had been resting on the door knob.

'Was that really necessary, House?' she said to no one in particular, shaking her hand gingerly to see if there was any permanent damage. Before Lucy could query once more as to who House was, she heard the sound of crashing and banging coming from the other side of the door. It sounded like heavy objects were literally being thrown across the room. Then, as suddenly as the crashing and banging had started, it stopped.

'Is someone in the room?' Lucy asked with alarm. 'Is House in there?'

Once again Eddy appeared to avoid the question.

'Let's try it again, shall we?' Eddy opened the door once more, this time much more cautiously. With a sigh of relief, she stepped through the entrance and into the room beyond. Lucy followed hesitantly behind her. Whoever or whatever had made the terrible banging and crashing noises must certainly still be inside.

Strangely, Eddy didn't seem to be the slightest bit concerned. She walked over to stand next to a large comfy looking bed in the middle of what, Lucy realised as she gazed around, was a perfectly round room. Lucy turned slowly, scanning the room. Everything in it was rounded. The curved cupboard fitted snugly against the wall and followed the bend of the room. A large stuffed armchair had a curved back so that it could be pushed up tight against the wall. A curved bookshelf stood alongside the armchair, bulging with its heavy load. The only thing that was square was the big four poster bed in the centre of the room.

Lucy looked around in awe. It was by far the prettiest room she'd ever seen. Everything was either white or shades of green. She must have just imagined that the room had been pink before. It was probably her mind playing tricks on her again. It had been a long day after all. All she needed was a good night's sleep and she'd be seeing things clearly again.

'What do you think?' Eddy looked at her eagerly. 'Do you like it?'

'I don't like green either,' Lucy replied flatly.

The smile faded from Eddy's face. Lucy didn't know why she had said that. It was an ugly thing to say and she really did like green. In fact, it was her favourite colour. She was just feeling so sad her dad had left and gone off without her, sad and hurt. No matter how nice her aunts seemed she couldn't help feeling just a little bit alarmed in this strange house filled with unexplained sounds and tremors.

Eddy studied Lucy's face intently, skimming back and forth across Lucy's features until she appeared to see something she liked and smiled brightly again.

'What a shame, I had a feeling you would really like green. Oh well, I hope you can put up with it while you stay with us. Oh, I almost forgot, there's one more thing.' Eddy walked towards the wall opposite the cupboard and, to Lucy's great astonishment, stepped right through it! Lucy's mouth slumped open in shock. She blinked and rubbed her eyes but her aunt was nowhere to be seen.

'Eddy, where are you?' she called out in a panic.

'I'm here silly.' Eddy's head appeared through the wall. Lucy gasped.

'Close your mouth and come and see your bathroom,' Eddy coaxed but Lucy stood stock still, her feet rooted to the floor.

Finally, realising Lucy wasn't following her, Eddy walked back into the room.

'It's an optical illusion.' Eddy pointed to the wall. 'There's actually a small opening and curved passage on the other side, but the wall and floor are painted to make it look like it's solid. Come, take my hand, I'll show you.'

Eddy guided Lucy forward and, sure enough, even though it looked like they were about to crash straight into a solid wall, they did in fact enter a small gap that curved to the left and then opened into a lovely light and airy bathroom that was also completely round, including the bath in the middle of the floor.

Lucy gazed in astonishment. This was by far the craziest house she had ever been in and her aunts were by far the craziest women she'd ever met. No wonder they lived out here in the middle of nowhere, all alone.

'George and I are completely happy out here in our beautiful home,' Eddy stated. Lucy's cheeks flushed brightly. It was almost as if Eddy had read her thoughts.

'Now why don't you wash up for supper and then come down to the kitchen. George will already be working her magic on the meal. Here, I've drawn you a little map so you can find your way,' Eddy handed Lucy a piece of paper with lots of arrows and squiggly lines on it. 'It might take a little time, but soon you'll know your way around this house like the back of your hand. Supper will be ready in half an hour. I'll leave you to unpack.' With that, Eddy swooped out of the room leaving Lucy staring after her in mute wonder. This had by far been the strangest day of her life. Surely nothing could get stranger than this.

CHAPTER 4

SOMETHING'S GOING ON

Lucy unpacked and hung her clothes up inside the little round cupboard. Although the cupboard appeared small on the outside, every time Lucy needed to hang up one more skirt, or put away one more pair of shorts, there always seemed to be plenty of room. She decided not to unpack her books. She had only really dragged the stupid old suitcase all the way out here to make her father feel bad. She wasn't even sure which books she had packed but couldn't imagine them being any good. They had been from her father's bookshelf and most of those books were old, dusty, falling apart and filled with boring stuff about fish. Besides, the bookcase in her new room was already bulging with books that looked much more interesting.

As Lucy left her bedroom to head down to supper, map in hand, she noticed the grandfather clock. It no longer stood next to George's door. Now it was positioned alongside her mother's. Perhaps one of her aunts had moved it, or maybe she simply wasn't remembering correctly. The time on the clock was also all wrong; both hands were on the nine. It almost looked like it was pointing at her mother's bedroom door.

Lucy had a sudden thought. Moving as quietly as she could, she tiptoed across the landing, turned the handle slowly and gave a little push. Nothing happened. She pushed a little harder. Still nothing. The door was locked tight. Before she could think of what to try next, Lucy heard George calling her for supper. The door would have to wait for now but Lucy was determined to try again. She knew nothing about her mother. All she had was one faded photograph of her mother holding Lucy moments after her birth, and nothing else. She needed more and maybe what she needed was inside her mother's old bedroom.

Lucy made her way to the kitchen, making sure to follow Eddy's instructions carefully but, even then, she was almost certain she went in and out of the same room at least three times, although each time by a different door. Eventually she opened a large heavy door and found herself in a cavernous room. A fire was roaring in the hearth, even though it was July and a lovely summer's evening outside. The kitchen floor was made of large irregular flagstones. A huge heavy square table stood in the middle of the room and was loaded with books, papers and odd shaped containers. One end of the table had been cleared to make room for three place settings. The table was surrounded by a number of chairs but not one matched.

George bustled over to her. 'Now, Lucy dear, what would you like to eat?'

Lucy's stomach rumbled loudly as she realised how hungry she was, the dry cheese sandwiches her dad had packed for the train journey had been finished hours ago. She was starving although, by the looks of things, supper was a long way off because there weren't any signs of cooking.

'What's your all time most favourite meal?' George continued putting her hands on Lucy's shoulders and crouching down to look in her eyes. After a few seconds she said, 'Wait! Don't tell me, I think I know just the thing'.

George turned back to the stove and picked up a big iron pot. She placed something in the pot but Lucy couldn't see what as George's body was in the way and her bellowing purple dress blocked Lucy's view. George started to mix the pot with a large wooden spoon and steam began to rise accompanied by the most amazing aroma. I know that smell, Lucy thought, just as George turned and carried the pot over to the table.

'Here you go. Sausages and mash with onion gravy.' George announced, presenting the pot with a flourish. Lucy looked at the pot, then at George, and then back at the pot in disbelief. The pot was filled with the fluffiest mashed potatoes and the biggest over-stuffed, juiciest, golden brown sausages Lucy had ever seen. Sausages and mash with onion gravy was her all time most favourite meal. What a coincidence.

'I almost forgot the gravy,' George said pulling out a small gravy pot from the folds of her skirt. George piled Lucy's plate high with generous amounts of all three.

'Don't forget to eat your greens,' she called over her shoulder as she returned the pot to the stove. Lucy looked at George and then back at her plate. There nestled next to her sausage and mash was a small pile of large green peas. When had those been put there? Lucy had watched George dish up and there had certainly been no peas in the pot. She shook her head. She really did need to get some sleep. It had been the weirdest day. Her mind was clearly playing tricks on her. Everything will appear normal after a good night's sleep, she told herself.

Eddy and George took their seats at the table as Lucy shovelled a large helping of food onto her fork.

'Now before we start eating,' George took Eddy's hand in hers, 'we have a tradition here to give thanks.'

Lucy guiltily lowered her fork that had been a millimetre from her mouth.

'I don't know any prayers.'

'You don't need to know any,' Eddy explained, 'you just need to say what comes from the heart. At the end of each day, Mother Nature has normally given us many gifts, whether it's the breeze that cools us down on a hot summer's day, the rain that falls on the flowers, or even the horse poo that becomes manure for my plants.'

'Ew!' Lucy exclaimed, although she put her fork down and reached to join hands with her aunts. As soon as their fingers touched, a shock coursed through her body as if she had been hit by bolt of lightning. Yelping in pain, Lucy fell back, knocking over her chair.

Rubbing her own hand, George scooped down to help her up, 'Goodness, what a lot of static there is in the air tonight.'

George's hair was sticking up wildly as if she'd put her finger in an electric socket and she tried in vain to smooth it down.

'Yes,' Eddy quickly agreed, looking shaken, 'plenty of static.'

George picked Lucy up off the floor while Eddy righted her chair. Lucy felt dazed. 'Did you feel the shock too?'

'Let's eat before the food gets cold,' George said without answering, as she sat back down and fidgeted with her cutlery.

'Hmm, this is delicious, George. You've out done yourself.' Eddy said with a grin, bits of sausage sticking out of her mouth.

Lucy slowly sat back down and looked at her aunts. They didn't seem at all bothered by the shock they had just experienced. Perhaps it was just static. Maybe Lucy had felt a worse jolt than her aunts, which is why they weren't making a fuss about it. Lucy reached for her fork again. Taking a bite, she momentarily forgot all about the static as the food melted in her mouth. Despite trying to eat like a lady, just like Mrs Kahn was always commanding, Lucy couldn't help herself. She quickly gobbled up every last mouthful, running her finger over the plate to catch the last bits of gravy. It was the most delicious sausage and mash she had ever tasted.

Lucy was just contemplating whether Mrs Kahn would ever forgive her if she actually picked up her plate and licked the last bit of gravy off, when a very large, very black cat landed with a thump right in the middle of the table, knocking over her empty glass of milk.

Quickly putting her hand out to catch the glass before it hit the ground, George looked at the cat with affection. 'Ah, Jack, I had a feeling we'd see you tonight. Curious about our new arrival are you?'

The cat hissed softly and paced back and forth across the table top, upsetting bowls and precariously stacked piles of books and papers as he went. Every so often, it paused to fix Lucy with a long stare. It had the biggest and brightest green eyes Lucy had ever seen. The cat was so big it was almost the size of a dog, and a big dog at that.

Eddy watched the cat prowling up and down with a twinkle in her eye.

'Lovely to see you again so soon, Jack.' She paused and tried to look apologetic. 'Listen, sorry about that last batch, I must have got the quantities a bit wrong.'

The cat hissed sharply, reached out a paw, nails flared, and swiped at Eddy.

'Now, now, Jack, was that really called for?' Eddy laughed as she easily dodged out of reach. 'We're only trying to help. We'll get it right one of these days.'

The cat hissed again but then sat down to lick his paws and clean his ears.

'Take no notice of Jack,' George said to Lucy. 'He's perpetually in a bad mood but that's not really his fault.'

George went over to the cat and stroked him fondly, although Jack appeared not to notice and continued with his ablutions. 'I've got something new I want to try which might just be the cure.'

The cat hissed once more, this time more quietly, but stayed still while George patted him.

'Is something wrong with the cat?' Lucy asked, unable to contain her curiosity.

George looked up absentmindedly as she continued to stroke Jack, who had finally begun to purr.

'Oh, um, Jack is suffering from a rather special and, um, unique ailment that we're trying to find a cure for. We just need to find the right ingredients and the right combination to fix him. We've had some positive results recently but none of them seem to last very long.'

'And every now and again there are some unanticipated side-effects that Jack doesn't appreciate,' Eddy interjected with a laugh.

The cat hissed quite viciously this time, as if in agreement.

George wiped her hands on her apron and turned to Lucy. 'Right, it's probably time for you to go to bed. It's been a long day and I imagine you're very tired.'

Lucy looked at the big clock above the hearth. Although she was feeling quite tired, it was only eight o'clock and normally her dad let her stay up a little later, especially during school holidays. Sometimes, if he got really engrossed in his dusty old fish books and research, he'd forget to come and tuck her in and she'd be able to read her own story books until late into the night.

'It's a bit too early for my bed time. Can I watch TV for a bit first? What channels do you have?' This thought perked Lucy right up. At the flat they only had four TV channels, if you counted the one that was permanently snowing. At least if her aunts had plenty of channels, she could spend the holiday watching TV and the time away from her dad might go a bit quicker.

'What's a TV?' George replied at the same time Eddy said 'We don't have a TV.'

'What,' Lucy cried in horror, 'no TV? Not even a small one?'

The aunts both shook their heads ruefully.

'Does that mean you don't have a DVD either?'

'I'm afraid we don't have a deeviwee, or whatever it was you said,' George replied.

'What about a computer?' Lucy asked, now feeling quite desperate.

'Nope,' Eddy shrugged apologetically.

'What?' Lucy yelped, 'You don't have a TV, you don't have a DVD and you don't even have a computer?'

'I'm afraid not my dear,' George replied gently.

'We've just never needed them you see,' Eddy explained, 'There's always so much going on here.'

Lucy looked around the large kitchen. It was so quiet she could almost hear the hair on her head growing. How could there be so much going on that they didn't want a TV or computer?

All of a sudden, it was too much for her. Lucy completely and utterly lost it.

'This is unbelievable,' she screeched. 'This has got to be the most boring house in the entire world. Nothing is going on here, absolutely nothing. What am I supposed to do all day? No TV? No computer? I'll have absolutely nothing to do. I'll be bored senseless. I'll hate every minute I'm here. I already hate every minute!' Lucy's anger hiccupped into a sob as she finished.

Rather than be cross at Lucy's rude outburst, Eddy just laughed, 'Oh you've got no idea how exciting it is to live here, you just wait and see.'

At her aunts' unruffled reaction to her outburst, Lucy felt her anger subside like a deflating balloon.

'Well, can you show me where I can plug in my iPod? It's run out of battery.' Lucy asked with a resigned sigh. At least she would have her music to distract her during the long boring days and nights ahead.

'Um,' Eddy now looked uncomfortably down at her feet. 'I guess you haven't noticed but we don't have electricity here either.'

There was nothing else to do. Lucy screamed. Never in her short life had she been more frustrated or more at loss for words. Then suddenly she realised something. Tears were starting to prick her eyes as she said in a small voice, 'If there's no electricity and no computer, how will my Dad get hold of me? How will I know when he is coming to get me?' A single silent tear trickled down her cheek. George reached out to fold Lucy into her arms. Lucy resisted for just a fraction before resting her head against George's ample comforting bosom. Lucy didn't want to be comforted but she couldn't help but feel safe and reassured in her aunt's embrace.

'We always hear the messages from the people who most need to reach us,' she told Lucy. 'If your Dad needs to get in touch, there will be a way, you'll see. Your dad telephoned us yesterday and no one's ever done that before.'

'But… but…' Lucy didn't know what to say. There was so much she could say but none of what she had seen or heard today made any sense. She was terribly confused. She suddenly felt weary to the bone – too tired and too confused to do or say anything more.

'Wait, I have an idea,' Eddy lifted Lucy's chin up with her finger. 'How badly do you want to speak to your dad right now?'

'Very, very badly,' Lucy let the sobs take over her body as she soaked George's dress with her tears.

'Well then that should work. Follow me.' Eddy led the way from the kitchen until all three of them arrived back in the hall, Lucy still enfolded in George's arms. While Lucy and George looked on, Eddy walked over to the cupboard beneath the stairs.

'Brilliant, it's still here.' Stepping back, Eddy revealed an old fashioned telephone sitting inside the cupboard.

Lucy stepped closer and peered in. She had seen telephones like this before but only ever in old movies. They were the ones where you stick your finger into a hole above each number and then rotate it in a circle to dial.

'Go on, give it a go,' Eddy urged.

'But I don't remember dad's phone number. It's stored in my iPod and that's out of battery.' Lucy stood defeated next to the cupboard.

'Just give it a go. You'd be surprised what you can remember when you really need to.' Eddy looked so determined that Lucy decided not to argue further. She sighed. Picking up the heavy receiver with one hand, she placed her finger in each number she thought might be the right one and rotated the dial slowly.

'This will be no good,' she muttered under her breath just

as she heard the phone make a connection and the sound of ringing come down the line. Lucy hastily placed the receiver to her ear.

'Hello?'

'Dad? Is that you?'

'Lucy?'

'Yes, yes, it's me Dad.'

'I can't believe it, I thought my phone was out of battery. I'm so happy to hear your voice.'

'I'm happy to hear your voice too, Dad.'

'Is everything okay, Lucy?'

'Yes, it's fine. I just miss you.' Lucy struggled to keep the emotion out of her voice.

'I miss you too, Lucy, so very much. I hated the way I left. I'm so very sorry but I will be back as soon as I can, I promise.'

Lucy had been cradling the phone to her ear while her dad talked. A silent tear slipped down her cheek but, strangely, she didn't feel sad. She actually felt happy. Happy to be talking to her father and happy to know that he was as sorry to leave her as she was to leave him.

'Lucy, the train is about to go into a tunnel so I might lose the signal. I love you and I will call you as often as I can.'

'I love you too, Dad.'

Lucy slowly replaced the receiver and then looked at her aunts who had been trying to stand at a discrete distance, although Eddy was doing a poor job of pretending she hadn't been listening.

Lucy smiled at both of them and they smiled back. No words were needed. They all knew the phone call had been the best thing for Lucy at that moment.

Lucy let her aunts guide her back to her new bedroom, only barely noticing that the return trip from the hall appeared to be shorter and take a different route to the one she had taken with Eddy earlier that afternoon. But she didn't think anything more of it.

She let her aunts help her get ready for bed and, no sooner

was her head resting on the large soft pillow, than she fell into a deep and peaceful sleep. She didn't see each of her aunts blow her a kiss and then blow another kiss around the room. She also didn't see the room briefly shimmer with a pale green light before returning to the night glow.

Nor did she hear Eddy whispering to George as they quietly closed the door behind them.

'Something is going on, George. I know you can feel it too. Ever since Lucy arrived, I feel different. My body feels all tingly and there are thoughts in my head I've never had before. It's like, all of a sudden, I know more than I ever did. I know things I didn't know I knew, if you know what I mean?' she looked at George expectantly but George didn't reply. 'And that electric shock we experienced at dinner? What was that about? Then there's House!' Eddy continued, 'I've never seen her behave this way before, she's no longer simply redecorating the rooms, she's moving them. I went into the sitting room earlier only to find myself in the toilet!'

George was silent.

'You feel it too, don't you George?'

George let out a long slow sigh. 'I do,' she finally admitted, 'and it's not the first time either.'

CHAPTER 5

THE WITCHFINDER GENERAL

A hundred miles away on a rundown road in the rundown part of town, a large sedan pulled up outside a shop with grubby windows, peeling paint and a fizzing neon sign that should read "Al's Dry Cleaners & Repairs" but some of the letters were missing so the sign currently said "A Dry leaner pair".

Sir Walter Witherbottom climbed out from the back seat and looked up and down the street to check no one was watching. He was dressed smartly in a dinner jacket that was buttoned a little too snuggly over his round little belly. Although a good looking man in his youth, years of over indulgence had taken an unfortunate toll on Sir Walter's appearance. His skin hung from certain parts of his body in gentle folds, most noticeably under his chin. Despite this, Sir Walter still thought himself to be quite the catch even though he had yet to find a woman who wanted the permanent honour of being Lady Walter Witherbottom. Nevertheless, he made sure his clothes were always made to measure and perfectly tailored. This would have been just fine if Sir Walter did not keep insisting his tailor make his suits two sizes smaller than what he actually was. As a result, his trousers stretched precariously across his rear end, and he was forever losing jacket buttons as they pinged away into the distance when he tried to fasten them after a particularly large meal, of which he had rather a lot, what with his important position in government and needing to entertain a constant stream of visiting foreign dignitaries.

Sir Walter entered the shop and the electronic doorbell chimed to the tune of 'The Wheels on the Bus.'

Behind the counter sat Phyllis Farley, a somewhat large lady of indeterminable age. Phyllis was munching oily French fries while watching her favourite soap opera on TV. Grease dripped down her chin which she wiped away with one hand while the other kept up a constant supply of fries to her mouth. Her eyes never left the TV. 'Don't let him speak to you like that, Margery,' she commanded the TV, totally ignoring the sound of 'The Wheels of the Bus' which had now started the chorus for a second time.

'Uh-hem.' Sir Walter cleared his throat to get Phyllis's attention.

'Be with you in a second, luvvie,' Phyllis replied without moving her eyes from the TV.

'I think you'll find I've come to pick up the red sequined dress,' Sir Walter's voice was clipped with suppressed irritation.

Phyllis froze, a French fry hanging loosely from her lips. Then she launched into action. She threw her fries down onto the greasy paper as if they were poison. Looking quickly for something to clean her hands on and finding nothing, she hurriedly wiped them on her dress and cleared her throat.

'Are you sure it's the red sequined dress you're after, and not the blue one?' she asked, having finally managed to swallow her mouthful of fries.

'I am most sure.'

'And when was the red sequined dress due to be picked up?'

'Today at precisely 1600 hours.'

'Are there any other garments with the dress?'

'Yes, a red feather boa,' Sir Walter said slowly through gritted teeth.

Without saying another word, Phyllis reached behind her and pressed a button. Instantly metal shutters clanged down and closed fast over the windows and door. Outside the neon sign flickered and went out.

'So sorry, sir, I didn't realise it was you. Right this way please.' Phyllis half bowed as she turned to lead Sir Walter towards the back of the shop.

'That was the most ridiculous password. Can someone please come up with something a bit more fitting of my status in the future,' Sir Walter grumbled. 'Red sequined dress indeed.'

'Yes, sir. Of course, sir. Sorry, sir.' Phyllis half bowed again as she reached a garment rail at the rear of the shop. She untwisted the end post to reveal a small scanner. 'Your badge, please sir.'

Sir Walter reached into his pocket and retrieved his wallet which was secured to his belt by a small chain. Opening the wallet, he pulled out a pink and green striped card with a microchip in the middle. The front of the card read 'Pooches & Poodles Grooming Salon' in big letters and 'Loyalty Card' in smaller letters underneath.

Phyllis took the card and swiped it across the scanner before returning it to Sir Walter. 'What a clever card,' Phyllis said admiringly, 'no one would guess what it actually was. I bet you get lots of people asking you where your dog grooming salon is.'

Sir Walter harrumphed in reply.

Phyllis tugged at a chain around her neck but nothing happened. She tugged again even harder. Still nothing. She gave it one final almighty tug and with a sticky squelching sound, the necklace rocketed out from between her generous cleavage. Catching the end in one hand, she revealed a locket.

'Some of my Bertie's ashes are kept inside in a tiny velvet pouch,' she tapped the side of her locket which appeared to have flakes of her sweaty skin sticking to it. Sir Walter wrinkled his nose in disgust.

'Just one moment while I get my microchip.' Phyllis opened the locket and a small cloud of dust emerged. 'Oh goodness me, it looks like my Bertie might have escaped.'

Sir Walter didn't know who Bertie was and didn't care.

'Can we get on with it, please?'

Phyllis blew on the locket and the dust cleared to reveal a small microchip secured to one side. She lifted it up to the scanner which beeped and a light flashed from red to green.

'That should do it.' She pushed back the clothes on the rail to reveal an elevator door that slid silently open.

Without so much as a "goodbye" or a "thank you", Sir Walter stepped through the rail and into the elevator with as much aloofness as he could manage, which was a bit tricky as his coat pocket got snagged on a loose wire hanger and he spent a few seconds wrestling with it before he was free.

No sooner had the elevator doors slid soundlessly closed than he was hurtling down into the bowels of the earth, ten stories below.

When the doors silently opened seconds later, Sir Walter stepped out into a room humming with activity. The room was lined with large screens and a small crowd of people were milling about, tapping on keyboards, adjusting equipment, checking read outs and generally looking very busy. This pleased Sir Walter. This operation cost a lot of money after all. A lot of tax payer money if the truth be told, but the tax payer doesn't need to know all the truth when it comes to government spending, do they?

Sir Walter spotted the man he had come to see. 'Right, Smith, what's this all about? Why have you summoned me here so urgently? I was just enjoying a rather delightful after dinner brandy with the Hungarian ambassador and Tiffany, the lead singer from Girls Gone Mad.'

Sir Walter did like to name drop and an evening with Tiffany, one of the hottest rising stars in the country, was certainly a name worth dropping. The fact that she had been sitting with friends at a separate table to that of himself and the

Hungarian ambassador was beside the point. Sir Walter thought that Tiffany might be a very worthy candidate for the role of Lady Walter Witherbottom and he was annoyed he was called away before he had the chance to use his charm and influence to get to meet her.

A young man with glasses sitting precariously on the end of his nose came scuttling up to Sir Walter after his summons.

'Witchfinder General, sir,' he attempted to salute but then seemed to change his mind half way and awkwardly extended his arm to shake Sir Walter's hand instead, which Sir Walter ignored. 'Thank you for coming at such short notice, and the name is Smittle, sir, not Smith. Steven Smittle.'

'Yes, that's what I said, Smit. Can we get on with it please? I don't have all night. I'm sure Tiffany will be wondering where I've got to.'

In reality, Tiffany had not even noticed Sir Walter had been dining in the same restaurant, let alone that he'd left.

'Yes sir. We knew you would want to see this immediately, which is why I issued the "Code Red".'

Smittle drew Sir Walter further into the room until they were both standing in front of the biggest screen. There were a lot of flashing red lights on the monitor and what looked like an aerial view of a map with increasingly larger concentric circles fanning out from a central black point.

Smittle let Sir Walter study the display for a bit, barely able to contain his excitement. Sir Walter studied the screen for a long time, trying to work out the significance of what it all meant. But the truth be told, he wasn't a man for technology. He preferred the old school techniques for spying and espionage. He also preferred the old school technique of people actually telling him what he needed to know rather than having to figure it out for himself.

Eventually Smittle couldn't contain his excitement any longer. 'Do you see what this means, sir?'

'Well of course I see it, Smythe, but why don't you prove to me why I pay you a salary and tell me what you think it means.'

'It's Smittle,' Smittle muttered under his breath so that Sir

Walter couldn't hear. Then, in a louder voice, he started to explain.

'It all started a few hours ago. The energy readings around the country have been going off the charts and we have been able to determine that they haven't been caused by a natural phenomenon.'

Sir Walter's expression quickly changed from highly annoyed to highly interested. 'Go on.'

'We've plotted all the readings and, based on the intensity, we are fairly certain that the energy surge epicentre originated in the village of Wickham.'

'Wickham? Why does that name sound familiar?'

'Wickham is the village where the witch was killed by one of our agents about twenty years ago.'

'Ah yes, that was a most unfortunate incident.'

'Yes, it is a shame that the witch died before we could study her,' Smittle agreed.

'Oh, I'm not referring to the witch. I don't give a jot about that scum. We also lost one of our best agents that day. It was most unfortunate. Operations were closed down after that incident, were they not?'

'Actually, our records show we didn't extract all our people from that location. A few 'sleeper' agents were left behind who were too well integrated into village life. It was thought that extracting them all at once would raise suspicion and the witch's death may have been looked into instead of being recorded as dying from natural causes.'

'Ah yes, good. An excellent decision. Must have been one of my own. Now, tell me more about this energy surge?'

'Well, first, it's the biggest surge we have registered since our records began. It was measured over thirty miles away from the epicentre in all directions. The Electricity Board recorded a series of complaints in the area including exploding light bulbs and appliances overheating. It was all over in less than a minute and the electric supply immediately resumed.'

'That is excellent information, excellent information indeed. Right, who's the local Councillor for the agency in Wickham?'

'Councillor Malys, sir.'

'That's right, I remember now, Malys had to take over after the unfortunate incident. Send a coded message to Malys. I want all the sleeper agents in Wickham reactivated immediately and send in reinforcements. I want our best agents on this. This is what we've been waiting for. It's time to harvest those powers for good and end these witches once and for all. Remember, we do this for crown and country, Smelt.'

'It's Smittle, sir.'

'What was that you said, Smide?'

'Nothing sir.'

'This needs to be a covert operation, do you hear me Smee? I don't want any agents crashing around, drawing attention to themselves. Not until we are absolutely sure what we are dealing with and not until we have perfected our extraction method. I don't want to lose another good agent and I also don't want the good people of Great Britain to get their knickers all in a knot if they suspect they are living amongst witches. We don't need a repeat of the hysteria-induced witch hunts of the 1600s. Everyone was accusing everyone else of being witches. There were so many supposed witches put on trial, it wasted a lot of time and the real filthy hags went to ground, disguising themselves as healers and the like. We need to be smart. We need to do this right.'

'Very good, sir. And there's one more thing, sir.'

'More?'

'Yes, sir. The energy surge appears to have had another effect too.'

'And what might that be, Smelt?'

'The captive in Cell B-7. Her energy readings are off the chart.'

'What? That old hag that was captured years ago? The one who's given us nothing but grief since she arrived?'

'Yes, sir, the energy surge appears to have reignited her, so to speak. She's giving out fairly powerful energy readings herself and there's something about her that's changed, something in her eyes is very different. I don't know how to explain it.'

Beyond the operations room, down the corridor, behind a twelve inch lead door reinforced with steel and inside a windowless padded cell, sat an old woman. Her grey hair hung almost to her waist. She was dressed in white overalls and her hands and feet were secured with chains. But if you looked closely, you could see a knowing sparkle in the depths of her dark blue eyes as she chuckled to herself with glee, 'The power of three. The power of three. It all begins with the power of three.'

CHAPTER 6

DOLORES MOONBEAM

Lucy yawned and slowly stretched. For a moment she couldn't remember where she was. Then it came back to her. Thinking of all the peculiar things that had happened the day before, Lucy smiled to herself. How silly she had been. In the bright morning sunshine of the new day, she was sure she would find nothing odd about the house, nothing odd about her aunts, and nothing odd about that big black cat with the strange green eyes.

She got up, dressed quickly and exited her bedroom. Something seemed different about the hallway. A grandfather clock stood next to her door and she couldn't quite remember if it had been there before. Quickly crossing the hallway, Lucy tested the door handle to her mother's old room. It was still locked. Determined to try again later, she headed down the stairs. Something seemed different about those too. There seemed to be more of them somehow. She felt as if it was taking her much longer to walk down the stairs than she remembered. But that couldn't be right. The stairs couldn't have changed overnight. She must have just been too tired and too distraught the previous day to remember properly. Lucy tut-tutted to herself; she really was being very silly. She had also forgotten to bring her instructions on how to get to the kitchen but, then again, how hard could it be?

As it turned out, it was very hard. Lucy just couldn't find her way. She seemed to be walking in circles. She walked through the same door at least twice and came upon a set of familiar stairs that she was convinced she should climb down to get to the kitchen, but the only way to go was up. Finally she found herself in a passage that came to a dead end with no possible way out other than a small trap door on the floor. Lucy started to worry. She also started to feel a little bit frightened. Just as she was about to turn around to retrace her steps, the trap door flew open with a bang and Eddy's grinning face appeared through it.

'Ah, there you are Lucy. I had a feeling I'd find you here. Come along, the kitchen is just below.'

Before Lucy could protest, Eddy's head disappeared and she had no choice but to follow her. Lucy walked over to the trap door and looked down. There was a wooden ladder leading to the room below, at the bottom of which stood Eddy. Once again dressed in shades of red from top to bottom, Eddy was smiling up at her and beckoning for her to climb down. Lucy sighed and swung her foot over onto the first rung. Clearly today was going to start out just as weirdly as yesterday had ended.

When Lucy's feet were firmly on the ground she looked around and, to her amazement, discovered that she was indeed right in the middle of the kitchen. How odd. She hadn't noticed the trap door nor the ladder the previous night.

Before she could comment on this, the sound of loud scuffling came from inside a kitchen cabinet. Lucy hung back as Eddy went over to investigate. The scuffling noise was replaced by sounds of bumping and bashing. Then George's distinctive, if somewhat muffled voice, exclaimed, 'This is not funny House!'

A noise, like rumbling low laughter, came from somewhere

deep within the house.

Eddy reached down and opened the cabinet door just in time to reveal George crawling backwards on all fours.

'Oh thank goodness you opened the door. It was so dark I couldn't see a thing.' George backed slowly and gingerly out of the cupboard, trying to free her flowing purple garments which were being snared on the door latch. Once freed, she quickly straightened up and brushed herself down.

'Ah Lucy, good morning to you, did you sleep well?' George enquired as if it was perfectly normal to enter the kitchen on all fours from inside a cupboard.

Lucy just stared at her aunt, her mouth hanging open.

'What would you like for breakfast?' George bustled over to the large range cooker, ignoring Lucy's gaping mouth. 'You can have anything you like.'

This statement caught Lucy's attention and she decided to ignore the mysterious cabinet business for now. Anything, thought Lucy, I bet I really can't.

Out loud she said in her most hoity-toity voice, 'Well, in London young ladies like myself like to watch what we eat, so I'll have wheat-free, sugar-free muesli topped with organic non-fat plain yoghurt and a glass of coconut milk please.'

Lucy wasn't sure what she was actually asking for but she had heard older girls in her school talk about these things. She was also pretty sure that out here in the country her aunts wouldn't know what any of this stuff was let alone have it available.

George looked at her sceptically, 'Are you sure that's what you'd really like?'

'Of course I'm sure,' replied Lucy feeling very unsure. 'I like to lead a healthy lifestyle.' Lucy knew she was being difficult but she couldn't help herself. The morning wasn't feeling so normal after all and she was still upset that her dad went off without her. So, if she couldn't take her frustrations out on him, well, her aunts would have to do. Maybe, if she was so difficult and unreasonable, they would have enough of her and demand that her father come back and take her away.

'Alright then, if you're really sure,' George replied. She picked up a large pot and put it on the stove. It looked like the same pot George had used the previous night to make supper. In fact, looking around the kitchen, Lucy suddenly realised what had been missing the night before. Pots and pans! She couldn't see any sign of there being any other pots or pans in the cluttered kitchen. There only seemed to be the one very large, very black pot. George picked up a wooden spoon, stirred the pot briefly and then ladled something into a bowl. She placed the dish in front of Lucy. There in the bowl was a small heap of pale brown muesli which looked more like a pile of wood chippings. On top of the muesli was a large blob of white gloopy stuff which Lucy could only assume was the organic non-fat plain yoghurt. Next to the bowl, George placed a glass containing a white insipid liquid.

Lucy gingerly spooned a small helping into her mouth. The moment the chippings passed her lips, she had to stop herself from spitting it straight out. It tasted disgusting. She then took a sip of the milk and gagged, just managing to swallow it down. The milk was no better than the muesli. Lucy didn't know what to do. Never in her wildest imagination did she think her aunts would actually know what this stuff was let alone have it in their kitchen. She was really rather hungry but she couldn't eat another mouthful. It was like chewing sawdust.

George was pretending not to notice Lucy's reaction. She went back to the pot and dipped her spoon into it again. Returning to the table, she placed an overflowing plate onto it.

'Lucy, I know you really want to eat your muesli but earlier I made scrambled eggs and bacon and there's simply too much for Eddy and I to eat. Just this once, would you help us eat it? I'd hate it to go to waste.'

Lucy looked up from staring bleakly at the uninviting contents of her bowl. She gazed at the pile of fluffy eggs and sizzling bacon. Her mouth began to water and her tummy rumbled loudly.

'Oh alright,' she said, trying not to sound too eager, 'I suppose just this once I can make an exception.' She quickly pushed her bowl aside and reached for the eggs before her aunt could insist she finished her muesli first.

'So, what would you like to do today?' George asked, sitting down next to her.

'I have no idea,' Lucy replied sullenly as she thought of the day stretching out endlessly before her. 'There's nothing for me to do. There's no TV, no computer, no DVD, no nothing.' Lucy's bottom lip stuck out of its own accord.

'You could go exploring?' Eddy suggested as she happily licked bacon juice from her fingers.

'Exploring? What? Like the Famous Five or Treasure Island or some other childish nonsense?' Lucy retorted sulkily.

Ignoring her rude outburst, George replied, 'Well, we thought you might want to get your bearings. You've seen a bit of the house but you haven't seen the gardens yet. There is also the woods and village beyond.'

'Oh,' Lucy exclaimed. She was trying hard to remain sulky but the idea of exploring more of this strange house and grounds certainly did intrigue her. 'I guess I wouldn't mind being shown around.'

'Oh, I'm afraid we can't show you around, Lucy. Eddy and I are working on... um... err... special projects and I'm afraid we can't spare any time at the moment, but you're free to go and explore on your own.'

'On my own,' Lucy retorted in surprise. 'You mean no one's coming with me?'

Lucy had never been anywhere on her own. Either her dad or Ali accompanied her everywhere she went in London, which wasn't many places. Normally it was just to school and back, and occasionally to the park. She spent most of her spare time either doing her homework in the flat, helping Mrs Kahn in the restaurant kitchen or accompanying Ali on his many mysterious errands where he would meet people in strange places, never letting her get out the car and never telling her what the meetings were about.

'You'll be perfectly safe, don't you worry,' Eddy reassured her. 'This is a very quiet village. Nothing exciting happens here.

Well not that often anyway. Besides, there are only two things you need to remember if you're feeling lost or alone or a little afraid. First, think really hard about where it is you want to go and you'll find your way. Second, if you need me, I will always find you. Always.'

Lucy wasn't sure what to make of this last statement. 'Um, ok then, so I can go and explore anywhere I want?'

'Absolutely anywhere,' Eddy agreed, munching her way through an apple.

'Actually, there's only one place you're not permitted,' George corrected, 'and that's our workshop. We promised your dad and we would like to keep our word.'

'Why doesn't my dad want me to see your workshop?'

'I'm afraid that's something you need to ask him,' George replied.

This was even more intriguing. Now Lucy felt she had two missions. The first was to get inside her mother's old bedroom and the second was to find her aunts' workshop and discover why her dad wanted to keep her out of it. Maybe this holiday wouldn't be so boring after all.

Eddy accompanied Lucy to the front of the house. Lucy was secretly pleased because she wasn't sure she would have been able to locate it on her own. Everything seemed different from the day before and she was struggling to get her bearings. As they emerged outside into the bright morning sunshine, Eddy turned to Lucy and, for the first time, looked serious. Crouching down, she placed both hands on Lucy's shoulders. 'Did you hear what I said before? Remember, think hard about where it is you want to go and you will find your way, and I will always be able to find you, no matter where you are, if you need me.'

'OK,' Lucy muttered, feeling a little uncomfortable by the intensity of her aunt's stare. Eddy straightened up. 'The woods are just beyond that wall,' she pointed to the end of the very long garden, 'and the village is beyond that. There's a path through the woods that is a shortcut to the village or you can take the long way round by road.'

As Eddy finished talking, a woman appeared at the bottom of the driveway, pushing a bright pink bicycle with a basket on the front.

Eddy groaned.

'Yoo-hoo! Edwina! Yoo-hoo!' the woman trilled. The woman was wearing a long flowing multi-coloured skirt and, as she walked, she jangled from an array of tiny bells and charms hanging from dozens of bangles, necklaces, belts and anklets. The resulting sound was quite deafening. Her mouse brown hair was streaked with grey and hung loose except for large sections twisted into beads or twine.

'Oh Edwina, I'm glad I caught you, I'm in a dreadful pickle. I was just in the middle of a tricky potion only to discover that I'm all out of Lovage. May I take a few snippets from your garden?' The lady brandished a large pair of secateurs and made a rapid snipping motion with them.

'But my, where are my manners? How very rude of me. I've only just noticed you've got company.' The lady turned her attention to Lucy. She had thick lashings of black eyeliner and a bright spot of pink blush was prominently displayed on each cheek. She reached out her hand towards Lucy. 'My name's Moonbeam Lotus Blossom. How do you do? And who are you?'

Lucy hesitantly shook Moonbeam's hand before dropping it quickly. 'Hello, I'm Lucy Sprat.'

'We must be getting on, Dolores,' Eddy interrupted hurriedly. 'You know where the herb garden is by now. Please help yourself to whatever you need.'

'Now, now, Edwina, you know Dolores is no longer a name that belongs to me. I have been reborn as Moonbeam Lotus Blossom,' Moonbeam chided. She turned to Lucy, 'You see, I used to be called Dolores but that's before I discovered my gifts. I then prayed to the universe and they gave me my new name of Moonbeam Lotus Blossom which reflects my inner spirit and makes me at one with the twelve planes of our subconscious worlds.'

Oh great, Lucy thought, another nut job. This place is

overrun with crazy ladies.

'Right,' said Eddy, 'good to see you Moonbeam. We must be going.'

But Moonbeam was not ready to say goodbye, 'So how do you know Edwina then Lucy? I don't think I've seen you around the village before?'

'Eddy's my aunt,' Lucy replied just as Eddy said 'Lucy's a friend.'

A look of pure amazement passed over Moonbeam's face. 'Oh my goodness!' she squeaked and then lowered her voice to a stage whisper. 'Does that mean you're one of us?'

'Can't talk now, Dolores, got to dash.' Eddy swiftly interjected before Lucy could ask Moonbeam what she meant. Eddy quickly steered Lucy down to the bottom of the garden. Lucy looked back to see that Moonbeam, or Dolores, or whatever the crazy lady's name was, was staring after them with a smile on her face and a strange look in her eyes.

Eddy finally stopped by a wooden door set in the tall red brick wall that surrounded the entire garden. 'Here you go, this leads to the woods. Don't rush back. Have fun!' With that she pushed Lucy unceremoniously through the door and quickly shut it behind her before Lucy could utter another sound.

CHAPTER 7

THE WHISPERING WOODS

Lucy looked around her. The garden wall backed right onto thick woodland that stretched out on either side as far as she could see. She wasn't sure what to do next. She had never really played outside on her own. It just wasn't advisable for a young girl to be wandering the streets of London by herself. Being a city girl, she had certainly never been in the woods before, let alone told to go and play in them alone. What was she supposed to do anyhow? She sighed, her initial enthusiasm quickly evaporating. This was going to be a long, dull day after all. She sighed again. Oh well, she might as well explore a bit of the woods, although she was sure there would be absolutely nothing to discover and even less to do.

Lucy walked a bit further. At first, she didn't really pay any attention to where she was going or what was around her. She was just feeling generally grumpy and a bit sorry for herself. But after a while, she started to notice things. The first thing she noticed was the silence. She was so used to the city noise – cars and sirens and people all around. Here there was nothing. Although, actually, that wasn't quite true. As her hearing adjusted and began to tune into the sounds of the woods, she realised that there were all sorts of noise around her. She could hear birds calling to each other in the dense tree branches and the tinkle of running water somewhere close by. She could hear clicks, twitches and small scuffles in the shrubs surrounding her and the hum of insects unseen. She looked at the ground and noticed a row of ants marching in a long orderly queue. Then her attention was caught by a flash of colour. She turned and saw at least a dozen butterflies dancing in the sunbeams that shone through the canopy of leaves above her. Lucy spun slowly around in amazement, her mouth involuntarily turning up in a smile. Just as she thought the moment couldn't be any more magical, a rabbit popped its head out of a burrow hole and hopped off out of sight. Without thinking, Lucy chased after it, trying to keep up. After a few moments she stumbled into a clearing. The clearing was almost perfectly circular with dense trees growing all around, like an interwoven wall of branches. The arms of the trees arched skywards as if trying to protect the glade from unwanted intruders. In the centre of the clearing was a small pool surrounded by lush green grass. Lucy thought it must be a pond but when she looked closer, the water was crystal clear and empty. No fish, no moss. Nothing but a solid rock bottom. Lucy straightened up and noticed something rather odd. Evenly spaced in a circle around the pond stood four stone pillars. Lucy started to walk towards the stone closest to her, when the sound of a branch snapping made her turn. A boy stepped into the clearing and stopped still, staring at her.

'Who are you?' Lucy called fearfully, backing up slowly towards the stones. She was suddenly aware that she was all alone in the woods.

The boy stepped closer. He was tall and looked to be a few years older than her. He had black hair and large green eyes. As he came nearer, Lucy noticed his clothes. There was something odd about them that she couldn't quite put her finger on. He was wearing grey tailored shorts with a collared check shirt tucked firmly into his waist belt. Perhaps boys dressed differently in the country. The boy stepped up to her and stretched out his hand in greeting.

'Hi, I'm Ja... er... Jake, pleased to meet you.'

Lucy shook his hand politely, too speechless to reply.

Jake laughed at her shocked expression.

'And you're Lucy,' he announced. Now Lucy was even more speechless. How did this strange boy know who she was?

As if reading her mind, he continued, 'I know your aunts.'

Ah, Lucy thought, that would explain it. All the strange occurrences over the last twenty-four hours seem to be somehow related to her aunts. Gathering her wits, Lucy retrieved her hand from where the boy was still firmly gripping it in his own.

'How do you know my aunts?'

'I guess you can say they're old family friends. Anyway, I heard you were staying with them all alone and thought you'd might like some company.'

Lucy tried to think of a haughty response but she couldn't deny it. She really did want some company, particularly someone her own age. Now that she could inspect him more closely, she figured the boy must be about fourteen or fifteen, and his clothes did appear to be a bit old fashioned. He probably had really old fashioned parents or possibly everyone in the countryside was simply old fashioned. Certainly her aunts didn't appear to have much fashion sense. They kept on wearing the same colour every day.

'So, would you like some company?'

'I'm perfectly fine on my own,' Lucy retorted, but then added quickly, 'but since you're here, you might as well stick around.'

She was trying to be cool but she was secretly delighted to have someone to talk to.

'So do you have a PlayStation or Xbox?' she asked hopefully.

'What kind of box?'

'Don't tell me you've never heard of it?' Lucy asked amazed.

The boy shook his head. Goodness, Lucy thought, we really are far away from civilization out here.

'How about a computer? Or TV?' The boy shook his head again.

'Surely you have heard of them?' Lucy asked in astonishment.

'Yes, I've heard of them, I just don't have them,' he replied scuffing the floor with his feet and avoiding her eyes.

'Well what do you have? What do you do for fun? Surely your parents must have some sort of computer. Most do.'

'I don't have parents,' the boy replied matter-of-fact, appearing unconcerned.

'Oh, I'm so sorry,' Lucy felt ashamed. 'Who looks after you then?'

'Well, I guess you could say I'm being looked after by two aunts,' he replied looking down at his feet and digging the toe of his shoe further into the ground.

'What a coincidence! I'm being looked after by two aunts too. I hope your aunts aren't as batty as mine.' Without waiting for a reply, Lucy continued, 'Have you lived here all your life?'

'Pretty much. I moved here when I was little but this village and these woods are all I know. Sometimes I think they are all I will ever know.' He sighed deeply and gave the ground an extra big dig.

'Well, this place is rather backwards but London is not far away. It only took about three hours to get here. You could move to London when you're older. That's where I'm from.'

The boy didn't seem too impressed. He looked like he was about to say something in reply but then changed his mind. 'So what do you think of the Whispering Woods?'

'Whispering Woods?' Lucy asked feeling a little alarmed by the slightly sinister sounding name.

'Well, their official name is the Wicker Woods but local folks call them the Whispering Woods because of all the noises and sounds that can be heard in them. Many a folk who have wandered out into the woods on their own at night have returned completely spooked and saying that they thought the trees and animals were whispering to each other. Of course, most of these folk had previously spent a merry night in the local pub so no one believes them. So what do you think of the woods?'

'Well, at first I wasn't sure but the longer I spend in these woods, the more I like them. I've never been in woods before.'

'Never? Goodness, well, you're in for a treat. These woods are special. Some people say they're magical, others say they are dangerous.'

'Dangerous,' Lucy couldn't help let out a little squeak. 'Why dangerous?'

'Well, about twenty-five years ago, a boy entered the woods with his friend. The friend returned but the boy was never seen again.'

'What happened to him?'

'Nobody knows. Some say he ran away. Some say that he was kidnapped by gypsies and others say that he was murdered right here in this very clearing.'

'What?' Lucy squeaked again looking around anxiously. The glade was dappled in sunlight. Birds twittered in the trees, butterflies danced in the sunshine and squirrels were jumping between the branches. It looked like the least dangerous place in the world.

'What do you think happened to him?' she whispered.

'Oh I think he's still here – he's just hiding,' he grinned.

'Oh that's just silly,' Lucy replied with a nervous laugh. 'Besides, he'd be all grown up by now.'

'That's true,' Jake agreed although his smile was no longer as wide. 'Most people think he simply ran away. His foster parents weren't the nicest of people so a lot of folk reckon he had just had enough. Anyway, did you know we're standing in the dead centre of Wicker Woods?'

'Cool!' Lucy turned slowly around and gazed at the clearing. 'So what are these four stones? They look really old.'

'They are. Legend has it that these four stones are all that remain from the first ever known witches' coven. The legend tells of four powerful witches, each with the ability to control one of the four elements – earth, air, water and fire. And the stones are laid out in a compass. Look.' Pointing to the largest stone at the top end of the clearing, Jake continued. 'That one's the north stone and it represents earth. The opposite one is the south stone and it represents water. The east stone is fire and the west stone is air.'

Lucy went to look more closely at the north stone. 'I think I can see some markings carved into it,' she exclaimed.

'That's right. Each stone bears the symbol of the element it represents. Although they are very faint these days, you don't notice them unless you know where to look.'

Lucy walked slowly from stone to stone, examining each in turn and running her hands across the strange markings. As she ran her hand across the pattern on the west stone, her hand started to feel warm and then rapidly became so hot she had to quickly withdraw it. 'Ouch! Come and feel this stone, Jake, it's really hot.'

Jake walked over and placed his hand on the stone. 'I don't feel anything. It just feels like a regular stone to me.'

Lucy placed her hand on the marking once more. 'Ow! That burns! How can you not feel that?' She turned to look suspiciously at Jake, thinking he must be making fun of her. But before she could challenge him further, she noticed something else.

'Hey, what's going on with your ear? How come it's twitching back and forth like that?'

Jake reached up to feel his ear then quickly covered it with his hand. 'Goodness is that the time, I must go.'

Turning, he ran out of the clearing before Lucy could utter another word. Only after he had vanished did Lucy realise he hadn't been wearing a watch. The next thing she realised is that she couldn't remember which way she had entered the clearing. So now she didn't know which way to leave. Not wanting to remain in the woods any longer on her own, she turned slowly in a circle, studying the edges of the clearing carefully, looking for something, anything that might look the slightest bit familiar. But nothing did. She could feel her panic rise as her heart began to beat rapidly and hot tears pricked her eyes.

She'd never felt so alone before, or so lost. How was she going to find her way back to her aunts' house? What was it that Eddy has said to her? Something about if ever she needed her, Eddy would always be there or some such nonsense. But it was worth a try.

'I need you now Aunt Eddy. I'm lost and I can't find my way back home,' she said out loud even though she felt foolish doing it. Lucy sat down with her back to a stone while she decided what to do next. She chose the one that had made her hand hot because, for some reason, she found it more comforting than the others. The clearing didn't seem so welcoming any more. Clouds covered the sun and now it looked gloomy with dark shadows in the crevices and beneath the trees, where anything could be hiding. The noises in the woods had changed too. No longer did they sound cheerful and happy. Now they sounded louder and more frantic, as if they were trying to sound a warning. The hairs on the back of Lucy's neck abruptly stood on end. She couldn't explain why but she suddenly got the sense that she was being watched.

Then the sound of something crashing its way through the woods started coming towards her. Lucy quickly stood up, looking all around, trying to figure out her best escape. Should she run or climb a tree or run and then climb a tree? She turned and started sprinting towards a large tree on the far side of the clearing. The crashing noise got louder and closer.

Just as Lucy reached the tree a voice called out. 'There you are.'

Lucy turned with relief to see Eddy burst into the clearing, twigs and leaves sticking to her hair and clothes which she was trying to brush off. 'I came the most direct route from the house which unfortunately, is through the densest part of the woods.'

Without thinking, Lucy rushed into her arms with relief but quickly regained her composure and pulled away. 'How did you know where I was?'

'You called me, silly.' Eddy chuckled as if Lucy had asked her the most ridiculous question in the world.

'Are you ready to go home? I think George is whipping up something special for lunch and, afterwards, I can show you the gardens and my greenhouse. But let's take the less direct route home. I've got enough twigs and leaves in my hair for one day.'

CHAPTER 8

CURES & CONCERNS

As soon as lunch was over, George left the table in a hurry, scurrying out of the kitchen through a set of large double doors Lucy hadn't noticed before. Eddy watched her go with a frown. Then she rearranged her face and grinned at Lucy. 'Come with me,' she beckoned, 'this door leads to the back garden, or at least it used to.'

Eddy turned the handle of a large gnarled wooden door, flung it open and peered warily around the corner. 'Ah yes, it's still here. That's handy.'

Lucy followed Eddy outside and gasped. The back garden was enormous. There were four large greenhouses standing side-by-side as well as row upon row of plants of every description.

'This is such a big garden. Do you look after it yourself?'

'At the moment I do, although old Mr Thomas used to do most of it. He's been our gardener for years. But he went missing two weeks ago so now I'm trying to manage on my own.'

'Gosh, do you think he died?'

'Who died? Oh, you mean Mr Thomas. No, he hasn't died. I would feel it if he had. It was just his time to leave us, that's all.'

This made no sense to Lucy but before she could probe further, a shrill voice interrupted them.

'Yoo-hoo, you two.'

Eddy groaned quietly and then raised her voice, 'Twice in one day, Dolores, sorry, Moonbeam. To what do we owe the pleasure this time?'

Dolores Moonbeam jangled up to meet them. She now had brightly coloured feathers sticking out at random angles in her hair.

'I am such a silly billy, Eddy, I forgot to ask earlier if you have any dried Kameria root? Only I have a client who has a strong case of diarrhoea and I'm all out.'

'Of course, Dolores.' Eddy was struggling to keep her voice pleasant. 'Although you do know that Blackberry root is just as effective?'

'Of course I know that, I'm an experienced Apothecary after all,' Dolores trilled with indignation. 'I simply find my gifts are stronger when I use Kameria and I naturally must provide my client with the best of my abilities.' Dolores swept back her hair in a clatter of beads.

'Why don't you stay here and enjoy the garden with Lucy while I fetch the Kameria.'

'No need for that, I'll come with you. It will be quicker that way.'

Eddy reluctantly inclined her head in agreement and moved towards another side door to the house, followed extremely closely by Dolores. Not to be left behind, Lucy hastily trailed after them.

The side door led into a cavernous room with floor to ceiling shelves stocked with carefully labelled glass jars of all shapes and sizes. A bulky wooden workbench dominated the room, on top of which stood a small gas burner and a large shallow stone bowl. There were smooth round stones of various sizes next to it.

Dolores looked around the room greedily. 'Oh my, what a fabulous collection of herbs. Quite similar to my own in fact. Ooh, and what's this fuzzy white stuff?' She picked up a jar and peered at the label. '"Angel's Heart"? I've never heard of it. What's it for?'

Sidestepping the question, Eddy offered up a small bag. 'Here you go Dolores, I've given you plenty of Kameria so you won't be running out again any time soon.'

Dolores Moonbeam wasn't listening. 'What a lovely little setup you have here, Eddy. We should compare notes. I'm sure we could both learn from each other.'

'That's a kind offer, although I'm a bit busy with orders at the moment.'

Eddy walked over to the door and held it open, 'After you, Dolores.'

But Dolores Moonbeam was still busy running her fingers hungrily over the jars, reading each label as she went.

'I am afraid I'm going to have to hurry you along, Dolores. Lucy and I have things we need to get on with.'

For a brief moment, Dolore's features pulled together in an ugly scowl but she quickly recovered her composure and smiled sweetly.

'As do I, Eddy, as do I. I need to sort out Mrs Peacock's diarrhoea before it gets too urgent. She is counting on me for a cure. Toodleloo you two.' With a jangle of bells and a swish of hair that dislodged two feathers, she swept out of the room.

Eddy closed the door behind her and leant against it, as if to make sure she couldn't return.

'I'm glad she's gone. That woman is a pain in the-you-know-where, spouting all this new age nonsense all of the time.'

Lucy was now studying the assortment of glass jars and odd shaped vessels as she made her way slowly around the room. 'So what are in all these jars then?'

'I make potions to order,' Eddy explained. 'I have a mail order service and also supply a few natural remedy shops. It's how I earn money to pay for the essentials we can't make ourselves. George and I used to do it together but she's been too focused on, well, other things lately. So I set up a separate workshop out here where I wouldn't disturb George with all my noise and mess.'

'I see,' said Lucy, although she wasn't sure she did.

'Would you like to help me make some potions? Today I need to make up a batch to treat smelly feet for a local herbal shop, another potion to cure chronic hiccups for a young man in Basingstoke and, for a poor sweet lady in Scotland, she would like to get over a lost love.'

'You can make potions to cure all that?'

'I certainly can. Should we start?'

Lucy nodded her head enthusiastically.

Eddy showed her which jars they needed for each potion and then how to carefully measure out the ingredients. 'If we add even a milligram more of the Bundlewheat Seeds, it will turn the feet blue so we must be very careful.'

Then Eddy showed Lucy how to grind the ingredients, using one of the smooth stones, so that it turned into fine powder. It was hard work and Lucy was sweating by the time they had ground up enough ingredients to make ten bags of the smelly feet cure.

'Now, the final part of the process is a bit special,' Eddy explained. She lifted down a very large, very old and very battered leather bound book. The spine was splitting in several places and some of the pages were coming loose.

'This book has been in our family for generations. It's been passed down from mother to daughter or sister for hundreds of years.'

Eddy laid it carefully on the workbench and Lucy stepped closer to inspect. On the cover in faded lettering were the words 'The Complete Compilation of Concoctions for Cures & Concerns'.

'This is where we find the recipes we need to treat the specific infliction or ailment. Now, I just need to locate the recipe to remember the exact words.'

Eddy flipped carefully through the book until she found the

page she was looking for. 'Right, here it is. So the last thing we do after making up this cure is repeat these words "Foetida pedes, cum hoc ego sanare vos".'

'What does that mean?'

'It's Latin and the basic translation goes something like this "Smelly feet, with this I treat".'

Lucy laughed, 'That's silly.'

'I agree, this particular one does sound silly but they can be a lot more serious, depending on the ailment. The words are a bit like giving a blessing. Each cure has its own and is not complete until we say the appropriate words. Would you like to say them with me now?'

Lucy shrugged her shoulders, 'Sure.'

It was clearly more of her aunt's hocus pocus nonsense but she didn't have anything better to do and the afternoon in her aunt's workshop had turned out to be surprisingly fun.

'Excellent. When more than one of us says the incantation, we join hands. It makes the effect stronger. George and I always do it together on the trickier cases. I'm not sure smelly feet really qualifies but why not, heh?'

Eddy walked to the other side of the workbench and positioned herself opposite Lucy, the batch of smelly feet potion in between them.

They linked hands and, as soon as they did, Lucy felt them tingle and zing like they were conducting a small electric current. The sensation spread up and outwards all over her body. But instead of it giving her a frightening shock, this time she actually quite liked the feeling. Her body was filled with a warm glow. It comforted her. It also made her feel strangely powerful, like she could do anything. She raised her head and by the look in her aunt's eyes, she could tell her aunt felt it too. They started to speak the incantation slowly together. Lucy found that the Latin words flowed off her tongue as if this wasn't the first time she had spoken them but rather as if she spoke the language every day. Oddly, she also found she didn't need to refer to the book to know what words to speak; they came without even thinking.

As the last word left their lips, the potion changed colour from pale yellow to deep red.

Eddy looked from the potion to Lucy. 'Well that's new.'

CHAPTER 9

SHEEP'S FEET AND HUMBUGS

'Oh bother, we're all out of sheep's feet.' Eddy had her head buried inside the belly of an old battered refrigerator that stood forlornly in the corner of her workshop. Every now and again the refrigerator let out a gurgle or a groan as if to protest against the strain of constantly trying to keep its innards cool.

'We're running low on a few other supplies too. I think now might be a good time to take a break.'

Lucy looked up from where she was grinding dried beetle wings into a fine powder. 'What do you need sheep's feet for?'

'We boil them up and then add the juice to a poultice which is particularly good at healing in-grown toe nails.'

'Ew!' Lucy finished grinding her powder and reluctantly stood up. She was surprised to realise two things. First, she was really enjoying herself and, second, she seemed to be unexpectedly good at preparing potions for cures and concerns. Almost instinctively, she appeared to know just what to do, whether it be how fine to grind certain ingredients so they form a soft powder or how to identify and delicately snip only the youngest leaves from a plant without disturbing the flowers. Eddy had only needed to show her once how to prepare a particular cure or potion and she had been able to replicate the steps exactly without needing to ask for help. This was a surprise because, at school, she was never normally this attentive or quick to grasp new information.

'I'm going to head into the village to restock some essentials? Do you want to come?' Eddy enquired.

Lucy didn't need asking twice. She quickly removed her apron and followed her aunt out the back door. Eddy led her to the garden shed where she retrieved two bicycles, both with large baskets on the front.

'Here, you can borrow George's, she never uses it and it's a bit smaller than mine. We'll go by the road. It's further but it's easier to ride our bikes on rather than taking the path through the woods.'

Eddy launched herself onto her bike and zoomed off leaving Lucy to frantically peddle after her.

'So what supplies do we need?' Lucy panted as she finally caught up.

'Oh, just the usual. Let's see, from the Butcher, I need sheep's trotters and pig's ears. From the Hardware store, I need ammonia, white spirit and some iron filings, and from the Grocer, I need castor oil and humbugs.'

'Humbugs? What potion do you use the humbugs for?'

'None, they are George's favourites. She likes to suck on them when she's working. She says they help her think. I say they help her get fat. She eats so many she'll look like a humbug one of these days,' Eddy chortled.

They cycled along the dusty lane until they reached the edge of the woods where it joined a tarred road.

'This is the main road into and out of the village. As you can see, it's quite busy.'

Lucy looked up and down the road. In the distance she could see what looked like the back of a bus retreating up the hill, black fumes puffing from its exhaust. In the opposite direction was an old man leading a donkey and cart piled high with cabbages. Other than that, the road was empty. If Eddy thought this was busy, she better not ever visit London.

Soon, they entered the village and pulled up beside a row of dilapidated shops with steep, sloping roofs, murky glass panelled windows and faded shop signs. Eddy leant her bicycle haphazardly against the wall of the first shop and breezed through the front door, accompanied by the sound of a chiming bell.

'Aren't you going to lock up the bikes?' Lucy called after her but the door had already closed. Lucy looked around. The street was eerily empty. The bicycles would probably be perfectly safe but, growing up in the dodgy end of London, Lucy had learnt to lock up everything if she wanted to keep it. As she was contemplating how best to secure the bicycles together, she suddenly felt a prickling sensation on the back of her neck and had the distinct feeling that she was being watched. She looked around again but the street was still empty. Then a movement caught her eye. She looked up just in time to see the curtain in a window above the shop twitch as if someone had closed it hurriedly. Forgetting the bikes, Lucy hastened after her aunt, launching herself through the shop door at considerable speed.

'There you are Lucy,' Eddy hailed her, 'I was just telling Mr Green all about you. Mr Green is the Grocer.'

Lucy turned to Mr Green. He was a small man, with wispy grey hair that touched his collar and ears that were just a bit too big for his face. He wore a pair of rimless glasses on his hooked nose and Lucy noticed that the back of his hands, which he was gleefully rubbing together, were astonishingly hairy. He wore a pristine green apron over his clothes.

'Welcome to Wickham, Lucy. Let me be the first to say how delighted we are that you've come to visit our humble village.' Mr Green stuck out his hand and, not wanting to be impolite, Lucy gingerly gave it a brief shake before hastily letting go.

'It's so wonderful to have another child in the village, there are not many of you, you know.'

Mr Green was staring greedily at Lucy which she found a

bit unnerving.

'What do we need from here, Eddy? I can help get the items for you.' Lucy asked, eager to be done as soon as possible so as to get away from Mr Green's unwavering gaze which now had taken on a slightly feverish quality.

'Oh what a sweet, delightful child. Such lovely manners you have, my dear,' Mr Green practically drooled at Lucy, 'but I have already gathered everything our Eddy needs in this basket. Come closer and have a look if you like.'

'No, you're alright, thank you.' Lucy took a step back and tucked herself behind Eddy who didn't seem to be finding Mr Green's behaviour remotely unusual.

'If you don't mind putting that onto our account, Mr Green, I'll settle up at the end of the month like usual.'

'Very good, Eddy, and I've popped in a little sweetie for the lovely Lucy to enjoy later, on the house.'

'Isn't that thoughtful, Mr Green. What do you say Lucy?'

Lucy mumbled her thanks but she knew she wasn't going to go anywhere near that "little sweetie". Maybe she'll offer it to George instead.

'It's exceptionally warm again today, don't you think Eddy?' Mr Green said as he wrapped their goods into neat little brown parcels. 'I don't remember the last time it rained.'

'That's true, Mr Green. Fortunately we have a well in our garden otherwise my plants would really be suffering. Right, time to get on, the butcher's next. Goodbye Mr Green,' Eddy called as she exited the shop.

'Toodleloo Eddy, toodleloo Lucy. Come and visit soon. I'm sure I'll always be able to find a little sweetie for you when you do.'

As Lucy rapidly departed the shop, she had to fight the urge to shake herself like a dog to get rid of the creepy, sickly sweetness that seemed to hang in the air of Mr Green's grocery.

Lucy followed Eddy into the next shop with a rusty sign above the door, displaying an ominous looking cleaver, which squeaked as it swayed in the warm breeze. 'Ah Mr Green, how are you today?'

Lucy groaned. Surely Mr Green hadn't followed them into the butchers. But to her dismay, there he was, behind the counter with a big cleaver knife in one hand and a slab of meat in the other. Although now, instead of his pristine green apron, he was wearing a white one smeared with blood!

'Hello Eddy, just one minute and I'll get your order,' Mr Green greeted them without looking up.

Putting the knife and meat down, he walked over to a large chest freezer and retrieved a parcel wrapped neatly in white paper. As he turned, he caught sight of Lucy trying to hide behind Eddy and stopped mid-motion.

'Who's this?' he asked suspiciously without taking his eyes off Lucy. Lucy was astounded. She had only just met him moments before in the grocery shop and now he was acting like he didn't know her. And how did he get into the butcher's so quickly? Perhaps there was some sort of back door that connects the two shops.

'Lucy is my niece, Mr Green. She's come to stay with us for a few weeks while her dad's away on business.'

Mr Green continued to stare at Lucy in a manner that made her feel like he really wasn't happy with what he was seeing.

'I shouldn't stay in these parts too long if I was you,' he said warningly. 'Not much for kids to do around here. You should leave as soon as you can.'

Lucy was taken aback. Only minutes before he seemed only too glad that she had come to visit and now he's telling her to leave. It didn't make any sense. Maybe he has some sort of split personality or something.

'Lucy's having a good time with us already, aren't you Lucy?' Eddy said cheerfully, not seeming at all bothered by Mr Green's sudden change of tune. 'Anyway, we better be off. We need to get to the hardware shop before it shuts.'

Mr Green grunted in reply and then started viciously chopping up the big slab of meat with his giant cleaver.

Eddy led Lucy out of the butcher's and into the last shop in the row.

'Oh hello, Eddy, good to see you again.'

Lucy couldn't believe it. Mr Green was coming forward from the back of the crowded room to greet them yet again. He had replaced his blood stained apron with a red striped one.

'Hello Mr Green, do you have my order?' Eddy asked, seemingly unperturbed by Mr Green's reappearance.

Mr Green pushed his glasses up his nose and scratched his head.

'An order, you say? Did you place an order?'

'I did, Mr Green. Remember, I placed it last week?'

'Ah yes, so you did. Let me take a look.'

Mr Green went over to a row of shelving that went from the floor to the ceiling. The shelves were crammed with an assortment of objects; packages wrapped in brown paper, cardboard boxes in various sizes and a collection of broken small appliances. He rummaged around inside a box and then pulled out a couple of bottles.

'Ah yes, here it is. I don't even remember this coming in. Did you want it now?'

'Well yes, if I may please Mr Green, it would be very helpful.'

'Right you are then,' said Mr Green handing over the bottles. 'Have you paid for them already?'

'No, I haven't. We agreed I would settle up my account at the end of the month with you as normal. Do you remember?'

'Right you are then, that's fine. Did you say you wanted to take them now?'

'Yes please, Mr Green,' Eddy patiently replied as she pried the bottles out of his hands.

Eventually letting go, Mr Green seemed to finally notice Lucy who had been trying to hide behind the overflowing shelves. 'Is that you, George? I didn't see you standing there.'

'No, Mr Green, this is my niece, Lucy,' Eddy explained tolerantly.

'I see,' Mr Green replied, although it was clear that he didn't.

'We must be going now. Goodbye Mr Green.' Eddy steered Lucy out of the shop.

'Goodbye, Eddy. Goodbye, George,' Mr Green called behind them.

When they were finally out on the street, Lucy couldn't contain herself any longer.

'What on earth is wrong with Mr Green? Why did he pretend he hadn't met me before in the butcher and hardware shops? And how did he get into those shops before we did? Can he walk through walls or something?'

Eddy frowned and looked momentarily confused but then she threw back her head and laughed.

'Oh Lucy, I am so sorry. That's completely my fault. I should have explained before we went in. Mr Green is not one man, he's three different men. They are all brothers, triplets in fact. Identical triplets, but you might have guessed that. Their names are Cecil, Cedrick and Cenwig. Although no one is quite sure which one is which anymore. We can only tell them apart by their different coloured aprons. They have been running those three shops side by side for as long as I can remember. They even live together in the same house although, strangely, they don't actually get on. As you might have guessed, one Mr Green is overly friendly, the other Mr Green is overly grumpy, and the third is overly forgetful.'

Finally it all made sense to Lucy. Well, at least some of it did.

'I need to make one final stop at the post office so I can get some of these orders in the mail.'

Lucy exhaled noisily. She was getting a bit bored of all this shop visiting business.

'You can wait for me outside if you prefer. There's a bench on the opposite side of the square that you can sit on while you wait.'

Lucy looked over at the bench. It backed onto a stone wall and the branches of a large oak tree stretched up and over the wall, casting the bench in shade from the scorching late afternoon sun. It looked much more inviting than yet another shop that was likely to be filled with more strange people, so she swiftly agreed.

* * *

Lucy definitely made the right decision because no sooner had Eddy entered the post office, than a tall man with floppy blonde hair came rushing towards her. It was almost as if he had been watching and waiting for Eddy to enter. He stopped in front of Eddy, scooping her hands up into his.

'Oh my goodness, Eddy, is it really you? Yes, yes it is!' he exclaimed before Eddy had a chance to reply. 'It's so good to see you again.' He squeezed her hands and looked deep into her eyes.

Eddy blushed and tried to gently tug her hands free but he held fast.

'Um, hello, do I know you?'

'It's me, Tom. Tom Winkle-Smith. We went to high school together, remember? I was a year ahead of you but we were in the same after school club at one point.'

'Were we? Gosh, I really don't remember. You do look a bit familiar though. You're not from Wickham are you? I would have remembered if we had taken the school bus to Snordom High every day.'

'No, no. I'm originally from Snordom myself so I didn't take the bus, which is a shame because we never got to spend that much time together.' He squeezed Eddy's hands again and tried to look meaningfully into her eyes while Eddy tried to avoid his.

'Anyway,' Tom continued not seeming to note Eddy's discomfort, 'I'm at university now training to be a lawyer. I'm just back for the holidays to help Aunt Ethel.'

'I don't need any help,' squawked the little old lady who stood behind the counter, who was carefully weighing up parcels and applying postage to them.

Tom just smiled at Aunt Ethel and then, lowering his voice, he said, 'She's awfully independent but she's not been too well lately so I offered to help.'

'I'm perfectly fine, there's nothing wrong with me and you

didn't offer. You just pitched up on my doorstep this morning, making a nuisance of yourself and getting in the way.'

Tom chuckled cheerfully at her outburst, 'Is there something I can help you with Eddy?'

'Actually, it's a question for Ethel really.' Eddy finally pried her hands free and edged around Tom so she could get to the counter. 'I have these parcels to post, please Ethel. Has my delivery come in?'

'Not yet, dearie, but I'm expecting it later today or first thing tomorrow.'

Tom had followed Eddy to the counter and was now standing a little too close for comfort. 'I can bring the delivery over to your house when it arrives. It will save you having to come back into the village.'

'Thanks, Tom, but there's no need. I'll come and get it. I enjoy my trips into the village.'

'Oh, it wouldn't be a bother,' Tom persisted, 'and it would give me a reason to see you again.'

Eddy was puzzled by Tom's attention. There was no denying he was good looking and she did feel a bit flattered but, for someone she barely remembered and hadn't seen in years, he seemed just a little too eager.

Meanwhile, Lucy was relaxing on the bench, swinging her legs lazily back and forth. She gazed about the sunlit square but there was still no one to be seen.

'Who are you and where do you come from?' a voice demanded.

Lucy jumped up in fright and turned around but there was no one there.

'I said, who are you and where do you come from?' the voice demanded again, more loudly this time.

Lucy forgot her fright. She was getting fed up with all the weirdness going on in this place.

'Who are *you*?' she demanded back. 'Show yourself.'

'Fair enough,' the voice replied as a rope ladder was thrown down from the branches of the tree above her. 'Come on up.'

Lucy gripped the ladder with one hand and looked up but

couldn't see anything other than branches and leaves. She hesitated, her new found bravery starting to ebb swiftly away as a strong gust of wind blew the leaves about vigorously. Just then, one of the Mr Green's came out of the grocery shop and looked over at Lucy with obvious interest. Without another thought, she grabbed the ladder with both hands and started to climb, the rope swaying wildly as she struggled from rung to rung. Despite her increasing anxiety, she kept on going and found herself climbing between the tree branches and arriving at a wooden platform. As she stretched out to grab hold of the ledge, two hands reached down and lifted her safely up. Lucy scrambled to her feet and found herself face-to-face with – well, she wasn't really sure. Standing before her were a girl and a boy. The girl was about her height but the boy was considerably taller. Both were wearing camouflage overalls, with bits of twigs and leaves stuck all over them. Their faces were painted green, brown and black to match their clothing. All Lucy could see were two sets of brown eyes and two big grins as they both stood facing her, mirroring each other with their legs apart and hands on their hips.

'Hello. I'm Beatrice.' The girl reached out her hand and shook Lucy's firmly. 'This is my brother Benjamin.'

'You can call me Ben,' the boy said, also shaking Lucy's hand firmly, 'and what Beatrice failed to mention is that I'm her much older brother.'

'Pah! Ben was born only ten minutes before me but he was born at five minutes to midnight. Which means his birthday is the day before mine and he never lets me forget it.'

'Too right,' Ben grinned.

'But I'm being rude. Come and sit down. Then you can tell us all about yourself. The suspense is killing me.'

Beatrice led Lucy further into the tree house that had big open windows providing an almost uninterrupted view over the village. Beatrice brushed some crumbs off an upturned wooden crate and gestured for Lucy to sit down. Beatrice and Ben then each acquired their own crate and sat watching Lucy with expectant looks on their faces.

'Why are you dressed like that?' Lucy blurted.

'We'll get to that in a minute,' Beatrice replied, 'but first, you have to tell us who you are and where you come from.'

'My name is Lucy and I'm staying with my aunts for a week or so while my father is away.'

'Where's your mother then?' asked Ben. Beatrice thumped him on the chest with the back of her hand.

'My mother died when I was a baby.'

'Oh I'm so sorry,' Beatrice replied just as Ben said 'How did she die?'

Beatrice thumped him again.

'Ow,' Ben rubbed his chest but grinned.

Beatrice quickly changed the subject, 'So who are your aunts?'

'George and Eddy. They live in an odd house at the edge of the woods.'

'The Wacky Wicks are your aunts?' Ben asked with a laugh.

Lucy looked confused.

'Georgina and Edwina Wick. They're your aunts, right?' Beatrice clarified.

'Oh right, I guess so. It's just, I didn't actually know their last name.'

Ben and Beatrice looked at each other quizzically. How odd not to know the names of your own family.

'Why did you call them "the Wacky Wicks"?'

'You have to ignore my brother, he can be very thoughtless sometimes.'

'Well, at least I didn't' call them "the Wick Weirdos" like some others do – Ow! Stop hitting me!'

'Some people in this village call your aunts weird or wacky,' Beatrice explained. 'It's mainly because your aunt George almost never leaves the house and, when she does, she's a bit scatty. People say they've seen her talking to a cat as if it was talking back. As for your aunt Eddy, well, she's just a bit eccentric, that's all.'

Lucy was quiet for a moment as she took all this in. It made sense to her. After all, she had thought her aunts were weird from the moment she had first met them.

'So why are you dressed up like that anyway?'

'Can we trust you?' Beatrice fixed Lucy with an unblinking stare. 'You've got to promise not to tell anyone what I'm about to tell you.'

'You can trust me. I won't tell anyone, I swear.'

'Very well. We're doing surveillance,' Beatrice replied importantly.

'You're what?'

'We're spying,' Ben clarified.

'Spying on who?'

'Everyone,' Beatrice lowered her voice, looking around to make sure no one could overhear even though they were high up in the tree and there was not a soul in sight.

'Why?'

'Well, there are some very odd things going on in this village and I'm trying to figure out who or what is behind it.'

'Like what?'

'Like, for instance, there are no children in the village.'

'But what about you two?'

'We don't count, we weren't born here. We moved here two years ago when our mother came back to look after our nan.'

'But what about Jake?'

'Who on earth is Jake?'

'He's a boy I met in the woods yesterday. He said he's lived here most of his life.'

'Ben and I know everyone there is to know in this village and there's certainly no boy called Jake living here. He was probably just a traveller weaving you a tall story.'

'But – '

'No buts, Lucy. The fact of the matter is, no children have been born in this village for years. In fact, as far as I can figure out, your aunt Eddy was one of the last babies to be born here.'

'Really, but she's so old.'

'I know! By my calculations, no babies have been born in

the village for at least twenty years.'

'Perhaps people in this village just don't like children so that's why they haven't had any.'

'Well, that might be one answer but our mother says it's the reason she left in the first place. She says the village is cursed and women living here can't fall pregnant. She moved away because she wanted to have children of her own. I personally don't believe the curse nonsense. I think there's some sort of conspiracy going on. I think this village could be a secret government scientific experiment.' Beatrice had lowered her voice further and finished her last sentence in a dramatic flourish.

'Do you have any of proof?'

'Not yet but later this week, Ben and I are going to break into the library.'

'Why the library?'

'Because that's the place where they keep all the village records, both the births and the deaths.'

'So that's it? Just because there are no children in the village, you think the government is responsible?'

'That's not all. I keep these log books of everyone's coming and goings,' Beatrice pulled out a large notebook from a metal box, 'and I've noticed that there have been some strange meetings happening at strange times and places between people.'

'Which people?'

'Well, we're not sure because they always wear hoods so we can't see their faces. But Ben and I plan to get closer to one of these meetings so we can get a better look. Then we'll be able to blow this government conspiracy sky high. All the newspapers in the country will be running the story as headline news.'

Lucy looked from Beatrice to Ben who had been swinging his binoculars back and forth while Beatrice talked, looking somewhat bored.

Ben noticed Lucy studying him. 'Don't look at me, I'm not the nut case who believes in conspiracy theories. I'm just here for something to do. It's pretty boring living in a village where the only other kid is your twin sister. There are only so many computer games even I can play.'

Lucy looked back at Beatrice. 'This all sounds a little far-fetched.'

'Well why don't you join us? I bet you, after just one day doing surveillance with us, you'll believe every word.'

Lucy thought about this for a moment. She didn't have anything better to do. 'Sure, why not?'

'Excellent. Meet us here at 10 o'clock tomorrow morning and we'll get you kitted up in your surveillance gear.'

Just then, Lucy heard her name being called. She looked down from her vantage point on the platform and saw Eddy standing next to the bench peering up.

'I knew I'd find you here,' Eddy smiled up at her.

How does she do it? Lucy thought, as she said goodbye to her new friends, threw the rope ladder over the edge and began to climb down.

CHAPTER 10

NEW ARRIVALS

By the time Eddy and Lucy had arrived home from the village, George was already in the kitchen serving up a roast chicken dinner, complete with potatoes, vegetables and delicious gravy, all from the same big pot she seemed to use for everything. As soon as the meal was over, George once again hurried off back to her workshop muttering, 'I wonder, if I just took half a pinch of badgers' toe…'

Eddy watched George go with a resigned sigh.

As there was no TV, Lucy helped Eddy prepare labels for the potions and cures they had made earlier that day. Each label needed to clearly spell out how to apply the potion. Too much could lead to disastrous effects, too little could be just as bad. Lucy found she didn't mind working in companionable silence, side by side with her aunt and was disappointed when Eddy said it was late and time for bed.

At the very moment Lucy was settling down to sleep, should anyone in Wickham have happened to glance away from their TVs, pulled back their heavy curtains and looked out their windows, they would have noticed another new arrival to their sleepy village. A long black car was silently driving down the main street. It had old fashioned headlights with chrome bumpers and trimmings. If someone had happened to notice the car gliding silently past, they may not have been certain, they may not have been sure but they might have thought they saw small puffs of green smoke coming out of the exhaust as it drove by.

The car came to a juddering stop outside a dishevelled single storey dwelling right at the bottom of Bottoms End Lane. Although no one really noticed that the bungalow was dishevelled or even that there was a house there at all. You see, all around the bungalow was an eight foot high Laurel hedge. The hedge was so thick and overgrown that, to the undiscerning eye, it was almost impossible to even see where the footpath to the house was, let alone the fact that there was a house behind the dense hedge.

A man with greying hair, wearing a faded blue blazer that had more than one patch on the elbows, climbed noiselessly out from behind the steering wheel. He walked around the car and opened the back door.

'Thank you, Harris,' a startling tall, pale thin man said as he unfolded himself out of the back seat. The man had a shock of black hair that was cemented to his head by a generous application of hair gel, creating two stiff waves on either side of his forehead that even the strongest breeze couldn't budge. He was impeccably dressed entirely in black from the top of the turned up collar of his long leather overcoat, to the tips of his shiny pointy shoes.

'Bring the bags would you, Harris, there's a good fellow,' he ordered as he stalked towards the house. He suddenly stopped mid stride and turned back to the car. Bending down to peer inside, he said in rather a bored voice, 'Coming Barry?'

Not waiting for a reply, he marched up the footpath to the front door, the hedge no longer appearing to block the entrance.

The sound of a small struggle came from the back seat as a short, stocky boy tried to squeeze past his bags so he could climb out of the car but, the more he squeezed, the more he became stuck. Eventually, after one final push there was a small popping sound and the boy landed in a heap on the floor, surrounded by bags. Harris wordlessly helped him up and then draped a bag over each of Barry's shoulders which had Barry staggering slightly under the weight as he teetered after the tall man up the footpath.

The front door of the bungalow opened as the tall man reached it. 'Take the bags to the usual rooms would you Harris? Then I'll have a brandy in the library.'

Now, there actually wasn't a library in the house. There just happened to be a room that had a single bookshelf in it that the man liked to refer to as the library. In fact, the bungalow was just a three bedroom brick house that he had purchased many years ago. The house had been empty and left to ruin when he bought it at a ridiculously low price. It had once been owned by a man and woman who used to foster a lot of children. The villagers had long known that the couple weren't the nicest people but had tolerated them because they gave foster children a roof over their heads, food and clothes. But when one of those children went missing and was never seen again, the villagers blamed the couple. No one would talk to them and no one would serve them in the shops. They eventually had no option but to move away. The problem was, no one would buy their house and it was left empty until the tall man had come along. The man liked the villagers to think the house was still empty. It suited his purposes just fine. He also liked to think he was much more important than he really was which is why he had a fancy black car and his own personal butler cum chauffeur cum house servant. The man had advertised for a butler over twenty years ago and Harris had applied. Harris had remained loyal and, for the most part, silent, throughout the years despite the tall man paying him very little and expecting him to do an awful lot. But he never questioned Harris' loyalty. He just assumed that Harris was honoured to work for a great man, such as himself.

'Come along, Barry,' he commanded, 'this house needs

cleaning and putting into order before you can go to bed. Harris can't do it all on his own.'

Barry groaned, 'But Uncle Nigel, if you're a magician, can't you just wave your magic wand and clean the house yourself?'

'I'll have no cheek from you, boy. A *great* magician never wastes his talents on such menial tasks. I'm doing your mother a huge favour by having you stay with me this summer, so you need to pull your weight.'

'Huh, what favour? My mother is paying you to have me,' Barry muttered under his breath as he reached for the bucket and mop.

* * *

The next morning, George once again disappeared into her workroom immediately after breakfast. Lucy joined Eddy in the greenhouse as it was still too early to meet up with Beatrice and Ben. Eddy was just showing Lucy how to repot some Wormwood seedlings when they heard raised voices float over the top of the walled garden.

'Are not!'

'Am too!'

'ARE NOT.'

'AM TOO.'

Abruptly downing tools, they ran to see who was causing the raucous.

Entering the walled garden, they discovered George, hands on hips, face flushed in anger and eyes flashing in fury. In front of her was a well-built man with black wavy hair and dark brown eyes. He had a large suitcase by his feet and also stood with his hands on his hips, face flushed in anger, and eyes flashing just as much fury as George's.

'What's going on?' Eddy looked from George to the strange man and back again.

'This… this man,' George spluttered waving a hand in the man's direction, 'claims to be our new gardener.'

'I am your new gardener,' the man replied slowly through gritted teeth, as if talking to an idiot. 'How many times do I have to tell you?'

'As I keep telling you, sir,' George spat the "sir" out like it was something highly distasteful on the tip of her tongue, 'we already have a gardener.'

'And as I keep telling you, madam, your gardener, my uncle, has retired and I'm here to take his place, as is my duty. How do you think I've got the garden gate key?' He shook a large bunch of keys menacingly at George.

'And as I keep telling you, Clifford would not have retired without telling me.'

'And as I keep –'

'Alright, alright!' Eddy bellowed, raising her hands. She turned to the strange man who was still staring daggers at George. 'Would you mind telling me who you are and explaining this from the beginning, if it's not too much trouble?'

The man's expression softened only marginally as he faced Eddy. 'Fine. My name is William Merchant. Clifford, my uncle, finally had to retire. He no longer had the stamina or strength to continue. Your garden is so big and the plant care so complex, he was just finding it too difficult to manage.'

'But he never mentioned any of this to me,' George complained dejectedly, 'and I talked to Clifford every day. We always had our afternoon cup of tea together.'

'My uncle did mention it to you. Many times in fact, but he was worried you hadn't really been listening. All you ever talked about was that bloomin' cat of yours. From the way my uncle tells it, you're obsessed with the animal.'

George had the decency to look abashed at the truth of this statement.

'Did Clifford really tell me he was retiring?'

'Yes. He told you every day for a month.'

'Actually, I knew he'd gone. I'd sensed it.' Eddy placed a comforting hand on George's arm. 'I'm sorry I didn't mention it. I thought you had sensed it too.'

'Oh dear, I can't believe he's gone.' George sagged against Eddy. 'We didn't even have the chance to say goodbye or give him some sort of retirement gift.'

'Getting to leave this place was gift enough, believe me. He's been counting the minutes since he first arrived. He's given the best years of his life to you people, just because of a mistake his grandfather made and the sacrifice he was prepared to make for our family. We owe him everything.'

'What sacrifice?' George straightened up. 'The way you talk, it makes it sound like Clifford wasn't happy here.'

William let out a bark of mirthless laughter. 'Of course he wasn't happy. Who would be happy being forced to do something you never wanted to do in the first place? Who would be happy having to ask permission every time you wanted to go outside the gates of this property? Why, it's practically modern day slavery.'

'How dare you!' George cried, her face once more flush with anger. 'We didn't force Clifford to do anything and he certainly was not our slave. He was free to leave anytime he wanted.'

'Really? Then why did he ask permission before he went out, huh? Answer me that.'

'Well, it's true, Clifford always asked if it was okay for him to leave but that's just because he's a gentleman with lovely manners. I told him many times he needn't ask but he just gave me an odd look as if I had somehow offended him. I'm sure that's because he felt it would not be fitting to come and go as he pleased. That was his rule, not ours.'

'Pah! That's utter nonsense and you know it. And as luck would have it, I'm the next oldest unmarried male in the family, so the responsibility now falls to me to complete the contract.'

'What contract?' Eddy interjected, looking confused.

'Oh you people are unbelievable. Are you really trying to trick me into adding more time to this confounded bond?' He reached into his pocket and pulled out an ancient silver timepiece attached to a long chain. George and Eddy immediately recognised it as the one they had seen Clifford consult daily. William flipped the lid open with a flick of his finger and looked at the face of the watch. Then he turned it around and shoved it towards them. 'Three years, six months, twenty-three days, two hours, fifty-five minutes and... fourteen seconds. That's how much time is left on this contract and I will not be giving you a second more of my life.'

Lucy strained to catch a glimpse of the watch. It was like nothing she had ever seen before. Rather than just the hour, minute and second hands of a normal watch, this one had three more, all moving at different speeds, all pointing to different circular planes around the perimeter of the watch face.

George looked from the strange watch back to William. 'I'm sorry, but I really don't understand. Clifford has been our gardener as long as I can remember. My mother once mentioned that he owed a debt to our family although she never explained what for. But why on earth do you have to take his place?'

William jabbed a finger at George, 'Don't play games with me, woman. You know as well as I do what will happen to my family if the terms of the contract are not fulfilled. Do you think I want to be here with you if I didn't have to? You're a bunch of cruel, twisted psychopaths.'

George was starting to get angry again, 'That's it. I've had enough of your insults and contempt. We didn't ask you to come. We didn't ask you to take Clifford's place. So you can just take your things and leave.'

'As if I could do that even if I wanted to. I will not take a single step off this property until this watch has wound down to a complete stop. My youngest sister is pregnant and, unlike you lot, I have a heart. I want that baby to live beyond its first year.'

As soon as the words left his mouth, the watch made a loud pinging sound and the hands starting whirling backwards. William stared in dismay. 'Oh that's just great. Now it's three years, seven months and eighteen days. Are you satisfied? Does it feel good to have tricked me into defying the terms of the contract?'

George squared up to him. 'I wasn't trying to trick you, you hateful man.'

'Likely story, you know as well as I do that neither my family nor I are allowed to breathe a single word to anyone about the terms of the agreement. If we do, at best it adds more time to the duration of the contract, at worse my family will suffer a lifetime of sorrow until my family line is no longer.'

The watch pinged and whirred again. 'Oh for heaven's sake! Three years, seven months and twenty-two days. Happy now, you witch?'

George leaped back as if she had been slapped. William glared at her. Lucy was sure she had never seen so much hatred ooze out of one person.

Eddy quickly stepped between them. 'Mr Merchant, as hard as it is for you to believe, my sister and I really do not know what any of this means but it's clear that you are unable to talk about it. It is also clear,' she paused looking meaningfully at George, 'that you are to be with us for a while and we are all going to have to try to get along. Three years is a long time for us to spend together if we can't.'

'Three years, seven months and twenty-two days,' William corrected sullenly.

'Precisely,' Eddy agreed. 'Now, let me show you to the garden cottage where Clifford used to live. I hope you'll be comfortable there.'

William grunted in agreement and picked up his suitcase. Lucy fell into step beside him.

'So have you always been a gardener?'

'Do I look like a gardener to you?'

Lucy looked him up and down. He was smartly dressed in a jacket and a crisp white open necked shirt.

'No, I guess not. What do you do?'

'I'm a doctor.'

'A doctor? Really? That's great. Maybe you can help Aunt George find a cure for her cat Jack. He's got some strange medical condition that she's been trying to cure for years.'

'Help your crazy aunt and her confounded cat? You have

got to be joking.' With that, Mr Merchant picked up his pace and stormed off after Eddy. Lucy decided not to try to catch him up. Here was yet another mystery to add to all the ones she had already discovered since arriving. Mr Merchant was certainly one angry man. He seemed to have a reason to hate Lucy's family but the real question was, what was this contract all about and why did it exist in the first place? And how was Lucy going to solve this particular mystery if Mr Merchant couldn't talk about it and her aunts clearly didn't have the first clue either?

As Lucy walked back towards the house, she noticed a climbing rose bush next to the back door that reached almost to the top of the roof. Most of the roses were a deep blood red colour but some of them were darker, almost black. As Lucy stared at the roses, a small cloud passed over the sun casting Lucy fleetingly in shadow and a shiver ran down her spine.

CHAPTER 11

THE BOY ON BOTTOM END LANE

Lucy borrowed George's bicycle to return to the village for her morning meeting with Beatrice and Ben. She could feel the excitement of seeing her new friends again building up inside her. As she entered the village, a strong gust of wind almost made her lose her balance. She screeched to a halt to narrowly avoid crushing a hat that was hurtling along the ground. A man was running after it and Lucy stooped to pick it up before it could blow away again.

'Thank you, oh thank you.' The man stopped beside her, panting heavily. He pulled out his handkerchief and dabbed at his mostly bald head.

'Confounded weather. Boiling hot, no rain for months and then these freak winds have started blowing up out of nowhere,' the man grumbled although he smiled warmly at Lucy.

'But where are my manners? Let me introduce myself, I'm Reverend Pickles and you must be Lucy.'

Lucy was astounded, 'How do you know my name?'

'Nothing much ever happens in Wickham, my dear, so a new arrival causes quite the kerfuffle, particularly if that new arrival is also a child. Besides Mr Green was telling everyone about you after your visit to his shop yesterday.'

Lucy briefly wondered which Mr Green it had been. It had to be the creepy Mr Green that she'd met first. The second Mr Green had been positively angry to see her and the third Mr Green had just been confused.

'So how are you enjoying your stay so far?'

'Actually, it's turning out better than I expected, although there are a few odd things about this place.'

'Cooee!' a voice trilled from the distance.

Reverend Pickles looked up and muttered something that sounded like "oh bother".

'I, um, just remembered a pressing appointment, I must be off. It was very nice meeting you, Lucy.' He spoke very quickly while trying to wedge his hat more firmly onto his head.

'Cooee! Cooee, Reverend!' The voice was now much closer and louder and was accompanied by a rather rotund lady who was flapping her hands wildly in their direction.

'It's too late for me but save yourself,' the Reverend whispered frantically before turning towards the rapidly advancing lady. 'Why Mrs Smite, how lovely to see you.'

Mrs Smite, who had by now reached them, bent over and lent heavily on the fence post, her large chest rising and falling rapidly as she inhaled big gulps of air.

'Goodness Reverend, did you not hear me calling? Anyone would think you were trying to avoid me if they didn't know better. You might want to get your hearing checked. I was calling rather loudly you know.'

'And how are you today Mrs Smite?' the Reverend asked smoothly.

'Well, as you ask Reverend, not good, not good at all.'

'I am sorry to hear that,' Reverend Pickles replied although he didn't look particularly sorry. 'Whatever is the matter?'

'Well it's the WI, Reverend.'

'The WI?'

'Yes, the Women's Institute.'

'I know what WI stands for, Mrs Smite, but what is the matter with it?'

'Meetings!' declared Mrs Smite.

'Meetings?' the Reverend looked confused. 'I don't understand Mrs Smite. Isn't that what the WI does? Have meetings?'

'Well yes, Reverend, it does but the problem is, someone is organising meetings!' Mrs Smite looked outraged.

'I'm still confused, Mrs Smite, why is that a problem?'

'Because,' Mrs Smite replied slowly as if explaining to a small child, 'I am the head of the local WI, Reverend, and I have *not* been organising these meetings.'

'I see,' replied the Reverend, although he really didn't.

Mrs Smite continued, her voice reverberating with indignity, 'I have discovered mysterious notices about forthcoming WI meetings all over the village, Reverend. Upon scrutiny, I found these notices to be complete fakes. Firstly, the dates and times did not make any sense. Can you believe that one meeting was listed for 8:65 PM and on the 31st of June no less? What nonsense. But it's not just made up times and days of the month that's the issue. The meeting places themselves don't exist. One was in the library basement. Another was supposedly in the anti-chamber of the village hall. Well, we all know that the library has no basement and there is no anti-chamber in the village hall. And if all that wasn't enough, Reverend,' Mrs Smite paused and took a deep breath, 'whoever wrote those notices didn't even have the decency to use the correct coloured paper!'

Mrs Smite was so infuriated her entire body was positively vibrating with it. Noticing Lucy for the first time, Mrs Smite stabbed an accusing finger at her, 'This is the kind of prank children would come up with.'

'Now now, Mrs Smite, let's not jump to any conclusions without knowing all the facts. Why don't you bring those notices to me and we can take a look at them together, see if there are any clues as to who might have put them up.'

'Well that's the problem, Reverend, they have disappeared.'

'Disappeared?'

'Yes, disappeared. I had tried to take them down when I first spotted them but they were stuck fast to the notice board. I immediately went to fetch my staple remover and scissors to try to pry them off but, when I returned, they were gone. No trace left behind whatsoever and this is the third day in a row.'

Mrs Smite turned once again to Lucy. 'You are new to these parts, aren't you girlie? How long have you been here?'

'Ah, um, this is my third day but it wasn't me, I swear. I've never even heard of the WI.'

'Well.' Mrs Smite puffed out her cheeks before letting out her breath all at once, her face red with indignation. Whether she was irate because she thought Lucy was lying or whether it was because Lucy had never heard of the WI was hard to say.

Reverend Pickles quickly stepped in, sensing that Mrs Smite was about to explode, at least verbally, if not literally. Gently grabbing her arm to regain her attention, he said soothingly, 'I am so pleased I've run into you today, Mrs Smite. Mrs Pickles has not stopped talking about that lovely Victorian Sponge you made for the last Ladies Cake & Coffee Morning. As light as a feather, she said it was. I don't suppose I could persuade you to divulge your secret recipe so that Mrs Pickles could make one for me?'

Mrs Smite's expression immediately softened. She playfully tapped Reverend Pickles on the arm although from the look on his face, it hadn't felt like a playful tap. 'Now, now Reverend, you know that I never reveal my baking secrets. However; I'd be more than happy to make you a Victorian Sponge myself. It's such a shame that Mrs Pickles doesn't seem to have the necessary skills in the kitchen. A busy man like yourself needs a lovely cake at afternoon tea to revive his spirits.'

'Quite right,' Reverend Pickles agreed although Lucy got the impression that perhaps he was simply agreeing in order to keep Mrs Smite agreeable. The Reverend steered Mrs Smite slowly away as he asked a question about scones which Mrs

Smite was more than happy to answer in detail. With Mrs Smite's attention diverted, Reverend Pickles put one hand behind his back and motioned for Lucy to go. Lucy didn't need any further encouragement. She climbed soundlessly back onto the bicycle and frantically peddled away in the opposite direction but not before she saw Reverend Pickles's eye close in a hint of a wink.

Lucy was out of breath by the time she reached the bench beneath the tree. She looked up but could see nothing but branches and leaves gently flapping in the breeze.

'I'm here,' she hollered.

Immediately the rope ladder lowered to the ground.

'Hang on, I'm coming down.'

Lucy watched as Beatrice swiftly scrambled down and landed with a flourish next to her.

'Where's Ben?' Lucy looked up at the ladder but no one else was climbing down.

'Dad brought him a new computer game so he wants to play that instead. We'll see him after he's played it to death for a few days, this happens all the time. So it's just you and me today. I thought we could do some on-foot surveillance and I can show you around the village at the same time.'

Beatrice fell into step alongside Lucy as they strolled towards the shops.

'You don't need to tell me if you don't want to, but what did happen to your mum?' Beatrice asked after a moment.

'That's okay, I don't mind talking about it. In fact, it's nice to talk about it for a change, my dad never wants to. He just changes the subject or he says it's too hard to talk about. All I know is that she became really sick after she had me. At least, that's what I think happened. My dad will only say that she "tried to hold on and stay in this world for us" but she wasn't strong enough and we lost her.'

'Oh gosh, I'm so sorry.'

'The worse thing is, he won't take me to her graveside or even tell me where she is buried.'

'That must be really hard for you.'

'In a way, although, I've never known anything different. It's always been just me and my dad so I'm used to it. I just wish he would stop avoiding my questions and tell me something straight for once. I'm not a kid anymore. I'm practically a grown up but he still treats me like a child.'

'Tell me about it, my mum is so annoying. I'm eleven but she still wants to do my hair and tries to tell me what clothes I should wear but our tastes are very different. She likes flowing skirts with lots of sparkles and, well, I like this.' Beatrice pointed to her jeans and plain coloured T-shirt. 'I've discovered that the plainer the clothes I wear, the less people tend to take notice of me, which is perfect for spying.'

'What does your dad do?' Lucy asked.

'He's a boring accountant. He travels a lot so we often only see him at weekends. He says he has to travel because of his work but I overheard him tell my mum that this village gives him the creeps. I don't think he was very happy to leave the city and move here but when my nan got really ill two years ago, we had to come. She's quite frail and she can't really be on her own and there's only my mum to take care of her.'

'How do you like living in a village? You must miss the city.'

'Not really, well, not anymore. It was tough at first but I didn't have a lot of friends in the city so it's not like I had many people to miss. Not many girls my age like to spend their time spying and uncovering secret government conspiracies. I think Ben's found it harder. He was very popular and had lots of friends but he soon made friends in our new school in Snordom, which is the closest town. It's only the school holidays that bug him because he doesn't get to see his mates as much. Our mum can't drive and the bus takes so long to get to Snordom.'

They had by now walked through the centre of the village and were ambling down a side road. There were less old stone cottages here and more modern brick houses.

'Hang on a minute,' Beatrice put her hand out to stop Lucy in her tracks. 'That car has never been on Bottom End Lane before.' She pointed to a long black car with chrome trimmings. 'I'm just going to write down its license plate number.' She pulled a notebook out of her jeans pocket and started to make notes with a pencil.

Just then they heard a door slam and a voice call out, 'I'm going exploring.'

A short, slightly chubby boy came into view between some tall hedges muttering, 'Not that you care,' as he looked down and kicked a stone with his shoe. The stone ricocheted off the pavement and hit him on the shin. 'Ow!' The boy bent down to rub it.

'Quick,' Beatrice whispered grabbing Lucy by the hand, 'we need to hide.' She pulled Lucy behind the nearest tree trunk but it wasn't big enough to conceal them both.

Don't let him see me. Don't let him see me, Lucy willed as she flattened herself against the tree and wished with all her might that the boy wouldn't notice her.

'Don't think I can't see you hiding behind that tree,' the boy called. Beatrice sighed and stepped out reluctantly to face him.

Lucy also pushed herself away from the tree.

'Whoa! Where did you come from?' the boy pointed an accusing finger at Lucy.

'From behind the tree. You saw us, you said so.'

'I only saw her,' the boy pointed at Beatrice. 'You just appeared out of thin air,' he exclaimed, clearly startled.

'Don't be silly, I was here all along,' Lucy replied but the boy just stared at her open mouthed as if she had two heads.

Taking charge of the situation, Beatrice extended her hand formally, 'My name is Beatrice Naran, and this is my new friend Lucy. Who are you?'

The boy reluctantly focused on Beatrice. Placing his hand in hers with a surprisingly firm shake he replied, 'My name is Barry Barrymore.'

'Barry Barrymore?'

'Yes, alright, get all your jokes out now. My mother thought she was being clever when she named me. It's a stupid name.'

Lucy immediately felt sorry for this boy. 'I think it's a very sophisticated name. Besides my last name is Spratt and all the kids at school call me Splat so I'm not going to be making fun of anyone's name.'

Barry smiled gratefully at Lucy.

'So then, Barry Barrymore, what brings you to the wonderful village of Wickham?' said Beatrice taking command of the conversation once more.

'I guess you could say I'm on holiday with my uncle, although it doesn't feel much like a holiday.'

'Why's that?'

'Well, because my mother has gone on a cruise for the summer. She's looking for husband number four and said I'd cramp her style if I went with her, whatever that means. So she sent me to stay with my Uncle Nigel instead. I think she's paying him to have me because he's certainly never been interested in spending time with me before. He says he'll train me to be his assistant but I don't believe him.'

'What does your uncle do?'

'He's a magician.'

'Is he any good?'

'Nah, he's rubbish, at least that's what my mum says. She says you can totally see him stick his hand up his sleeve to make things disappear. I haven't seen his magic show in years so he might be a bit better now but I doubt it.'

'What's a magician doing in a small out of the way village like Wickham?' Beatrice mused.

'He's got some sort of magician's gig, so he tells me. He says we'll be here for a couple of weeks, maybe longer, depending on how things pan out.'

'Do you know any tricks then?'

'Nah. I've asked my uncle to teach me but he won't. It's really lame. Not much fun for school holidays, that's for sure. What about you guys? What are you doing?'

'We're going spying,' Lucy replied at the same time as Beatrice declared, 'We're not doing anything.'

Barry laughed good-naturedly, 'So which one are you doing

then, spying or nothing?'

Beatrice steadily looked him up and down and then slowly walked around him. Barry's smile fell off his face as he followed her movements nervously with his head whilst remaining rooted to the spot.

'I suppose you will do,' Beatrice finally declared, 'but can you be trusted? Can you keep a secret?' She pushed her face up close to Barry's so he had to look cross eyed to focus on her.

'Ye-e-ss,' he stuttered and then once again more assuredly, 'yes, I can definitely be trusted.'

Beatrice stood back, this time with an approving look on her face, 'I think you'll do just fine. Welcome to the club.'

'There's a club?' Barry enquired enthusiastically, 'I've always wanted to be in a club.'

'Yes, of course there's a club,' Beatrice replied importantly, 'and I'm the leader.'

'What's it called?'

'Um, it's called…' Beatrice looked around for inspiration, 'it's called… Wickham's Undercover Spy & Surveillance Agency,' she finished with a flourish.

'Ha ha ha, that's hilarious,' came a voice from behind them. They turned to see Ben walking casually down the road towards them.

'What's so funny about that?' Beatrice asked hands on hips.

'Wickhams Undercover Spy & Surveillance Agency. WUSSA for short. You really are a WUSSA sometimes Beatrice.'

'Oh shut up. Besides, what are you doing here? I thought I wouldn't see you for days.'

'Well, I figured I can play my new game anytime but it's not everyday someone our age comes to the village and now there's another one. You alright mate? Ben's the name.'

'I'm Barry,' Barry muttered, suddenly feeling self-conscious in front of this confident character.

'Excellent, good to meet you Barry and good to see you again Lucy. It looks like we've got quite a party going on here. What are we all going to do now, Bea? I'm guessing you're trying to be in charge again.' Beatrice scowled at her brother but stepped forward in front of him to face the others.

'Well, Lucy and I were going to do some spying but there's too many of us now and we'll be noticed so I think perhaps we should initiate the latest member of our crew into the club.'

'Ooh, an initiation ceremony, sounds like fun.' Ben rubbed his hands together with a mischievous twinkle in his eye.

'Is it going to hurt?' Barry asked in a quiet voice, wrapping his arms around himself for comfort.

'Of course not,' Beatrice reassured him, 'we would never hurt you, you're our friend now. Besides, I haven't made up my mind what the initiation ceremony should consist of. The first point of order is where to have it? The tree house will be a bit crowded.'

'I know,' Lucy put up her hand as if she was in the classroom and then quickly lowered it but not before she saw Ben smirk.

'What do you have in mind, Lucy?'

'There's a clearing in the woods. It has four stone pillars laid out in a circle, like four points of a compass. In the middle is a small pond with crystal clear water. That would be perfect for an initiation ceremony.'

'Are you sure you remember correctly, Lucy? Beatrice and I know every inch of the woods and we've never come across a clearing like the one you've described.'

'Ben is right, Lucy. We really do know every inch of this village and the woods and we've never seen anything that matches your description.'

'I'm not lying, I promise you. I was only there yesterday, I can show you.'

'I've not seen the woods, with or without stone pillars, so I'm up for some exploring,' Barry declared giving Lucy a supportive smile.

'Sure, why not,' Ben shrugged, 'it's not like we've got anything better to do. Come on Bea, we're bound to find a good place in the woods for the initiation ceremony anyway.'

CHAPTER 12

STONE PILLARS

The group of new friends chatted all the way to the woods. Ben seemed genuinely delighted to have company other than his sister. He played the fool, flicking Beatrice's hair, doing silly jigs and telling lame jokes. Lucy liked Ben a lot but she was also really starting to warm to Barry. He had a quiet but clever wit and was happy making himself the butt end of a joke. As for Beatrice, she was clearly enjoying being in charge of a bigger group for a change. She hustled them along, chiding anyone who didn't keep up and, in no time, they had arrived at the edge of the woods.

As they entered, Lucy looked around to get her bearings but the little tracks disappearing into the woods all looked identical to her.

'Which way,' Ben asked with a laugh, 'or are you finally going to admit you made that bit up about the stone pillars?'

'I didn't make it up,' Lucy declared crossly. She looked around again but still nothing seemed familiar. Then she remembered Eddy's instructions so she closed her eyes and concentrated very hard on what she wanted to find. In her mind, she could see the clearing with the stone pillars as if she was floating above it. Then the image shifted and travelled at speed above the woods until the picture stopped and floated over the exact spot where the four of them stood. Lucy could clearly see the tops of each of their heads and then, in an instant, the image disappeared. She opened her eyes and blinked hard. That was strange.

'Are you okay?' Beatrice reached out for her arm, 'You've gone very pale.'

'I'm fine. Come on, it's this way.' Lucy beckoned to the others as she led them through the woods. After a short while, they emerged into the clearing.

'There you are,' Lucy pointed triumphantly over to where the four pillars stood shrouded in mist, 'the perfect place for an initiation ceremony.'

'You've gone batty,' Ben replied.

'There's nothing here,' Barry scratched his head in confusion.

'Are you sure you're okay?' Beatrice put a comforting arm around her.

Lucy shrugged it off. 'What are you all on about? There are the four pillars, right there in the centre of the clearing, can't you see them? They're there in that big patch of mist.' She stood with one hand on her hip and the other pointing wildly at the pillars.

The three looked at Lucy, looked towards where she was pointing, looked at each other and shook their heads.

'She's clearly as barmy as her aunts,' Ben murmured.

Beatrice, noticing the crestfallen look on Lucy's face, clapped her hands together to get everyone's attention.

'This clearing will work perfectly anyway. Why don't you boys gather some sticks to make an altar we can use to pledge our allegiance to the club. In the meantime, I will work on the ceremony to make it all official.'

'Sure thing Bea, just make sure you don't bore us all to an early death with your fondness for using very long words and for taking a very long time to say them.'

Beatrice tried to swat her brother but he leapt out of reach, laughing, as he and Barry moved across the clearing in search of sticks and twigs.

Lucy looked at them dejectedly as they moved away. She didn't understand. Why were they pretending they couldn't see the pillars? How could they possibly not see them?

A rustling in the trees made Lucy turn just in time to see Jake step out into the clearing. His face lit up when he saw her.

'I knew you would come back. I've been waiting –' he stopped midsentence as he realised that Lucy was not alone. He looked suspiciously at the three children on the other side of the clearing. Ben and Barry were busy gathering sticks and Beatrice was busy giving them instructions.

'Who are they?' he hissed as he jabbed an accusing finger in their direction.

'They're my friends.' Lucy couldn't help feeling a little bit proud that she could use the word "friends" having spent so many years without any.

'That didn't take long.' There was a hint of spite in Jake's voice. 'You've been here all of three days and you already have three friends.'

'Four,' Lucy replied.

'What?'

'Four. I have four friends. You were my first.'

Jake's expression softened slightly. 'Well who are these *friends* anyway?'

'Beatrice and Ben are brother and sister, twins actually, from the village. I met them when I went to the shops with Eddy.'

'I thought they looked familiar. What about that chubby boy, I've not seen him before?' Jake pointed at Barry.

'That's not a very nice thing to say. Barry is just visiting. He arrived yesterday with his uncle. He's a little bit like me that way, having to spend his holiday with a relative.'

Jake grunted but didn't say anything further.

'What I don't understand, Jake, is why they can't see the pillars? Either they can't see them or they are pretending not to, which would be cruel and I didn't think they were the cruel type.'

Jake was studying each of her new friends with intensity. 'They can't see the pillars because they haven't been invited to see them,' he said distractedly.

Lucy looked at Jake with a confused frown, 'What does that mean?'

Jake suddenly looked guilty, 'Actually never mind. Forget I said anything.'

'Well, I can't forget. You need to tell me. What do you mean I need to invite them to see the pillars?'

Jake sighed and ran his fingers through his thick black hair. 'This is probably something you should talk to your aunts about.'

'Well, I'm talking to you. I'm sick of all this weird stuff going on and nobody speaking to me about it.'

Jake sighed again but remained obstinately silent.

Lucy tried a different tact, 'How come you and I can see the pillars but the others can't?'

'Well, you can see them because everyone in your family can, always have, always will. And I can see them because I was invited to see them.'

'Who invited you?'

'George.'

'My aunt George?'

'Yes.'

'When did she do that?'

'Er, a long time ago. Long before you arrived.'

'So all I have to do is to invite Ben, Beatrice and Barry to see the pillars and they will?' Lucy asked hopefully.

'Yes, but Lucy, you need to be sure you can trust them.'

'Of course I can trust them, they're my friends.'

Before Jake could protest further, Lucy raised her voice and called out to the others. When they looked up and noticed Lucy was not alone, they quickly ran over.

'Who do we have here?' Ben asked with an impish grin, 'Have you picked up yet another stray Lucy?'

Jake bristled. 'I'm not a stray.'

'What a week this has turned out to be, hey Bea? First Lucy arrives, then Barry and now we have a new stray.'

'Just ignore him,' Beatrice interjected. 'He's only trying to get a rise out of you. I'm Beatrice.'

'This is Jake,' Lucy began, 'He's the one I told you about.'

Beatrice gazed at Jake with interest. 'I've not seen you around before, Jake, and I spend a lot of time exploring the village. Where do you live?'

'I think Lucy has something she wants to tell you,' Jake blurted out, changing the subject. Beatrice gave him a suspicious look but turned to Lucy.

'What is it Lucy?'

Lucy felt her face flush with embarrassment as she realised everyone was now staring at her. 'I, um, well...'

Jake quickly stepped in front of her, 'Lucy, forget what I said, this is a really bad idea.'

Defiantly, Lucy straightened her shoulders and looked at Beatrice with more confidence than she felt, 'Beatrice, I'd like to invite you to see the pillars.'

Beatrice started to smirk at this bizarre announcement but her eyes followed Lucy's hand pointing towards the pillars and her mouth dropped open.

'Pillars! Stone pillars! Where did they come from?'

Lucy quickly turned to Barry who was looking from Beatrice to Lucy and back again as if they were mad. 'Barry, I invite *you* to see the pillars.'

Barry's mouth also fell open as the mist cleared and four aged stone pillars emerged before him. 'I see them! I see them!' he exclaimed excitedly.

Ben laughed dryly. 'Ha ha. You guys are hilarious. There are no pillars.'

'And Ben, I would like to invite *you* to see the pillars too.'

It was Ben's turn to gape as the stones appeared before him.

Lucy was overjoyed that her new friends could finally see the pillars and would no longer think she was some sort of lying lunatic. Jake stepped up behind her and whispered in your ear, 'I hope you know what you've done.'

She turned around feeling cross he was trying to ruin her moment. 'I know exactly what I've done. My friends didn't believe me before and now they do. It's very simple.'

'Is it? Are you sure you can trust them?'

'Why do you keep going on about trust? What's the big deal about four stone pillars anyway?'

'Oh Lucy, you have no idea. You really need to speak with your aunts.' With that, he moved to the edge of the clearing and quickly disappeared into the woods.

Lucy stared after Jake and a feeling close to dread started to form in the pit of her belly but, before she could dwell on it, Ben rushed over.

'Come on, Lucy, tell us your secret? How did you make the mist just disappear like that? It was so thick we couldn't see the stones before.'

Lucy shrugged, 'I guess you just weren't looking properly.' The truth was, Lucy really didn't know. None of this made sense to her. She was trying to think of a logical explanation but was coming up empty.

Beatrice gave her a quizzical look. 'Perhaps but there's something else you're right about, this is the perfect place for our ceremony,' she pronounced.

* * *

Later that evening, after the WUSSA initiation ceremony was over and the four new friends were all officially members, Beatrice crept into Ben's room after lights out and they whispered excitedly about how they had never seen those stone pillars before even though they had explored every inch of the woods many times over. And wasn't it almost like magic how the mist lifted and the pillars appeared? Although of course Ben scoffed at the idea of magic and Beatrice quickly agreed that there must be some sort of scientific explanation. A few streets away, Barry couldn't believe that, for the first time in his life, he had the undivided attention of an adult. He had been so excited about his day, making new friends the moment he stepped outside the house and being part of an initiation ceremony in the middle of a mysterious clearing, that he simply had to share it with his uncle, even though he knew Uncle Nigel was never the slightest bit interested in Barry or what he did. But, as Barry had started to recount his day over a dinner of sausage, egg and chips, his uncle had laid down his knife and fork, folded his hands in front of him and listened intently. He even asked Barry a few questions which Barry tried to answer in as much detail as possible. At the end of the retelling, his uncle had said "Good boy" which made Barry's cheeks flush with pleasure. All the while, Harris sat silently in the corner, shining Uncle Nigel's shoes until his face reflected in them.

Over on the other side of the woods, as Lucy snuggled down under her covers, she couldn't quite shake the feeling of unease that maybe she had done the wrong thing today. But for the life of her, she couldn't figure out why it would have been wrong. It was just a feeling she had inside.

CHAPTER 13

A MEETING IN THE DARK

Nigel straightened his tie, adjusted the red carnation in his lapel, and looked nervously over his shoulder. The confidence he had felt when requesting this meeting was rapidly evaporating. He attempted to lean casually against the bridge wall, feigning great interest in the stream running beneath it although the light of the summer day had almost faded to blackness so it was pretty hard to see anything really. A small vein beneath his left eye twitched in time to his accelerated heartbeat. He looked around again but couldn't see anything in the growing gloom so made a show of smoothing down his trouser pants instead, although he was actually trying to wipe the sweat off of his clammy palms. He kept checking his watch. The longer he waited the less certain he was of what he should do. Barry's revelations had initially confirmed the need for this meeting but now he wasn't so sure. There wasn't anyone around as far as the eye could see, which wasn't very far, and he was starting to feel increasingly uneasy about waiting out here, all alone, in this secluded spot outside of the village.

'Right then, what's all this about, Nigel?' A voice boomed from behind him.

'Aah!' Nigel was so startled his feet physically left the ground as a hooded cloaked figure emerged out of shadows.

'Councillor, you came.' Nigel half bowed and didn't know if he felt relieved or anxious now that his wait had finally come to an end.

'Well of course I did, Nigel, you summoned me using the emergency protocol, which is most irregular, I can assure you. This had better be good.'

'Yes, um, yes, well you see, there's something you need to know, something important.'

'Fluffy! Fluffy, stop that this instant!' the Councillor retorted.

Confused, Nigel glanced down and saw a very small, very white and very fluffy dog at the end of a lead the Councillor was tugging. Fluffy, it appeared, had taken objection to the Councillor's ankle and had its teeth firmly planted around it.

'Geroff.' The Councillor's leg shook backwards and forwards violently sending Fluffy into the air before falling to the ground with a yelp.

'Pick that dog up, Nigel, I can't stand the beast. I just brought it along as a cover. It's very risky us meeting out in the open like this where everyone can see.'

Nigel picked up the squirming little dog and looked around again. There was still not a soul in sight and night was almost fully upon them so the chances of being spotted were very slim.

'So come on, get on with it, I haven't got all night.'

'Um, yes, of course, certainly.' Nigel shifted Fluffy, who was still squirming frantically, to his other hip. 'Well, the thing is –'

'What I can't understand,' the Councillor interrupted, 'is why headquarters sent you of all people? They said they were sending reinforcements but I was expecting a higher calibre than you. The energy readings are off the chart since that wicked little girl arrived. I would have expected HQ to have sent their best people for this one.'

'Well, that's the thing, HQ didn't send for me.'

'Whatever do you mean, Nigel? Why on earth are you here if HQ didn't send you?'

'Well, it's because I *felt* it, Councillor.'

'Felt what? What on earth are you talking about? Talk sense man.'

'I *felt* the energy surge,' Nigel confessed sheepishly, not daring to meet the Councillor's eyes.

'You felt it? You *felt* it? How on earth did you feel it? Explain yourself. Spit it out. Well, I'm waiting.'

Nigel was starting to wish he hadn't called this meeting. It wasn't going the way he had rehearsed in his head.

'It started that night twenty years ago, the night Cybil and I went to Wicker House.'

'Ah yes,' the Councillor sighed, 'that was a most unfortunate incident.'

'It was indeed. It had never been our intention for the mother to die.'

'I'm not talking about the mother you fool!' the Councillor hissed. 'I don't give two hoots about the death of that filthy witch, Josephine. No, what was unfortunate is that Cybil died too. If only she lived and you had died instead, that would have been a much better outcome. Cybil was so much cleverer, so very talented. She was a master at deception and she had only just had her hair done too. Such a waste, such a loss to our cause.'

'Yes Councillor,' Nigel replied apologetically.

'Well, we have to make the best of a bad situation. It has been twenty years since the last energy spike. I've been in touch with HQ and they've activated all the existing agents in the area and the new recruits have arrived.'

The Councillor started to tug on Fluffy's lead, trying to pull the dog out of Nigel's arms, indicating the conversation was over. Nigel tightened his grip.

'Should I go on telling you about how I felt the energy

surge?'

'What? Oh alright then, if you must.' The annoyance in the Councillor's voice was clear and Nigel's necktie suddenly felt too tight.

He tugged on it nervously. 'Well, at first, I didn't realise anything had happened. After the energy pulse killed both the witch and Cybil, I felt rather strange for weeks but I just put it down to the shock. You know, literally the shock of almost being electrocuted. But then peculiar things started to happen.' Nigel looked expectantly at the Councillor.

The Councillor was picking at some dead moss which clung to the bridge wall and couldn't have looked any more disinterested in what Nigel was saying but finally replied, 'Oh alright then, I'll bite, what peculiar things happened?'

Nigel perked up, 'Well, you know how I've always been an illusionist in my spare time when not on WI business, performing magic tricks at holiday resorts, that sort of thing?'

'You are hardly ever called on WI business, Nigel, but I'll humour you. Go on.'

'Well, it's just that they are not tricks anymore?'

'What do you mean? Can you please get to the point, this is becoming tiresome and I need to get Fluffy home before anyone notices he's missing.'

'Well, I mean, I can actually perform magic now, not just pretend to perform it.'

'*What?*' the Councillor's voice came out in a low, menacing hiss. 'Are you saying you're a *witch?*' The last word was spat out with all the disgust the Councillor could muster.

Nigel staggered back as if he'd been slapped, 'No, no, I'm just saying that I seem to have inherited it – I think when Josephine died her powers were somehow transferred to me.'

'I'm finding this very hard to believe, Nigel, but if what you're saying is true then we've been able to successfully extract a witch's powers. We've been able to transfer a witch's power to a WI member who's survived.' The Chancellor's hands rubbed together gleefully. 'Oh this is good news, Nigel. Wait until I tell the Witchfinder General, he's going to be so pleased with me. This could be the breakthrough we've been waiting for to finally get rid of this magical pestilence once and for all.'

Nigel wasn't sure why the Witchfinder General would be pleased with the Councillor when it was he, Nigel, who had the powers but he didn't like to disagree. He was just happy the Councillor appeared to approve of him for once.

'Yes, indeed and, if you permit me, I can now begin a small demonstration of my abilities –'

The Councillor waved an impatient hand, 'I haven't got time to see a silly magic show, Nigel. Besides, as you well know magic is an abomination on this earth and needs to be wiped out for the greater good of all humanity!'

'Er, yes, Councillor, of course,' Nigel stammered, 'but for us to eliminate magic isn't it better that we know how it works. Ever since that night twenty years ago, I have felt a strange kind of power pulsating through my blood. It gets stronger when I'm near water. And it's been a lot stronger since I arrived in the village.'

'Hmm, this is all very interesting, Nigel, very interesting indeed. So you say your powers have got stronger now that you are physically closer to those filthy hags, eh? Well, this is quite a discovery I've made.'

'So what's the plan, Councillor? What would you like me to do?'

'*You?*' the Councillor looked Nigel up and down with undisguised contempt. 'Well Nigel, right now, I need *you* to keep a low profile. I'll let you know if you're needed. I need to report my findings to HQ straight away. I'm sure they will want to question you, probably run a few tests too. If what you say is true, then this is the first known instant where a witch's powers have transferred to another human. Normally, as you know, when a witch is killed, the poor blighter doing the killing meets the exact same death. We need to figure out how come Cybil was electrocuted and not you and how come the witch's powers were transferred to you. Then we need to figure out how to replicate it. I want to strip each one of those evil sorceresses of their depraved powers. Then, if we still need to kill them, we can without killing ourselves in the process. Instructions will follow Nigel. I won't risk another meeting out in the open like this so be on the lookout for a message.'

The Councillor grabbed Fluffy out of Nigel's arms and slipped back into the shadows, melting into the darkness before Nigel could utter another sound, his revelations about what Barry had unwittingly discovered still unspoken.

This had definitely not gone according to plan. Nigel had imagined the Councillor being delighted with his announcement and showering him with praise and rewards; a more senior position perhaps; a meeting with the Witchfinder General himself even. Instead, Nigel felt like even more of an outcast than he had before.

Nigel was just a new recruit when the whole unfortunate incident with Cybil had happened. It had been his first assignment for the Witchfinder Institute, known as the WI for short, both for convenience and for the handy confusion with the Women's Institute. It had also been Nigel's last assignment. The WI had seemed to conveniently forget all about him after he handed in his report following the deaths of Cybil and the witch. Cybil had been his senior agent for the few months leading up to the incident. He knew Cybil's own reports about his performance had been less than glowing. She had told him so many times. So it hadn't surprised Nigel when he received a letter shortly after advising him to relocate to Swansea and wait further instructions. Those further instructions never came, which frustrated and angered Nigel in equal measure. Ever since he was a young trainee magician and had stumbled into a secret WI meeting, he had wanted to be a part of the WI. He could scarcely believe what he had overheard. Real witches using real magic roaming freely around the country, using their powers for no good and to further their own diabolical causes. As an illusionist who prided himself with misdirection and the sleight of hand to convince his audience that he was using magic, the thought of people actually being magical, of being able to perform magic, had unsettled him greatly. He had volunteered there and then to join this secret society. Three months later, after completing his initiation training, he had been sent to Wickham. And three months after that, he had effectively been kicked out of the WI. He had been plotting his glorious return ever since. He wanted to prove his worth to the WI. Show them what a mistake they had made by summarily dismissing him all those years ago. He wanted to be the one who finally put an end to the vile witches. And, now that he had powers of his own, he knew he could do it too. He would show them. He would show them all and then they would be coming to him, begging him to tell them what to do. They would finally show him the respect he deserved. He certainly wasn't going to tell any of the WI about how his very own nephew had befriended the witch-child. Oh no, he would keep that bit of tantalising information to himself. He didn't want to reveal all his tricks after all. Not yet, anyway. With a satisfied smile, Nigel headed back towards the village.

CHAPTER 14

HOUSE STOLE MY DOORS

Lucy woke up the next morning to the sun streaming through her windows. She swiftly dressed and made her way to the bathroom to wash her face and brush her teeth. She was only just getting used to the bathroom entrance. This morning, more than any time before, the wall of her bedroom looked like exactly that, just a wall. But she knew it was an optical illusion so she walked confidently towards the entrance.

'Ow!' Lucy banged straight into the wall. She must have misjudged it. Rubbing her nose, which had taken the brunt of the collision, she felt along the surface to find the gap, but the wall was solid beneath her fingers. She spread her arms wider and kept on groping but still couldn't find the opening. Feeling a little alarmed, she started to run her hand along the length of her entire bedroom, even where she absolutely knew the bathroom couldn't be, but all she felt was solid wall. When she had made a full circle and was back to the spot she had started from, panic really started to swell within her. She pushed on the wall with all her might. Perhaps the entrance had closed somehow. Eddy hadn't said there was a bathroom door but maybe she had forgotten to mention it. Perhaps the door looked exactly like the wall and it had somehow closed in the night. Lucy carefully inched herself around the room once more, this time feeling up and down the wall with both hands, trying to find anything that resembled a door, like a handle or even some hinges. She found nothing. The panic that had been slowly rising accelerated into full scale terror. It was time to find her aunts. She ran across the room and threw open the bedroom door. Then she screamed.

Behind her bedroom door was a solid brick wall. Lucy pounded her fists against it. 'Help! Let me out! Let me out!'

She couldn't ever remember feeling so scared. She was sealed shut inside her own bedroom. She ran over to the window to see if there was a way to climb down, even though she was more than three stories above ground, just as a loud thud came from inside her wardrobe.

Lucy frantically looked around for a weapon, for something she could use to protect herself. Grabbing the heaviest book off the shelf, she swiftly crouched beside the wardrobe, book raised ready to bring it down on whoever or whatever emerged.

More thomps and thumps came from inside the wardrobe, this time accompanied by grunts and groans. Lucy raised the book higher just as the cupboard door burst open and Eddy tumbled out onto the floor.

Startled, Lucy dropped the book as Eddy picked herself up and dusted off her clothes.

'House, this is just going from the absurd to the ridiculous!' Eddy shouted out.

The windows rattled in response.

Eddy spotted Lucy cowering behind the wardrobe. 'Ah, Lucy, there you are. I had a sense that you needed me. Sorry it took me so long to get here. House has been up to her tricks overnight and it took me a while to figure out how to get to you. Are you ready for breakfast?'

Lucy was so stunned by her aunt's astonishing appearance

she was momentarily tongue-tied. 'I haven't been able to wash yet,' she eventually stammered. 'My bathroom's gone.'

Eddy looked around the room slowly. 'Ah yes, so it is. I'm sure I can find where it has got to on the way to the kitchen. Come on.' With that, she turned and climbed back into the wardrobe leaving Lucy with no option but to follow her.

Lucy soon discovered that where the back of the wardrobe had once been was now a narrow wooden rickety staircase that led down a dark and dingy stairwell, through many twists and turns, to a small hallway adjoining the kitchen. Curiously, off one of these twists and turns, Lucy had found the tell-tale optical illusion entrance to her bathroom although, without the rest of her bedroom wall next to it, the entrance was pretty obvious standing out against the dusty, cob-webbed covered crumbling brick wall of the stairwell.

After a quick wash, they arrived at the kitchen. Following the dinginess of the stairwell, Lucy had to blink a few times before her eyes adjusted to the brightness of the room. The sun was spilling through the windows and Lucy could hear birds singing outside. The pot was bubbling away on the stove and a welcoming aroma drifted across the room. The kitchen was filled with light and Lucy felt her spirits lift after the frightening start to the day.

'Today you have porridge with cinnamon and syrup for your breakfast. George sensed that you might need something a bit more substantial and comforting this morning.'

Eddy filled a bowl to the brim and Lucy sat down at the table, suddenly realising how hungry she was. After a few quick mouthfuls, Lucy asked, 'Where is Aunt George?'

A disapproving frown flittered over Eddy's face before she smiled brightly. 'She was up early this morning as usual. She took a cup of tea to Mr Merchant but he didn't want it and, ever since, she's shut herself away in the workshop where she always is,' Eddy said with a hint of bitterness.

Lucy put her spoon down. It was time to get some answers.

'Aunt Eddy? What happened this morning? There is something odd going on and I can't keep ignoring it. I can't keep finding excuses for the strange things that have happened ever since I arrived or keep thinking it's a figment of my imagination because it's not is it?'

Eddy exhaled slowly and smoothed out the folds of her crimson red skirt.

'It's difficult to explain, Lucy. Your dad made us promise.'

'But he's not here now and this is just getting bonkers. I mean, come on, the door of my bedroom is walled up overnight and a new entrance appears in my wardrobe? I didn't imagine that and there's no logical explanation for how it happened. You have to tell me the truth.'

Eddy sighed again. 'You're right, Lucy. I think it's time you —'

But she never got to finish her sentence. A blood curdling scream rang out from deep within the house.

Eddy jumped to her feet. 'Wait here,' she cried as she ran off in the direction of the scream.

For once Lucy decided not to do as she was told and hastened after her aunt as silently as she could. But she soon lost sight of her as Eddy raced through rooms, down corridors and across hall ways that Lucy had never seen before.

Just when Lucy thought she would have to give up and try to find her way back to the kitchen, she heard a commotion coming from somewhere close by. It sounded like George shouting. She followed the sound along the corridor. As she turned the corner, she came across George pounding her fists against a bare wall. George had tears of frustration running down her cheeks. Not sure what to do, Lucy stepped back, crouching down behind a chest of drawers.

'Let me in! Let me in!' George banged her fists even harder against the wall. 'This is not funny, House, you let me in this instance. You bring back the door!' George was banging her fists so hard, plaster dust flew in the air.

Eddy was trying to put her arms around her but George kept shaking her off as she pounded against the wall.

Eventually George turned around and slowly sank to the floor.

'House won't let me in,' she whimpered into her hands.

'House won't let you into where?' Eddy was trying to get her bearings as to what part of the house they were now in.

'The workshop!' George cried. 'House stole my doors. I only left for a minute to get some more Mouldy Mouse Droppings from the store room and, when I came back, House had removed all the doors and all the windows. I've been looking for hours and all I can find are solid bare walls where the doors should be. I know it's in there Eddy, I can feel it, I can feel it!' Eddy nodded her head. If George said she could sense something, she was always right.

'How am I supposed to help Jack now?' George's eyes shimmered with a fresh batch of unshed tears. 'How can I fix what I did if I can't work on the cure?'

George started to moan and slumped against Eddy. Eddy cradled her head as she gently rocked her back and forth.

'Look, George, I know you might not want to hear this but perhaps it's a good thing. You know as well as I do that things have changed ever since Lucy arrived. We simply can't ignore it anymore. Something is happening, something is coming and it doesn't feel good. House clearly knows it too otherwise why would she be acting so strangely? We can't carry on pretending that everything is fine when it's clearly not.'

George whimpered a little louder and buried her head further into Eddy's arms.

'Look at me, George.' Eddy tenderly lifted her head in both hands until they were eye to eye. 'You know it's true. It's time to stop burying our heads in the sand, you with your cure for Jack and me with my potions. We need to stop all that and focus on Lucy. We need to figure out what's going on before it's too late.'

George tried to look away but Eddy's grip was firm. George sniffed loudly, wiped a hand across her nose and then along her clothes.

'Well,' she hiccupped, 'it may have something to do with the prophecy.'

Eddy abruptly dropped her hands.

'Prophecy! What prophecy?'

George fiddled with the hemline of her shirt and avoided Eddy's eyes. 'There's an ancient prophecy to do with our family. I can't really remember. It's something about being keepers of something or other.'

Eddy leapt up in disbelief. 'And you've never thought to tell me? When all this weird stuff started happening, you thought it best just to carry on shutting yourself away in your workshop trying to find a cure for your cat!'

'Well, I, um, didn't think it was important, not as important as finding a cure for Jack and he's not just my cat. That's a hurtful thing to say.' George continued to fiddle with her hemline, bowing her head low.

'You didn't *think* it was important. George! How could you? I can sense something is wrong and if I can sense it, then you must be in sensory overload yet you've said nothing.' George whimpered in response to the fierce tone of Eddy's voice. Eddy got up in disgust and started to pace up and down the hallway, turning around just before she got to the chest of drawers. Lucy willed herself to be still, she prayed her aunts wouldn't spot her hiding place. Eddy paced back again, this time walking beyond the chest of drawers. Lucy was now in plain sight. She knew she would be spotted this time. As Eddy turned around her eyes swept across Lucy crouched down low but, strangely, she didn't appear to notice her at all. Eddy walked back to George as Lucy slowly let out her breath.

Eddy crouched down. 'Right, you need to tell me everything. Start from the beginning. Don't leave anything out. What do you know about this prophecy?'

George dropped her hem and slowly heaved herself to her feet. She smoothed down her skirt and put her shoulders back. 'Let's go to the kitchen. I think we might need a strong cup of tea for this.'

Lucy, not wanting to miss a single word, carefully followed them making sure to stay out of sight so her aunts didn't catch her eavesdropping. Talk about a prophecy was definitely not something she wanted to miss. Fortunately the return journey to the kitchen was rather straightforward. No ladders to climb or cupboards to clamber through, just a few twists of the corridor and they were there.

Lucy snuck in through the kitchen door and hid behind the broom closet while her aunts' backs were turned.

Once they were settled with steaming mugs of tea in front of them, George began her story. 'It was a short while before my twenty-first birthday so Sam was almost eleven and you were just coming up to your first birthday. Mother was preparing for my "Celebration" as she called it. She had been busy for weeks in the workshop. She had said it was important for everything to be ready because it was the beginning of the prophecy. She said we were the Keepers and our time was almost here.'

'But what does all that mean, George? What are we the keepers of?'

George hung her head. 'I don't know, Eddy. I wasn't paying much attention. By then I was already trying to find a cure for Jack and, back then, I was so obsessed with it, working day and night trying to figure out how to help him.'

'Not much has changed then,' Eddy muttered.

George either didn't hear her or chose not to. 'Anyway, it wasn't that long afterwards that mother died. At which point, I was so focused on getting through that and looking after you and Sam that I forgot all about it, until now.'

'What with all your forgetfulness it's a wonder that Sam and I survived our upbringing at all.'

'Hey, that's not fair. I did the best I could.'

'You're right, you did. Thank goodness Sam was a grown up long before her time otherwise I don't know what would have happened to us.'

'True,' George grudgingly admitted, 'I miss Sam.'

'Me too,' Eddy squeezed her sister's hand. 'Anyway, what about this prophecy? How are we going to find out about it with mother gone?'

'Well, I suppose we could try to find The Book and see if there's anything in there about it.'

'Wait a minute. What book?'

'The book of all the ceremonies and rituals. The one mother had. The one that was passed down from one generation to the other for hundreds of years. That book.'

Eddy looked at George dumbfounded. 'Nope, never heard of it. It seems to be another thing you forgot to mention over these last twenty years.'

George looked sheepish. 'I suppose I have, I'm sorry, I honestly just forgot about it. Mother would bring it out from time to time when I was growing up, particularly around certain full moons or a solstice. I had a look at it once. I couldn't understand a lot of the writing but it was full of stories written by the women in our family going back hundreds of years and it was also full of their own potions and charms, and, well, magic.'

'Magic?'

'Yes, the women in our family are magical, you must have realised. It's more than just my ability to sense things and your ability to find people who need your help. And it's more than just the fact we can make potions that help people because if other people try to make the same potion, they are useless. There's something bigger than that and the women in our family have it. It's all written in The Book.'

'So where is The Book now?'

'That's the thing, I don't know. In the last few months she was alive, mother became very secretive. She kept on saying we must be careful but she never said why. She also said "they are watching" but she never said who. And again, I wasn't paying much attention. I thought mother was going a little loopy like Aunt Harry had so I ignored most of what she was saying. The only thing I remember is that she said we must always look after The Book and that it must never leave our family. She had it a few days before she died to help prepare for my celebration, then she said she needed to hide it. That was when House went crazy for the first time, adding floors and stairs and towers and extensions.'

'Hang on a minute. You mean to say that House has done

this before? And you never thought to mention it?'

George looked even more uncomfortable. 'Look, I realise I haven't handled this well but since House has made sure I can't get into my workshop, you're right, it's time to start figuring out what's going on here and we can start by finding The Book.'

'What about Lucy? We need to tell her what's going on.'

'We can't, Eddy, we promised her father. We can't go back on our word.'

'I know George, but it just doesn't feel right to keep this from her. You say House was going crazy twenty years ago when mother was worried we were being watched and House is going crazy now.' Eddy got up from the table, and walked over to the back door which was opened wide onto the sunny garden beyond. She turned back to George, 'Do you think we could be in danger?'

'In danger? Why would we be in danger?'

'I'm not sure but, for one thing, our roses have turned black.'

George walked over to join Eddy by the back door as they both gazed at the huge climbing rose bush. Every single one of its formerly red rose blossoms was now a dark, velvety black.

'You know the name of this particular rose bush, don't you?' Eddy asked.

'Yes, it's the Periculum Rose. The danger flower.'

CHAPTER 15

UNWELCOME VISITORS

Lucy could no longer hear her aunts as they talked by the back door, finishing their mugs of tea. As she edged out from behind the broom cupboard, the sound of the doorbell echoed through the house. Lucy scurried back into the hallway hollering, 'I'll get it'.

'Lucy, wait!' George called out but Lucy ignored her as she hurried to the front door. She had heard so much this morning, she needed time to think, time to try to figure out what it all meant.

She swung open the big, heavy front door to discover a tall man standing on the steps.

'Well hello there young lady,' the man bowed in greeting, 'my name is Tom Winkle-Smith.'

Lucy looked him up and down and decided there was something about the way his eyes were shining almost feverishly bright and the way his smile appeared just a bit too wide that made her wary. 'My dad told me never to talk to strangers.'

'Oh don't be silly, I'm no stranger. I'm a good friend of your aunt Eddy. You must be Lucy.'

'How do you know my name?'

'Your aunt told me of course, silly, now where is the lovely Eddy? I have a package for her. I work at the post office. Shall I come in?'

Not liking being called silly once, let alone twice, Lucy decided she wasn't going to make it easy for this Tom Winkle-Smith. Besides, something about him made her feel distinctly on edge.

'My aunt's not here right now. You can give the package to me and I'll give it to her later.'

Tom Winkle-Smith's smile faltered just a little, 'I don't mind waiting.'

'Don't be *silly*,' Lucy replied sweetly, matching his wide false smile, 'you must be needed back at the post office to look after all those other packages.'

'Who's at the door, Lucy?' Eddy walked up behind her. 'Oh, it's you Tom.'

'So you are here.' Tom gave Lucy a meaningful look and there was a glint of something in his eyes that Lucy didn't like, even though he continued to smile broadly. 'I'm delivering your package.'

'There was no need. I normally pick up my parcels. Your aunt knows that.'

'Oh, it was no bother. Besides, it gave me an excuse to see you again.'

Eddy looked perplexed. 'In that case, thank you.' She reached out for the package but Tom clutched it tightly to his chest.

'It's heavy. Why don't I carry it in for you?'

'Really, there's no need. I'm used to heaving around heavy things.'

'I insist. It's the gentlemanly thing to do.' Tom took a step over the threshold forcing Eddy to step backwards. He looked around the entrance hall, taking it all in. He seemed to be studying it closely, as if making mental notes.

'What an interesting home you have. Why don't you show me where to put this package for you?'

Eddy took another step back as Tom advanced closer, then she shrugged and turned around. 'Okay, follow me.'

Tom followed eagerly behind her. Eddy took two large steps across the hallway and abruptly halted. She pointed to the sturdy hall table. 'You can put it here.'

Tom was startled, clearly thinking he was about to follow Eddy further into the house.

'Here? But that's hardly any help. I'm sure this isn't where your package needs to be. Let me carry it all the way for you.'

'Here is fine, here is where I want it,' Eddy replied firmly.

Tom's smile faltered before he quickly regained his composure, 'No problem, anything for the lovely lady.' He placed the package down on the table with a flourish.

'So when can I see you again?'

Eddy took his arm and steered him back to the front door.

'Tomorrow,' she replied.

'Really?' Tom's face lit up with hope.

'Yes, I have to come to the post office tomorrow so no doubt I'll see you then.' With that, Eddy closed the door sharply on Tom's still smiling face.

Leaning against it, she looked at Lucy and smiled, 'He's a little intense, isn't he?'

'Just a bit.'

Eddy picked up the package, which wasn't heavy at all, just as the sound of breaking glass and raised voices could be heard coming from the garden.

'Now what?' Eddy hurried towards the commotion with Lucy following quickly behind. They followed the sounds of shouting until they came to the greenhouse where they found Dolores Moonbeam and Mr Merchant in a heated squabbling match.

'Just let me have those herbs and I'll be on my way,' Dolores said through gritted teeth as she tugged on a large seedling tray filled with spikey green and silver leaves.

'I'm not letting you have anything, you thieving hippy. Let

go.' Mr Merchant yanked hard on the tray making Dolores almost lose her footing but she clung on to the seedlings.

'What's going on here?' George had arrived at the same time as Eddy and Lucy.

'I caught this burglar helping herself to the contents of your greenhouse.'

'I am no burglar! Eddy, tell him,' Dolores pleaded.

'Oh so you know this criminal?' Mr Merchant said as he held firm to the tray.

'Eddy, George,' Dolores implored, 'I do apologise for this little hullabaloo. It appears there has been a misunderstanding or, rather, this gentleman has misunderstood.' She sniffed as she looked down her nose at Mr Merchant.

'What brings you here today, Dolores? We didn't realise you had come to visit yet again,' Eddy asked with barely concealed vexation.

'Well, um, yes, I didn't want to disturb you, Eddy. The last time I was here you told me to just help myself so I thought I would do just that and not be any bother. But then this, this man started yelling at me and grabbed the seedling tray and, I'm afraid, there's been a small accident.' Dolores inclined her head towards one of the large glass greenhouse panels which had been completely smashed.

'What are you after this time, Dolores?' Eddy took a step closer and pried the seedling tray out of her reluctant fingers.

Eddy studied the tray. 'This is Silver Nightweed, one of the most difficult herbs to cultivate. It's very rare, as I'm sure you know. It also has only a few very specific uses and can be deadly if not handled correctly. What did you want with it?'

Dolores looked flustered. 'Oh goodness, silly me, Silver Nightweed you say? I mistook it for, um, Silver Tanglenot, for the bunion case I'm treating. What a silly billy I am. So sorry to have disturbed you, I'll be on my way.'

She scurried past Eddy in a jangle of bells.

Eddy gently grabbed her arm as she passed, 'Please ask next time. That way I can help you find exactly what it is you're looking for.'

Dolores nodded her head wordlessly and scuttled away. The four of them watched her depart in silence, listening as her bells faded into the distance.

Mr Merchant looked at Eddy and George and snorted. 'I'll get back to work then,' and promptly turned his back on them.

George was about to call out after him but, before she could, another set of bells sounded, this time much larger and louder. It was the bells hanging outside the back door which were attached to a pulley system of thin rope that disappeared into the house.

'Gosh, someone's at the front door again, it's like Piccadilly Circus here today.' George hurried away while Eddy carefully placed the tray of Silver Nightweed back into its protective cage, muttering to herself. 'Silver Nightweed and Silver Tanglenot look nothing alike. Funny thing to mix them up.'

'Lucy,' George called moments later, 'Look who's come to visit?' She escorted Beatrice, Ben and Barry out to the greenhouse.

'Hello kids,' Eddy greeted. 'Now Ben and Beatrice I recognise but who's this charming young man?'

Barry's face flushed pink with delight as Eddy smiled warmly at him, 'I'm Barry.'

'Barry you say? So that makes Ben, Beatrice and Barry. We could call you "Triple B" or, even better, "B to the power of three"!' Eddy proclaimed, pleased with herself.

'You just missed your mother,' George informed Ben and Beatrice.

Lucy gaped, 'Dolores Moonbeam is your mother?'

Ben groaned, 'Oh no, you've met our mother? She's a nut job.'

'Ben, you can't say things like that about our mum. She's not a nut job, she just gets a little carried away sometimes and right now she's getting carried away with natural healing remedies. You can't blame her really. Dad's not here all week, gran can't leave the house and we're older now, we don't want to hang out with our mum all day. She's got to find something to keep her busy.'

'I suppose so,' Ben mumbled unconvinced.

Barry had been looking all around him in awe. 'Wow, what a crazy house you've got.' He noted the look George gave him and quickly corrected himself, 'Nice crazy. I've never seen a house like it. Can you show us around Lucy?'

Lucy, remembering her walled up bedroom door from this morning, replied, 'Maybe another time Barry. It's such a lovely day, let's explore the gardens instead. Even I haven't had a chance to see everything yet, it's so big. There's even a maze.'

All the children agreed and, making sure to steer well clear of Mr Merchant, Lucy waved goodbye to her aunts and led her friends further into the garden. As soon as they were out of earshot, Lucy hurriedly told them about the events of this morning although she left out a few things, like how Eddy had to rescue her through her bedroom wardrobe and the bit about magic because, well, she didn't really believe in all that stuff. But she did tell them what she had overheard about a special book, how her aunts sensed danger and how her grandmother, before she had died, had claimed the house was being watched and had hidden the book.

Beatrice was beyond excited. Finally she had a real mystery to solve. Even Ben seemed to be intrigued. And Barry, well, he was just happy to be included.

'Right, the first thing we need to do is visit the library,' Beatrice announced.

Lucy was confused, 'Why the library? The book must surely be hidden somewhere here in the house or the gardens.'

'Yes but don't you think it's a bit strange that your grandmother would die mysteriously just days after saying they were being watched?'

'Who said she died mysteriously?' Ben enquired.

'I did,' Beatrice said.

Barry scratched his head. 'I still don't get it, why do we have to go to the library? It's just going to be filled with smelly books. How's that going to help discover what happened to Lucy's grandmother.'

'Well,' Beatrice explained, 'in Wickham, the library is not

just the library, it also doubles as the central registry office for the entire village. All births, marriages and deaths are recorded and stored there. The librarian, Mrs Smite, is also the local registrar. So we need to break into the library, find Lucy's grandmother's death certificate and see what's listed as her cause of death.'

'Is that the same Mrs Smite who runs the local WI?' Lucy recalled her encounter with the angry lady and didn't relish the thought of a repeat experience.

'Also,' Beatrice ignored Lucy's question, 'maybe it's not such a crazy idea that the book is in the library. What better place to hide a book then amongst other books. It's hiding in plain sight.'

The other three looked at Beatrice in silence for a moment. Then one by one they slowly nodded their heads in agreement.

'I'm in,' Ben voiced, 'particularly for the breaking in bit. That sounds like fun.'

'Thinking about it, we probably don't actually need to break in. We just need to find a way to distract Mrs Smite long enough for one of us to check the records.'

'Well,' Lucy ventured, 'I'm pretty sure Mrs Smite doesn't like me and she definitely doesn't trust me. She thinks I put up phoney WI posters around the village. If I'm the one who distracts her, she'll be so focused on me that you'll be able to slip past her undetected.'

'She doesn't trust me either, and for good reason too,' Ben added. 'After all, I once rearranged her entire library index cards on the carpet so that they spelled out rude words. I also enjoy reordering the library books whenever I get the chance. One time I was able to swap the entire contents of the A shelf with the Z shelf undetected, one of my proudest moments. I can definitely help distract that old bat.'

Beatrice looked at them both and a slow smile spread across her face, 'I think I've got just the plan.'

CHAPTER 16

THE LIBRARY

The children met up in the village square and watched from a distance as Mrs Smite waddled over to the library door and laboriously unlocked it following her lunch break. They waited a few minutes before Beatrice followed after her.

'Good afternoon, Mrs Smite, you're wearing a lovely frock today.' Beatrice breezed in giving Mrs Smite her most winning smile. Mrs Smite looked up, her brow creasing when she discovered who was talking.

'Oh it's you Beatrice Naran. I see you're not with your troublemaker brother today.'

'I've just come to find a new book to read,' Beatrice announced innocently.

'Just remember to keep the noise down,' Mrs Smite instructed.

Beatrice smiled sweetly, readjusted her shoulder bag and sauntered as casually as she could to the back of the room. The library was housed in an old Victorian school building. The main room was filled with rows of book shelves reaching over seven feet high but still not tall enough to touch the vaulted ceiling. The floor was covered in thick carpet which absorbed the sound of Beatrice's footfall. At the rear of the library was the door leading to the records room and Beatrice positioned herself by the shelves closest to it, feigning interest in reading the book titles as she slowly worked her way down the row.

Exactly five minutes after Beatrice entered the library, Barry burst in, having opened the door with more force than intended. It flew back violently and hit the inside wall with a loud bang.

Mrs Smite looked up and frowned as Barry made his way nervously into the library.

'Who the dickens are you?'

Barry jumped. He hadn't expected Mrs Smite to speak to him. This was not what they had rehearsed.

'I, um, I'm Barry,' he replied in an anxious whisper looking extremely guilty as he shifted from one foot to the other.

'Speak up boy, I can't hear you,' commanded Mrs Smite.

'My name's Barry. Barry Barrymore.'

'Barry Barrymore? Is this some sort of childish joke? I wasn't born yesterday you know sonny. What's your real name?'

'My real name really is Barry Barrymore,' Barry insisted.

'I'm not going to be drawn in to your silly little game, young man, so let's just pretend your name really is Barry Barrymore.' Mrs Smite spat out his name as if there was something distasteful on her tongue. 'Where have you come from, Barry Barrymore? You're not from around here.'

'Cardiff,' Barry explained helpfully but Mrs Smite looked even less impressed.

'And when did you arrive from Cardiff, Barry Barrymore?'

'About a week ago,' Barry replied apologetically. He was becoming more and more agitated and shuffled from foot to foot with increasing speed.

'A week you say?' Mrs Smite stood up from her desk and peered closer at Barry. 'Know anything about posters? Are you handy with pen, paper and glue?'

'I don't know anything about posters or paper or pens or anything,' Barry promised earnestly while beads of sweat popped out on his brow, 'I've just come to get a book.' He pointed to the shelves.

'You don't fool me for a moment, Barry Barrymore. I've got my eye on you and remember, no noise!'

Mrs Smite sat down with a thud and waved her hand imperiously towards the bookshelves. Not waiting for a second invitation, Barry scampered over to the shelves at the front of the room and the opposite end to Beatrice, taking pains not to look at her or to show in any way that they knew each other, as Beatrice had instructed.

Barry had just positioned himself in front of a bookshelf as Lucy entered quietly through the front door. Keeping her head down she tried to slip in between the two nearest bookshelves without Mrs Smite spotting her but it was too late.

'You!' Mrs Smite's voice echoed around the library. The "no noise" rule clearly didn't apply to her.

Lucy froze and slowly turned to face Mrs Smite.

'What do you think *you're* doing?' Mrs Smite said accusingly.

'I've come to borrow a book. There are no good books to read at my aunts' house.'

'Pfft.' Mrs Smite's nose screwed up as if she'd just smelt something unpleasant.

'Likely story. Well, I've got my eye on you too.' She raised her voice, 'I've got my eye on all of you.'

No sooner were the words out of her mouth than the door flew open once more and Ben burst in.

'Mrs Smite! You're a vision to behold,' he declared with a broad grin on his face.

'Stop right there Benjamin Naran. You can just turn yourself around and leave by the way you came in.'

'Now, now Mrs Smite, I know you don't really mean that. You wouldn't deprive a child desperate to read one of the many fine books you have in your library, would you?'

'Pfft!'

'In fact, I have a few books that I'm really interested in.

Could you look them up on the computer for me to see if you have them?'

'Why don't you just look through the bookshelves yourself Mr Naran, the books are all in alphabetical order or, should I say, they were before you arrived.'

'What are you trying to say, Mrs Smite?' Ben's face was a picture of innocence.

'You know exactly what I'm saying, Mr Naran, now be off with you, I've got work to do.'

'Mrs Smite, I beg you, all I want is to read a good book and, while you hold an excellent stock here, I've got a feeling that the books I'm after may be more unique and I might need to request them from the main library in Snordom.'

This got Mrs Smite's interest. She was very proud of the range of books she had to offer in her little library and how seldom any of her customers ever had to request a book to be sent from the Snordom Town Library because they couldn't find what they wanted.

'Very well, Mr Naran, give me the details of the book you're after.' Mrs Smite wheeled her chair over to the computer.

This was Beatrice's cue and she quickly made her way over to the door leading to the records room while Mrs Smite couldn't see her.

'The first book I'm after,' Ben stated in a loud voice reading from a piece of paper he pulled out of his rucksack, 'is "101 ways to escape from prison" by J.L. Brake.'

Mrs Smite looked up from the computer keyboard. 'Is that really a suitable book for a child to be reading, Mr Naran?' Disapproval radiated from her body as she stared at Ben over the rim of her reading glasses.

'Isn't it better, Mrs Smite, that I read a book like that rather than nothing at all?' Ben grinned back at her.

'Pfft,' she replied as she tapped the keys. After a moment she turned back to Ben, 'This book is not listed in the Snordom Town Library. In fact, it's not listed at any library within 20 miles of here. Is it actually a real book, Mr Naran?'

'How very strange,' replied Ben innocently, 'perhaps J.L.

Brake hasn't been released yet. Can you try another one for me? The title is "The Black Market: What sells, what doesn't" and the author is Count E. Fitt.'

Mrs Smite had just turned back to her computer when a loud bang sounded through the library as a stack of books hit the floor near Beatrice.

'Shhhhh,' Mrs Smite admonished loudly.

'Sorry,' Beatrice mouthed back as she stooped to pick up the books.

This was the children's cue. Clearly Beatrice was switching to Plan B.

Lucy quickly walked over to Barry, who had been pretending to study the same book since he arrived. She pulled out a few sheets of brightly coloured poster paper and giggled loudly as she gave a couple to Barry, who also attempted to giggle although his came out like a snort which actually made Lucy giggle properly this time. Then they hastily left the library.

'I know exactly what those two are up to,' Mrs Smite declared in outrage as she followed after them as swiftly as her large frame would allow.

As soon as the door had closed behind Mrs Smite, Beatrice ran over to Ben. 'Quick, we need to find the keys. The door to the records room is locked.'

Without another word, Ben vaulted over the desk and started rummaging through the drawers.

'Found them.' He threw a bunch of keys to Beatrice who ran back to the records room. 'Keep a look out Ben, we won't have long.'

Outside, in the village square, Mrs Smite was doubled over, her hands resting heavily on her knees as she gulped in big lungfuls of air. She had attempted to run after the children but her large bulk and her level of unfitness put a rapid stop to her sprint. Lifting her head, she saw the two of them huddled together in front of the village notice board. Deciding that stealth was a better tactic than speed, she crept up behind them as quietly as she could and brought down a beefy hand on each of their shoulders.

'Caught you,' she crowed in triumph.

Lucy and Barry turned slowly to face Mrs Smite.

'I knew it,' Mrs Smite continued, 'I knew you were the ones putting up the fake WI posters. Hand them over.' She stretched her hands out, waiting.

Reluctantly, Lucy and Barry turned their posters around to show Mrs Smite. Lucy's was a drawing of brightly coloured flowers; Barry's was covered in boats.

Mrs Smite's triumphant smile collapsed.

'What the blazers are these?'

'Our drawings,' Lucy replied for both of them because Barry was frozen solid in fear. 'We wanted to share them with the villagers. We thought they might help to brighten up the notice boards.' Lucy tried to arrange her features in a virtuous expression.

'Pah!' Mrs Smite stared in outrage and then snatched the posters, tearing them up into little bits and letting the pieces drop to the ground.

'Clean up this mess,' she commanded as she swivelled on her heels and laboured slowly back to the library.

'She's coming, Bea, hurry!' Ben yelled from his position next to the window.

Beatrice, who had been frantically looking through the filing cabinet drawers, slammed them shut and grabbed the book that lay open on the official register desk. She shoved it into her shoulder bag and quickly exited the room, pulling the door closed behind her. She tried to turn the key in the lock but it wouldn't turn. With no time to spare, she threw the keys to Ben who managed to return them to the drawer and vault back over the desk moments before Mrs Smite banged the library door open with such force the hinges visibly bulged.

'Are you two still here,' she declared with loathing.

'I think we were just leaving, weren't we Bea? I'll come back another day to follow up on those books.'

'Pfft,' was the reply as they scurried out the door, making sure to give Mrs Smite a wide berth as they went.

The four friends reunited at the top of the tree house.

'That was so much fun,' Beatrice declared.

'It was wicked,' Ben agreed. 'Did you see the look on Smite-the-Fright's face when you two started giggling over poster paper?'

'I don't know,' Barry was very pale, 'that woman is proper scary.'

'Why do you think we call her Smite-the-Fright?' Ben grinned.

'Did you get my grandmother's death certificate?' Lucy asked eager to get back to the task at hand.

'Unfortunately not. I just didn't have long enough to search, but I did get this.' Beatrice pulled the book out of her shoulder bag.

'What is it?' Barry peered closer.

'It's the Register book. It records the date and time of every birth, death and marriage in the village.'

'Mrs Smite will definitely notice something as large as that missing. She will know it was us.' Lucy clenched her hands together nervously.

'Don't worry about that, the book will be back by morning. Mrs Smite will never even know it was missing.' Beatrice started thumbing through the pages, scanning the information.

'But how are we going to get it back? It was hard enough getting it out in the first place. Mrs Smite will know we're up to something if we all go back again.'

'Don't worry about it, Lucy, we'll do it the way I had wanted to do it all along,' Ben reassured her.

'And how's that?'

'I'll break in of course. There's a window with a dodgy latch. I do it all the time. It's how I amuse myself when it's just me and Bea. I sneak in and nab an item, usually something small that I can fit in my pocket, like a stapler or the library stamp. Then the next day I watch while Smite-the-Fright hunts high and low for it and then I return it the following night. I just love the look on her face when she finds the missing item exactly where she originally left it. She thinks she's losing her mind.'

'That seems a little mean, even for Mrs Smite,' Lucy said.

'I think it's brilliant,' Barry's face was lit up with admiration. 'My only question is, why didn't we just do it Ben's way in the first place? Surely that would have been easier and would have given us more time to search for the death certificate?'

'Excellent question, my man,' Ben slapped Barry on the back, 'but unfortunately my sister had an elaborate plan in her head and there's no shifting her when she's made up her mind.'

'Enough about that,' Beatrice said with excitement, flapping her hands at them. 'Look, I've found something. Here's the record of your grandmother's death, Lucy. It says she died twenty years ago.' Beatrice checked her watch that also displayed today's date. 'In fact, the twentieth anniversary of her death is in ten days' time.'

'Ten days, you say?' Lucy looked astonished, 'What a coincidence, that's my birthday.'

Beatrice was flipping through the pages of the register. 'Aha! Here's my proof. A birth was registered a week before your grandmother's death but, since then, not a single baby has been born in Wickham.'

'Oh that's just another coincidence,' Ben scoffed, 'you look for conspiracy theories everywhere.'

'The facts speak for themselves, Ben. Lucy's grandmother dies in mysterious circumstances after which no children are born in Wickham.'

'How do you know she died in mysterious circumstances?' Ben challenged.

'Because of this,' Beatrice brandished a thin notebook that had been tucked away in the back page of the register book.

'It confirms my hunch. It appears that Mrs Smite has a bit of a morbid curiosity for deaths in the village. Look, she's carefully copied out the names and dates of death of everyone who has died in the village in the last thirty years, but she has also included their cause of death. Mrs Smite must be awfully friendly with Doctor Diggley to have access to this type of information. It says here that the cause of death was unexplained but was, in all likelihood, a result of natural causes.

No foul play was suspected despite an unexplained scorch mark surrounding the entire body when it was discovered!'

As the children sat back in stunned silence trying to digest this revelation, over at the library, Mrs Smite was busying herself righting the shelves after the children had been rifling through them. If truth be told, there wasn't a single book out of place but Mrs Smite wouldn't have been convinced of that. Oh no, she knew those children had come into the library with the sole purpose to play a trick on her but she had been too clever for them. They hadn't got away with it. As she finished straightening the already perfectly straight row of books, something caught her attention. The door to the registrar office was ajar. She hurried over to her desk to check her keys but they were where she had left them. Surely she hadn't forgotten to lock the door the last time she was in the office? She was normally so careful. She was about to investigate further when the soft chime of the door announced that she had another customer. Convinced it was the children returning to harass her, she quickly shut and locked the office door and rushed to the front of the library only to have her scowl replaced by a coquettish smile.

'Why Reverend Pickles, how wonderful to see you again, let me help you with those books.'

Fortunately for the children, Mrs Smite's delight to see Reverend Pickles completely put out of her mind any thoughts she had had to inspect the registrar office. In fact, she only remembered half way through the following morning and when she did a thorough top to toe inspection, twice, she could not find a single thing out of place. Even the register book was opened to the exact same page and her secret little notebook was still safely tucked away in the back. So perhaps she had indeed forgotten to lock the office door. As unlikely as that explanation was to Mrs Smite, it was the only one that could possibly be true.

CHAPTER 17

EXTRAORDINARY WI MEETING

Barry was excited to tell his uncle all about the latest adventure he and his friends had been up to. He still couldn't quite believe the change in his uncle. Nigel had been so attentive to Barry recently, asking him lots of questions about his day and his new friends. Barry had never had such undivided attention, especially from a grown up and one related to him no less, that he practically glowed from the effects.

But this evening was different. Uncle Nigel was distracted. Barry was telling him all about their library adventure and happily expanding on his role which became bigger and bigger as he exaggerated the story, trying to get his uncle's attention, but to no avail. Uncle Nigel only grunted in response. In the middle of Barry's third retelling, by which point he had such a leading role that one could have assumed the entire caper was his idea, Uncle Nigel abruptly pushed his chair back and stood up.

'I have to go out now. Be a good boy and get yourself off to bed.'

'But Uncle, it's not even eight o'clock. It's much too early for bedtime.'

'Well then, read a book or something. I'll see you in the morning.'

Nigel made to leave but Barry quickly trailed after him. 'Where are you going?'

Nigel was momentarily put off his stride, 'I, um, I'm performing a magic show this evening.'

'I haven't seen one of your shows for ages. Can I come?'

'I, er, well, it's not that kind of show. I, um, am going to give a magic talk. Yes, that's it, a magic demonstration to, um, the local amateur magician's society. Quite a large group of them actually, there won't be room for you.'

'Wow, I had no idea Wickham had so many magicians. I'm sure they won't mind you bringing your nephew along, would they? You can say I want to be a magician too.'

'No, that's out of the question. It wouldn't be, um, professional. Now Barry, stop pestering me, stay here and help Harris tidy up the supper, there's a good boy.' And with no more than an anxious look at his watch, Nigel dashed out of the house.

'I guess it's just you and me tonight, Harris,' Barry said dejectedly turning to his uncle's man servant only to find Harris about to step out the door himself.

'Um, your uncle left his lucky cape behind.' Harris quickly grabbed the cape from the coat rack. 'I'd better take it to him; he doesn't like to do his magic shows without it. Lock the door behind me, Barry, I won't be long.' And with that, Harris also hastened out of the house.

Barry stood in the middle of the hallway for a moment, bemused by the sudden exit of first his uncle and then Harris. But after a minute, he came to a conclusion. Harris clearly was going to watch the magic show himself. Well, there was no way Barry was going to miss out. He grabbed his hoody and quickly followed after them.

Once out on the lane, Barry at first couldn't figure out which way they'd gone. Then he noticed his uncle a little way off at the end of the road, but there was no sign of Harris. Just before his uncle turned the corner, he looked back over his shoulder and Barry swiftly stepped back behind the hedge. If his uncle saw him, he knew he'd make him go back inside. Barry peeped around the hedge to see if the coast was clear and spotted something odd. Harris was also peering after his uncle from behind a tree on the opposite side of the lane. Clearly Harris didn't want his uncle noticing him either. How strange.

Harris waited until the coast was clear and then skulked after Nigel, ducking into a doorway just as Nigel checked over his shoulder once more. Something was very odd indeed and Barry was determined to find out what. He felt he had stumbled across his very own mystery. Already, he couldn't wait to tell the others all about it.

As stealthily as he could, Barry followed Harris as Harris furtively followed Nigel. Nigel was taking them on the strangest route. He doubled back through the village twice, he did a complete about turn once and appeared to walk in increasingly large circles through the village on three separate occasions. Harris followed at a discreet distance and seemed to instinctively know moments before Nigel would check over his shoulder or do an abrupt about turn. Harris ducked out of site each time and Barry did the same. Harris's attention was fully focused on Nigel so he never noticed Barry shadowing him.

Eventually, as dusk was settling in, Nigel came to the front of a large formidable stone wall with big wrought iron gates guarding the grand house that lay beyond. The gates were flanked by two enormous sleeping dragons made of stone although, on closer inspection, each dragon had one eye open which seemed to stare straight at Barry in his hiding place. Nigel looked up and down the road three times. He then reached inside his jacket and pulled out a large black bundle which he quickly unfolded to reveal a cloak. He swept the cloak around his body and pulled the hood down low over his brow. It was now impossible to see his face hidden beneath. Rather than heading for the main gates, Nigel paced sixteen steps to the right where the wall was covered in waves of trailing ivy. He faced the stone wall and, checking once more to make sure no one was watching, started counting the stones. Finding the one he wanted, he pressed on it firmly. Nothing happened. He pressed again even more firmly, this time putting the full weight of his body behind it. Still nothing. Reaching into his pocket, he withdrew a crumpled piece of paper and checked his notes. Shaking his head, he groped his jacket with one hand to return the paper to his pocket, while counting the stones again. This time, he finished on the stone immediately below the one he'd previously leant on. He pressed hard and it gave way. Even shrouded by his cloak, Barry could sense Nigel's relief as he lifted back the ivy curtain and disappeared through it, not noticing that the scrap of paper had not been securely returned to his pocket and was now floating to the ground. Before Barry could think what to do next, Harris emerged from the encroaching darkness and swiftly followed behind Nigel.

Barry was, in all honesty, so shocked to have just seen his uncle walk through a solid stone wall, not to mention his man servant perform the same disappearing act, that it took him a moment to breathe, let alone move.

He hesitated. His natural instinct was to turn around and run all the way back home before his uncle could catch him snooping. But then he imagined what it would be like to tell his new friends all about this evening's big adventure. And then he imagined the disappointed look on Beatrice's face if he confessed to running away. He had no choice, he simply had to follow. He had to find out what his uncle was really up to. This was definitely no ordinary magic show.

Barry left the safety of his hiding place behind a large bush and hurried over to where the piece of paper lay discarded on the path.

He opened it up and saw his uncle's untidy hand writing…

16 paces right of gate
2 across
5 down
press hard

Barry looked up at the wall. He was definitely standing in front of the section that was covered in ivy. The ivy stopped short of a big stone pillar dividing the wall into two large sections. Barry counted two stones from the pillar and then five down. The stone was just by his head. He reached up and pressed hard but nothing happened. Maybe he needed to include the first row when he counted down. This got him to a stone that was even higher than his head. He pressed it but again, nothing happened. Barry tried one more time. This time, he counted two stones across, then five down and finally he pressed hard on the one below stone number five. At first nothing seemed to happen. Then Barry heard a click and a low rumble. A doorway had opened beneath the ivy. Taking a deep steadying breath, he cautiously stepped through it.

He found himself inside a high walled garden. Flower beds, flanked by wide pathways were laid out in neat formation. Barry heard the muted murmuring of distant voices that sounded like angry whispers.

He crept low along the pathway towards the sound. As he rounded a corner, he saw Harris crouched down behind a row of bushes sculptured into mini pyramids. Beyond the pyramids was a tall, circular hedge which was broken by two stone archways, standing opposite each other like sentries. And just beyond the first archway, Barry could make out the lanky form of his uncle, even disguised in his long black hooded cloak.

Barry hastily stepped out of sight as a short hooded figure came into view and spoke to Nigel sternly, 'Are you quite sure you weren't followed?'

'Yes, Councillor, quite sure. I devised a cunning route which allowed me to catch anyone in the act long before I reached here.'

'Pfft, well, this better be important, Nigel, you put us all at great risk by summoning us here.' The small hooded figure waved a piece of bright yellow paper in front of Nigel. From his hiding place, Barry could just about make out the words printed in large black letters at the top of the page. It read:
EXTRAORDINARY WI MEETING.

Barry's eyes were starting to adjust to the gloom, and he realised his uncle and the short hooded figure were not the only ones meeting here tonight. In the shadows he made out at least half a dozen cloaked figures flanking the pair on either side.

'I was left with no choice, Councillor,' Nigel squeaked, 'you hadn't replied to any of my meeting requests.' Nigel pulled a handful of coloured poster paper from his pocket. 'I had to invoke the emergency gathering procedures.'

'Well, get on with it then, we haven't got all day. The longer we are out in the open, the greater the chance of detection.'

'Right, certainly Councillor. Well, the thing is, I've found the Whispering Stones.'

'What? *You? You* of all people have found the Whispering Stones when we've had our best team searching for years to no avail? The very stones our research determined are the key to the witches' powers?'

Uncle Nigel looked apologetic. 'Yes, I'm afraid I have.'

'Explain yourself, man, this should be a good story.' The other hooded figures sniggered, catching the incredulous tone in the Councillor's voice.

'Well, actually, it wasn't me who found the stones. It was my nephew, Barry.'

Barry inhaled so sharply when he heard his name that one of the hooded figures turned around and looked in the direction of where he was crouched, hidden behind a stone carving. He clapped a hand over his mouth and forced himself to breathe normally, straining to hear what his uncle said next.

Nigel pulled himself up straighter. 'Yes, that's right. My nephew has become friends with that foul witchling, Lucy. She took Barry and their other friends to the clearing in the woods and revealed the stones to them. She said something like "I invite you to see" and Barry said the stones then appeared out of thin air as if by magic.'

The Councillor pushed passed Nigel and started pacing up and down in front of the hooded gathering. 'Well, this is very interesting. We've searched all over this village and woods for decades but never discovered the location of those wretched stones. Now we know they are in the clearing. This is a good result. For the first time we have a chance of stopping any more of those wretched Wick witchlings from ascending to their full powers. If we can find out when they will next gather at the stones, we can take them all out once and for all. The Witchfinder General is going to be most pleased when I inform him I've discovered the stones.'

'Er, well, it was actually me who made the discovery,' Nigel corrected hesitantly.

The Councillor rounded on him. 'We are not in this for personal recognition, Nigel. This is a noble cause, greater than any one of us. You'll do well to remember that.'

'Yes, Councillor, of course, Councillor, humblest apologies, Councillor.'

The Councillor turned to the others, 'Right, we've risked ourselves long enough thanks to Nigel. Make your way back to your individual stations and await my instructions. I will get word to the Witchfinder General. Be ready, the end is near.'

The hooded figures nodded and quietly dispersed, melting into the shadows and appearing to disappear before Barry's very eyes. Barry looked over to where Harris had been hiding, but he too had vanished. Nigel and the Councillor were the last to leave. It looked like Nigel wanted to say something more, but the Councillor raised a hand to quiet him and brushed passed him haughtily. Barry watched the short hooded figure of the Councillor until it rounded a corner and disappeared. When he looked back, his uncle was gone.

Barry gasped for air, realising he'd been holding his breath through the whole exchange.

Then he looked around the garden in the growing darkness and realised something else. He had no idea how to get out.

He headed in the direction he thought he'd come from but, when he rounded a bend, all he saw was more formal gardens stretched out ahead of him.

He was about to turn back and try the other way when a voice spoke behind him.

'Who are you and what are you doing here?'

The voice was stern and Barry started to tremble. It must be the person his uncle had been speaking to, the person he referred to as "Councillor".

Barry turned around slowly and then breathed a sigh of relief. Before him sat an elderly lady in a wheel chair. While her face was set in a fierce expression to match her stern voice, Barry spotted a twinkle in her eye.

'I repeat, who are you and what are you doing in my garden?'

Barry decided the truth was perhaps not the best way to go at this time. Besides, he could barely understand all that he had seen and heard this evening.

'I'm very sorry, Madam. I, um, found an open gate in your wall and decided to explore. But then I became lost and couldn't find my way out.'

'An open gate in my wall, you say? How odd. I must get my housekeeper to investigate. I can't risk just any old ruffian finding their way into my garden, can I?' The lady looked pointedly at Barry, although a smile tugged at her lips.

'Now then, young man, let's make our way over to the main gate and, while we do that, we can get to know each other a little better. I will start. My name is Lady Elizabeth. My friends call me Lizzy. Perhaps one day you might call me Lizzy too, but for now, Lady Elizabeth will do.'

Barry proceeded to tell Lady Elizabeth who he was and how he came to be in Wickham as they slowly made their way to the gate, even telling her about his new friends. Lady Elizabeth seemed genuinely interested and when she made him promise that he'll bring them all to meet her soon, Barry eagerly agreed.

CHAPTER 18

YOU'RE A WITCH!

'You're a witch!'

An accusing finger pointed at Lucy and she gasped in surprise. The finger belonged to Barry who burst out laughing at the expression on her face.

'It's true. You are a witch or rather, a witchling.'

'What are you talking about?' Lucy asked in alarm.

'Yes, what are you talking about Barry?' Ben's head popped up through the treehouse hatch as he joined them. Beatrice followed closely behind, carrying a bag of apples.

Once they were all settled, Barry retold the events of the previous evening, stopping to go back over details again for Beatrice, who was taking copious notes.

Lucy sat in silence, hanging on to every word. After Barry had told them everything, twice, she finally burst out, 'There's definitely some sort of mistake here. I can't be a witch. I don't have any magic powers. There's nothing special about me.'

'Well, you did make those stone pillars appear,' Barry offered.

'No I didn't. They'd just been hidden by the mist. I simply

helped you focus on what was already there.'

'Maybe,' Barry agreed unconvinced.

Beatrice looked Lucy up and down slowly. 'Have you ever tried to do anything witch-like?'

'I wouldn't even know what to do or where to begin. Honestly, guys, I'm not a witch. I'm a very, very ordinary girl from London.'

Barry bit into an apple and chewed thoughtfully. 'Well, you can disappear.'

The other three looked at him with astonishment.

'It's true. Lucy disappears. One minute she's not there, the next she is. She did that the first day I met you both, do you remember, Beatrice? I practically jumped out of my skin.'

'Oh that,' Lucy scoffed, 'I had just managed to hide myself behind the tree better, that's all.'

'No, no, that's not it at all, Lucy. I was staring right at Beatrice and could see her clearly, even though she was mostly hidden behind the tree. At first, Beatrice was all alone and then, suddenly, you just appeared next to her, as if from thin air. I thought I had imagined it at the time, but now they say you're a witch, it makes sense.'

Ben, who was crunching on an apple, looked slowly from Barry to Lucy. 'There's only one thing for it, Lucy. You have to disappear.'

'I can't disappear, I don't know how. Honest, believe me, I am not a witch. I cannot do magic. There is nothing special about me. I am as ordinary as ordinary can be.'

'Well, I'm afraid I'm going to need proof of your ordinariness,' Ben said chewing happily. 'Go on, prove to us you can't disappear. But you have to prove it by trying really hard to disappear. I won't believe you if I think you're faking.'

'Oh Ben, you're impossible. Don't listen to him, Lucy, you don't have to prove a thing to me, I believe you.' Beatrice put her hand on Lucy's arm reassuringly.

'But you weren't there, Beatrice, a bunch of hooded people really do believe that Lucy is a witch.' Barry turned to Lucy, 'I think you and your aunts could be in danger. I didn't like the sound of the person they called Councillor one bit. So, if you are a witch, you need to find that out pretty quickly. You may have magical powers you don't even know about that could help protect you.'

Ben started laughing so hard he began choking on the apple still stuffed in his mouth, 'Oh this is going to be a good day. I almost decided to play my video games today but I'm really glad I didn't. I would have missed all this fun. Well, how are you going to prove that Lucy is a witch, Barry?'

Barry thought for a moment. 'Ben's right, you need to make yourself disappear again,' he suggested.

'Honestly, I can't. I was just hidden behind the tree,' Lucy protested. 'You simply didn't see me.'

'Nah, that tree was never big enough to hide all of you. You made yourself vanish!'

'I can't, really, I can't. This is all ridiculous, I'm not a witch and I can't make myself disappear.' Lucy was starting to feel hot and flustered.

'Well,' Beatrice began, always the practical one, 'the only way to know for sure is to prove it, one way or the other.'

'But how am I supposed to prove it? I don't even know how to make myself disappear, because I can't do it. I am not a witch. This is all just silly.'

Barry wasn't giving up, 'Lucy, think back to that time when we met. Did you do anything special or different that you can recall? Try to remember, before I noticed you, what were you thinking?'

'I don't know, I guess I was thinking that I really hoped you wouldn't see me.'

'Is that it?' Ben scoffed, 'Is that *the magic*? Doesn't sound very magical to me.'

'I suppose the only thing for it is to give it a go,' Beatrice said, ignoring Ben.

'What, *now*?' Lucy looked at the expectant faces staring back at her.

All three nodded eagerly. Barry's eyes were full of hope and faith that she could do it. Beatrice had her notebook in hand, ready to record any important observations. And Ben was leaning back against the post, a small frown of doubt crinkling his forehead, ready to laugh out loud when nothing happened.

Lucy looked at them looking at her and wished she could be anywhere but here. She wished she could be far away from their prying eyes. She wished the floor would just open and swallow her up so she could disappear.

Beatrice dropped her notebook.

'Whoa,' Ben stood up straight, blinking rapidly.

'Yes!' Barry punched the air. 'I knew you could do it.'

* * *

Lucy found her aunts drinking tea in the sitting room while they talked to each other in low, urgent voices. Today, two of the walls were decorated in black and white striped wallpaper, another was painted grey and the fourth in a blue so dark it looked like ink. George was sitting rather uncomfortably on a wooden bench, her favourite overstuffed armchair nowhere in sight. Eddy was perched on the edge of a hard metal chair, the only other seating in the room. The room was stark and sombre, which matched George and Eddy's mood perfectly.

Jack, the big black cat, lay sprawled between them on a ragged mat, purring ever so slightly as George absentmindedly stroked his head. Suddenly, he leapt to his feet, the hackles of his fur standing on edge, just as Lucy cleared her throat and both her aunts visibly jumped.

'Goodness, Lucy, you startled us, we didn't see you come in,' George proclaimed as she steadied her cup before slurping some of the spilt tea out of the saucer.

'That's because you didn't see me,' Lucy replied.

'What do you mean?' Eddy peered at her curiously.

'I have something to show you,' Lucy explained, 'and then I think it's time you stopped hiding things from me and told me everything.'

'I don't understand, Lucy, what is it you think we're keeping from you?' George responded but without conviction as she avoided eye contact.

'Just watch first.'

Lucy stood before them and took a deep calming breath. Then she closed her eyes and wished very hard that her aunts couldn't see her.

'Oh,' said Eddy.

'I see,' said George.

Lucy opened her eyes and reappeared before them, 'So, are we witches or what?'

George heaved a sigh. 'Well, I guess that's one way of describing it,' she reluctantly agreed.

'I knew it,' Lucy cried. 'Well, actually, I've only just found out. Why didn't you tell me? Why have you kept this a secret? This is huge! It explains everything that's been going on since I arrived. Well, actually it doesn't fully explain it. There's been *a lot* of weird stuff happening that I've just ignored or dismissed but it's got to be all connected, right? It's all got to do with the fact that we're witches!' Lucy was talking at top speed as she paced rapidly to and fro in front of her aunts. She was giddy with excitement. If she was honest with herself, she was giddy with a little bit of fear too. She didn't know why but all of a sudden she felt as if she should be afraid. But afraid of what, she didn't know.

Eddy stood up and gently took both of Lucy's hands in an attempt to still her.

'You're right, Lucy, we should have told you sooner. We thought we were doing the right thing by not telling you. But, you have to admit, it's a strange thing to tell someone and you weren't ready to hear it when you first arrived. We had to wait for you to come to the realisation on your own but I'm glad you now know because a change is coming, I can feel it. We need to be ready and we can only be ready if we are united.'

'Eddy's right,' George stood and joined them. 'We have to prepare. It's time that I started focussing on us and not Jack for a while. Ow!' George cradled her hand which now sported a nasty scratch made by Jack's claws. Jack hissed at George before turning and fastening his startling green eyes on Lucy.

'I'm sorry, Jack,' George implored, 'it's not for long and you know I need to do this.'

Jack hissed again but then paced over to Lucy and briefly rubbed against her legs before stalking out the room, his ears twitching madly.

Lucy watched him leave, 'It's almost as if Jack can understand every word you're saying.'

'So we know a change is coming and we know we have to prepare, but prepare what? That's the big question,' Eddy mused.

'I think I can help with that,' a voice said from the doorway.

This time, George was so startled she dropped her cup and saucer and they smashed to the floor.

'Who are you?' George barked.

'My name is Harris. I live with young Barry and his uncle, Nigel,' Harris explained as he took a cautious step further into the sitting room. George leaped in front of Lucy, small sparks flying out from her hands.

Eddy also took a step closer so that Lucy was now shielded by both aunts.

'How did you get in here?' Eddy demanded. 'There are alarm triggers all around this house. No unwelcome visitors could ever get in here undetected.'

'I think I had a bit of help from this.' Harris held up a lady's handkerchief.

George peered at it and then stifled a small cry before launching herself at the dainty cloth and ripping it out of Harris' hand.

'How did you get this?' she demanded as she gently fingered the silky cloth embroidered with the letter J for Josephine.

'Your mother gave it to me a long time ago,' Harris answered softly.

George looked up at him suspiciously. 'Why would she have done that?'

'We were close. I was assigned to be her Guardian. As a Guardian, you're not supposed to get close but I broke the rules. Your mother was so special; I just couldn't keep my distance. We were very happy until the Guardian Council found out and reassigned me.'

'Wait, what? A Guardian? The Guardian Council? What are you talking about?' Eddy asked.

'It's probably best that I start from the beginning. Do you think we could possibly sit down? This may take a while.'

'Of course,' George replied, 'although there isn't much seating available today. Oh...'

A plush three seater sofa suddenly appeared next to the ragged mat. 'I see House has provided seating for everyone. This sofa looks much more comfy than that wooden bench. Oof!' George hit the floor with a bump as the sofa jerked out the way just as she was sitting down.

George pushed herself up.

'I guess House would like Lucy and our guest to sit here instead.'

George raised her voice, 'I'll just go back to the hard-as-nails bench, shall I House?'

A low rumble, like a faraway chuckle, came from somewhere within the house.

Once everyone was seated, Harris began. 'I met your mother forty-two years ago. She was my first Guardian assignment.'

Eddy opened her mouth to ask a question but Harris raised his hand to stop her.

'There are things that you all should know and things you should have been taught a long time ago. I'm breaking protocol by being here but I feel my duty to you is more important than my duty to the Guardian Council.'

Eddy closed her mouth and nodded her head for Harris to continue.

'As I was saying, I met your mother before you were born. Every Custos Elementums is assigned a Guardian.'

'What on earth is a Custos Elementums?' George stumbled over the pronunciation.

'It's what you are. You are Keepers of the Elements; earth, wind, water and fire. Some people think you are witches, but that's just ancient folklore. It's true, you do have special gifts, you have certain powers and your greatest power is to keep nature in balance by holding your element in check. If the elements aren't kept in check, eventually one or more starts to dominate leading to major natural disasters, even loss of life. Have you noticed how we've had no rain for months? And how unseasonably hot it's been all year?'

'But surely that's just a heatwave,' Lucy protested. 'It can't have anything to do with us. It's bound to pass soon.'

'Not unless the Keepers intervene. Without an intervention, there could be a never ending drought or worse. You were all born to be Keepers but, without proper training and without your Ascension Ceremony, you won't be able to fully realise your powers. And, unless you have fully fledged powers, you won't be able to control your element properly.'

'What's the Ascension Ceremony?' Eddy asked.

'It's a special ceremony that can only take place at midnight on or around your twenty-first birthday. The Book of Ascension is used to guide the ceremony. Once the ceremony is complete, the Keeper comes into his or her full powers.'

'That's what mother was planning for me,' George whispered almost to herself. 'Twenty years ago, that's what she was preparing for before she… died.'

George looked at Harris, realisation dawning, 'Does that mean I can never get my full powers, because I didn't have my Ascension Ceremony?'

'I'm afraid so, George. But, the good news is, your powers will grow as those of the Keepers around you grow. You may have noticed that, since Lucy arrived, your powers have felt stronger? As long as you stay together, you are able to feed off each other's powers and the collective strength makes you each stronger.'

Eddy interjected, 'So how do you know all of this?'

'I'm a Guardian. It's my job to know.'

'So what's a Guardian anyway?' Lucy asked.

'There have been Guardians almost as long as there have been Keepers. Long ago, people feared Keepers and became suspicious of them, believing them to be doing the devil's work. Then the witch hunts began and Keepers started being accused of witchcraft. Suspected witches were thrown into a lake. If they drowned they were innocent but if they floated it confirmed their guilt and they were burnt at the stake. Dozens of Keepers were lost during the witch hunts and serious imbalances in nature resulted – earthquakes, tornadoes, tidal waves. It was at that time that the Guardians of the Keepers were formed. Our mission is to guard over and protect the Keepers as much as we can without interfering with the true order of things.'

'What does that mean?' George asked.

'Of utmost importance is that we Guardians don't do anything to change the future. We have to keep our distance and allow the natural order of life to unfold. We can't tell a Keeper what to do or where to go. A Keeper must have free will at all times and decide on the course of events for him or herself. But a Guardian can try to influence events around the Keeper to try to make sure the right path is followed. I know this all sounds a bit complicated but, Lucy, it was no coincidence that your father was invited on that expedition and you landed up here. Those were carefully orchestrated events to make sure the right outcome came about. You were nearing your eleventh birthday and you didn't even know your aunts existed. It was time that you met them.'

'So it's your fault my dad went away?'

'Well, not me specifically but the Guardian Council would have arranged it somehow. There are Guardians all over the country. Each Keeper typically has at least one assigned to look after them. A Keeper should never know who their Guardian is. In fact, they shouldn't even know they have Guardians. I'm breaking so many rules by telling you this. But I guess I broke the rules all those years ago when I fell in love with Jo.'

'You were in love with our mother? She never mentioned you, not once. There was never a man in her life, I would have remembered,' George exclaimed.

'We had to keep it secret, George. If we were found out, I would have been reassigned, possibly to the opposite end of the country, and we couldn't risk that.'

'Why didn't you just leave the Guardians and be with our mother if you loved her so much?'

Harris looked forlorn, 'Actually, I wanted to but Jo wouldn't let me. She felt the work of the Guardians was too important and keeping nature in balance had to take priority over our love. We managed to keep it a secret for many years. I got to see you grow up, George. You were named after me, you know?'

It was at this point that George fell off the bench. Once she righted herself, she took a hesitant step towards Harris, 'You mean you're my father?'

Harris looked sheepish, 'Yes. In fact, I'm Sam's father and yours too, Eddy.'

It was Eddy's turn to be shocked. 'This can't be true. Why keep it a secret all these years? We needed someone after mother died. I was just a baby, George was in her own little world trying to fix Jack and it was up to Sam to try to keep us together and look after the household when she was just a child herself. We struggled for years on our own. How could you abandon us like that?'

'I didn't abandon you. I know it might look like I did but your mother never wanted anyone to know who the father of her children was. She said bad things always happened to men who fell in love with Wick women and she wanted to protect me. She thought if no one knew I was the father, then that would keep me safe. She also didn't want the Guardian Council to find out because she thought they might take you children away for safe keeping. Eventually, they got suspicious anyway and reassigned me when Eddy was only days old. The reassignment was supposed to be punishment although it turned out lucky for me in the end. My new mission was to get inside information on the WI and they assigned me to be Nigel Jones's butler, who was a wannabe WI member. Nigel always had airs above his station and had advertised for a butler cum man servant so I was made to apply.'

George looked confused, 'Wait, did you say they wanted

information on the Women's Institute?'

'No, WI in this case actually stands for Witchfinder Institute. Ever since the witch hunts in the sixteen hundreds, there has been a Witchfinder Institute headed up by the Witchfinder General. The WI went underground after the 1700s ruling that witches could no longer be punished by law. But they have been growing in power ever since, funded by a secret division of government that not even the prime minister knows about.'

'So are the WI still hunting witches, I mean Keepers, to kill them?' Lucy asked a little fretfully.

'Not exactly. You see, it's impossible to kill a Keeper without being killed yourself. The WI found this out very early on. If they drowned a Keeper, the people involved would die the same death, even if they were standing on dry land. Of course, it took them a while to figure this out because they killed more innocent people than actual Keepers during the witch hunts. But eventually they realised there was no way to kill a real Keeper without being killed. So for years they've been working on ways to extract the Keeper's powers. Once a Keeper is without power, he or she can be killed without any repercussions.'

'How on earth can they extract our powers?' Eddy demanded.

'Advances in science and technology have finally given them the tools they need. They are close to perfecting a weapon that can render a Keeper powerless and helpless. The problem is that the WI is no longer just this ideological organisation that thinks that the Keepers are doing the devil's work. Although I think most WI members still think this is what they're doing. But the Witchfinder General and the people above him are now more interested in how they can use the powers they extract for their own gain. If anything, this is more dangerous than when they just thought Keepers were unnatural and shouldn't be walking about unchecked amongst regular humans.'

'So Barry's uncle is part of the WI. Is that why you were

following him the other night?' Lucy asked.

'Yes,' Harris admitted. 'Nigel is trying hard to integrate himself into the WI but he's not really accepted. Nigel and Cybil, who was the head of the local WI at the time, were there when Jo was killed. Nigel wasn't supposed to have been there but he wanted to prove himself. He showed up just as Jo and Cybil were at a stand-off. Cybil was about to use a power extraction device on Jo when Nigel arrived and startled her. She accidently switched the device to the incorrect setting, killing Jo and herself almost instantly. Nigel was protected because he had taken this handkerchief Jo had given me and put it in his pocket for decoration. Jo had given it to me for protection and I had carelessly left it on the hall table where Nigel found it. Not only did the handkerchief shield him but somehow Jo's powers were transferred to Nigel too. I can only guess this had something to do with the protection charm Jo had placed on it.

Nigel didn't realise anything had happened at first. He was immediately banished by the WI for causing Cybil's death and I had to go with him. Over the coming months, we both began to realise he could do things he had never done before but he was too afraid to say anything in case the WI put him on their most wanted list too. He only returned because Lucy's arrival changed everything.'

'What do you mean?' George enquired, looking protectively at Lucy.

'As I mentioned earlier, Keepers have some powers on their own; however, they get most of their powers from each other. But it needs the power of three Keepers to really liven things up. That's why George and Eddy lived together quite peacefully without anything truly remarkable happening. When Jo died, your collective powers were diminished. For a while, your powers built up again when Sam was with you but young Keepers don't have a lot of energy in them until they are approaching their eleventh birthday. After that, their powers gradually increase until they're twenty-one. Then, when they go through the ascension, they transform into a fully-fledged

Keeper. Sam left home long before Eddy's eleventh birthday so you never got to feel the energy that the power of three or more can bring. But you must have noticed, as soon as Lucy arrived, things started to change. You must have felt different.'

George and Eddy looked at each other in silent agreement.

'Anyway, Nigel began feeling this too. Because a portion of Jo's powers transferred to him, he felt the energy surge when Lucy arrived and it compelled him to come back. He didn't want to bring Barry but he's never been able to say no to his sister, particularly when she offers him money. Never did he imagine that Barry would actually give him all the inside information he needed to help raise his position with the WI. Unfortunately, because of Barry, he now knows where the Ascension Stones are?'

'What are the Ascension Stones?' Lucy asked.

'They are the stones in the clearing in the woods. The WI call them the Whispering Stones. You showed them to Barry and the others, and then Barry told Nigel.'

Lucy gasped in dismay, 'Oh no, I had no idea. I just wanted my friends to believe me. Jake told me how to make them see the stones, I'm so sorry.'

'Who's Jake?' George enquired.

'He's another boy I've met. He says he knows you. He's got black hair and the strangest green eyes you've ever seen.'

'Is that so?' George, who had been stroking Jack again, suddenly pulled his tail sharply. The cat meowed loudly but looked almost pleased with himself.

'Never mind that now,' Eddy intervened. 'What do we need to do, Harris?'

'The only thing that can be done. We need to make sure your Ascension Ceremony takes place. Your twenty-first birthday is approaching. The Book of Ascension has everything in it. It will tell us not just how to perform the ceremony but the preparations that need to happen beforehand.'

'There's just one problem,' George said sheepishly. 'We don't know where the book is.'

CHAPTER 19

LADY ELIZABETH

Ben, Beatrice and Barry sat in stunned silence. The four friends were once again reunited in the tree house and Lucy had just finished telling them all about Harris and his big revelations. Eventually Beatrice spoke, 'We figured you might be a witch but we had no idea it would be this serious or this dangerous.'

'And this cool!' Ben added, grinning. 'This is awesome. It's the best summer ever! What's our first mission, Lucy?'

'Well, if by "mission" you mean what do we do next? Then the answer is absolutely nothing.'

'What?' Ben's face fell. 'Nothing? What's the point of that?'

'My aunts are seriously concerned that I might be in danger and, since we don't know who the WI are other than Barry's uncle, we don't know who we can trust except for Harris that is.'

'I'm really sorry about my uncle. I can't believe I told him everything. I'm such a fool. I should have known a grown up couldn't be interested in me.'

Lucy patted Barry's arm reassuringly. 'It's not your fault. Besides, Harris hopes Nigel will reveal who the WI members are so good may come from this yet. In the meantime, my aunts think it's better if we just carry on like normal. They don't want us to do anything out of the ordinary in case it raises suspicion.'

Ben hit the wall of the tree house in frustration. 'It's the worse summer ever,' he muttered sulkily. 'What are we supposed to do now?'

'Actually, I have an idea,' Barry pulled a cream coloured card out of his back pocket. 'This was on the doormat this morning.'

'What is it?' Beatrice plucked the card out of Barry's hand and studied it.

'It's an invitation from Lady Elizabeth. You know, the one from the garden the other night. She's invited us for afternoon tea.'

'This day keeps getting worse and worse,' Ben grumbled. 'First there's nothing to do, and then we're asked to visit with a boring old lady. No thanks.'

'Actually,' Beatrice quickly cut in, 'this is perfect. If we visit Lady Elizabeth, we may get the chance to explore her gardens. It can't be a coincidence that the WI chose her garden to meet in. Maybe there's a connection somewhere. Maybe Lady Elizabeth is the connection.'

Barry started to protest but Beatrice held up a hand, 'I know you think she is nice, Barry, but sometimes people can pretend to be one thing just to get what they want.'

'True,' Barry admitted glumly, 'look at my uncle. He never was interested in me. He was only interested in my friendship with Lucy.'

'I'm with Beatrice,' Lucy agreed, 'I think we should visit Lady Elizabeth and see what we can discover. I'm tired of everyone trying to protect me all the time. I want to find out what's going on. I say we go.'

'Fine,' Ben agreed begrudgingly.

* * *

At the appointed time, the four friends, who had made a bit of an effort to tidy themselves up and didn't have a dirty hand or face between them, stood on the doorstep in front of the big imposing black doors. Barry had been relieved to find the wrought iron gates standing wide open when they arrived so they didn't have to figure out how to get in but now they all stood nervously fidgeting on the threshold of this large stately home.

'You knock, Barry,' Beatrice whispered. 'It was you she invited in the first place.'

Just as Barry hesitantly raised his hand towards the large brass knocker, one of the doors flew open with a bang and Mr Green pushed rudely past them without pausing to apologise.

'Oh and thank you for the delivery, Mr Green,' a voice called after him.

The children turned towards the voice only to discover a tiny woman dressed all in black save for a white pinafore staring back at them. The woman's face was stern with beady little eyes peering at them over a hooked nose, like a bird might scrutinise a worm just before devouring it.

'What are you doing here? You'd better not be playing one of those silly games where you ring people's doorbells and then run and hide. I've no time for silly little games today.'

The children got the distinct impression that this woman would not have time for silly little games on any day. The woman stared hard at Lucy in particular.

'Lady Elizabeth invited us.' Barry stepped forward, acting more confidently than he felt, and extended his invitation for inspection. 'Could you please tell her we're here?'

'Well, Lady Elizabeth may have invited you but she's not taking visitors today. She's had one of her little turns and needs to rest so run along. Off you go.'

The woman made to close the door when a gentle voice called out from behind her, 'Let them in Malys.'

Malys scowled briefly before rearranging her features. 'Of course, milady, I was just about to.' Malys opened the door wide with a smile that didn't quite reach her eyes.

'Thank you, Malys. I think we'll have tea in the Garden Room and make sure we have plenty of cakes and sandwiches too. This lot look hungry.'

'Yes, milady,' Malys replied still smiling tightly.

The children explored the Garden Room while Malys went to make the tea. The room was light and airy with large glass paned windows running from floor to ceiling across one side, giving a panoramic view of the garden below. The room was cluttered with weird and wondrous objects. Noticing the children's curious looks, Lady Elizabeth said, 'Please go ahead and touch anything you want. I gathered these during the years of my travels and the most precious thing about them is the memories they bring back.'

The children picked eagerly through the objects while Lady Elizabeth explained where they were from. After a short while Malys wheeled in a hostess trolley laden with tea, cakes and sandwiches.

'Shall I pour, milady?' Malys spoke to Lady Elizabeth but looked at Lucy.

'That's okay, Malys, I'll manage.'

Malys looked as if she wanted to protest. 'Very well, milady,' she eventually replied before slowly backing out of the room, all the while keeping her eyes on Lucy.

'She gives me the creeps,' Beatrice whispered.

'Yum.' Ben and Barry, who hadn't noticed anything but the trolley since it arrived, were already piling their plates high.

'What kind of travelling did you do, Lady Elizabeth?' Beatrice slowly turned over what looked like a wooden African sculpture as she studied it from all angles.

'I was a pilot when I was younger. I was very lucky coming from a family with money. I had my own plane and spent years travelling across all five continents.'

'Wow, a pilot, that's cool.' Ben, who had been gorging himself on cake, perked up with interest.

'Yes, it was very… cool… indeed,' Lady Elizabeth laughed softly as she adopted Ben's language. 'At least, it was until the plane ran into trouble.'

'What happened?'

'I was about an hour into my flight when the engine cut

out. I only just managed to bail out with my parachute in time.'

'Then what happened?'

'Fortunately, I survived the jump but, unfortunately, I landed badly. I hit the ground too hard and the impact shattered my spine. I've been in this confounded wheel chair ever since.'

Ben was by now enraptured and had moved closer to Lady Elizabeth as she told her story.

'Is it difficult learning to fly? How many countries did you visit? Could you do any stunts?' Ben fired questions eagerly.

Lady Elizabeth chuckled. 'Which question would you like me to answer first?'

'Excuse me,' Beatrice interrupted, 'may I use your bathroom?'

'Of course, dear, it's the third door down the hall on the right.'

Beatrice kicked Lucy's foot as she walked past.

'Oh, I need to go too, I'll come with you.' Lucy stood up and hurried after Beatrice.

Exiting the room, they almost tripped over Malys who was purposefully dusting an already very clean and shiny hall table immediately next to the Garden Room door.

'Goodness, that table is so shiny you can see your face in it. You've clearly been polishing it for some time, Malys.' Beatrice smiled sweetly at her.

Malys glared back and muttered something under her breath that sounded like "pesky children" before stomping off down the passage and disappearing around the corner.

'I think she was eavesdropping. Come on, she's gone now, let's explore.' Beatrice crept down the corridor trying each door as she came to it.

'Gosh there are a lot of rooms in this house that don't do a particular lot,' she exclaimed having just closed a third door to a room that was filled with yet more chairs and strange objects. 'Lady Elizabeth sure did a lot of travelling.'

'And collecting,' Lucy agreed.

They came to a door at the end of the passage. Beatrice

twisted the handle and pushed only to find it wouldn't budge.

'How curious! There must be something very interesting behind this door if Lady Elizabeth keeps it locked,' Beatrice mused.

'Yes, but how are we going to find out? We can't very well break in.'

'Maybe we don't need to break in. Maybe we just need to walk through it. Or rather, you need to walk through it.'

'What? I'm not some sort of magician. I can't simply walk through a door.'

'Have you ever tried?'

'Of course not. I've only just discovered I can make myself invisible after all.'

'So now's as good a time as any to give it a go. What if, when you disappear, you become transparent? Like a ghost.'

'I don't know. I feel pretty real when I disappear. In fact, I can still see myself plainly so I never quite believe that no one else can. But I suppose I could give it a try.'

Lucy turned to face the door and willed herself not to be seen.

'You've done it, Lucy, I can't see you anymore. Now try to walk through the door.'

A loud thud filled the passageway.

'Ow!' Lucy reappeared rubbing her nose. 'At least we know I'm not a ghost. What do we do now?'

Beatrice thought for a moment. 'I think you should sneak up on Malys. She's definitely acting suspiciously. Perhaps she's connected with this WI business somehow. Either that or she's just a really grumpy person who doesn't like children.'

'My money is on grumpy but why not, I'm getting the hang of this disappearing act. Let's see if we can find where she went. But we'd better be quick. If we're gone too long, we're the ones who will start to look suspicious.'

They sidled down the passage in the direction Malys had hastened off in. Turning a corner they found another shorter hallway leading to what looked like a back staircase. Tiptoeing closer, they heard the sound of low urgent voices.

'This is it,' whispered Beatrice, 'time for you to do your thing.'

'Okay, wish me luck.'

Lucy disappeared and made her way down the stairs as silently as she could. Rounding a corner, she had to quickly step back behind a door when she almost stumbled into Malys talking to a man. At first, Lucy couldn't see who Malys was speaking to from her position behind the door but, reminding herself they couldn't see her, she took a steadying breath and stepped out from her hiding place. For a moment, her heart stopped when the man looked away from Malys and straight at Lucy, as she stared back at the face of Mr Green. But which one? And hadn't he just been leaving when they arrived? So what was he doing back so soon?

Mr Green turned back to Malys, 'I just want to be clear of the plan.'

'We've just been through it, Green. You're taking a great risk coming back here like this. What if the children spotted you again?'

'I was very careful. They definitely don't know I'm here.'

'Fine, well, as I told you less than hour ago,' Malys paused to ensure her displeasure at Mr Green's sudden return didn't go unnoticed, 'in a nutshell, it will all happen on the Night of Ascension. New equipment is coming from head office. The Witchfinder General is sending it along with extra reinforcements. We will hit those repulsive witches so hard their heads will spin, perhaps literally if the new equipment is as good as promised.'

'And what about the fledgling witch?'

'That little nose wipe? We plan to capture her. We've never had a witchling before. The Witchfinder General thinks we might learn all kinds of things from a fledgling. And we'll be able to experiment on her without fear of the same level of repercussions as she hasn't come of age yet. If the prophecy can be believed, then this fledgling is the one they've been writing about for hundreds of years. The one who will be all powerful. The one we have to stop. For good.'

Lucy gasped in shock.

Malys swivelled on her heels, her beady eyes peering all around.

'Did you hear that, Green?'

'Hear what?'

'That sound, man, did you hear that sound?'

'I didn't hear anything but I'd better go, as you say, it's a risk being here. I'll let myself out the back into the garden so no one sees me from the front of the house.'

'Well of course no one will see you from the front, you'll be using the secret door in the wall as usual, Green.' Malys peered at him curiously, a distrustful frown beginning to crease her brow.

'What's this month's code word, Green?' Malys asked suspiciously, taking a step closer to Mr Green.

Mr Green looked momentarily stricken. 'Bubblegum,' he eventually offered.

'That was last month's code word,' Malys took another step forward menacingly.

Before Mr Green could respond, the servant bell above the lettering "Garden Room" tolled back and forth.

'Right, that will be the mad old bat upstairs summoning me to tidy up after her and those brats. I can't believe the Witchfinder General gave me this post as my undercover assignment. I've been that woman's bloomin' servant and nursemaid for almost twenty years. But it won't be for much longer. Once we've rid Wickham of this ungodly vermin, I'll be moving on to better things, you mark my words, Green. A successful outcome could mean that I'm the one who's next in line to be Witchfinder General.'

'And a marvellous one you would make too, Councillor.'

Slightly mollified, Malys waved him away. 'Off you go, Green, and try to remember your code words in the future.'

Mr Green nodded and then made his way silently out the back door.

Lucy quickly hurried away up the stairs as Malys turned to follow her.

She rounded the corner and bumped into Beatrice.

'You need to look where you're going when you're invisible,' Beatrice said rubbing her arm.

'Sorry,' Lucy grabbed Beatrice by her other arm, 'but we need to move. Malys is on the way.'

They hurried back to the Garden Room. Lady Elizabeth looked up as they entered and greeted them with a knowing smile and a half raised eyebrow, as if she knew exactly what they had been up to.

The girls only just managed to position themselves on two armchairs, as casually as their heaving breaths would allow them, when Malys burst into the room.

'Time for your afternoon nap, milady. These children will have tired you out.'

'Oh, I think I can go one day without my nap, Malys. The children are a delight. They are not tiring me one bit.'

'Sorry, milady, your son's orders. He only wants what's best for you.'

'My step-son,' Lady Elizabeth corrected, but she sighed in resignation.

'Very well but you children must promise to come and see me again. Next time Malys can make us a picnic for the garden.'

Malys scowled at the suggestion she would do any such thing but kept quiet. Instead, she held the door open and gestured with her hand for the children to leave.

'Do shake my hand farewell before you go, children. I've had such a wonderful time having you here,' Lady Elizabeth implored.

The children took it in turn to shake her hand, starting with Ben and ending with Barry.

They were then herded out the front entrance by Malys who looked down her nose, sniffed loudly, and shut the door firmly behind them without another word.

The children walked in silence until they reached the front gates.

'Malys!' squeaked Lucy.

'What about her?' Beatrice asked.

'She's the one. She's the head of the local WI, I'm sure of it. Mr Green is involved too. At least, one of them is. I bet it's the butcher. He seemed to take such an instant disliking to me.'

'I'll never think that having tea with an old lady is boring ever again. First I find out Lady E was a pilot adventurer. Then we discover the heart of the WI is beating right inside her house! It's back to being the best summer ever,' Ben grinned from ear to ear.

'Well, that's not all that happened,' Barry spoke urgently. 'Lady Elizabeth pressed this into my palm as she was shaking my hand and she whispered "give Harris my regards".'

Barry held up a small cream card. Printed on it was a small symbol of an eye inside a triangle.

CHAPTER 20

THE SECRET ROOM

'Argh!' Eddy slammed a book down in frustration, sending a cloud of dust rising up to her head. She and George were in the main workshop surrounded by a mountain of books. 'That's it. We have searched every nook and cranny of this house and have looked at everything that remotely resembles a book. The Book of Ascension is definitely not here.'

George heaved a sigh and wiped her brow, leaving a smudge of dirt behind as she picked up yet another book covered in a thick coat of dust. 'We have to keep looking. What choice do we have? If we are going to protect this family and help keep nature in balance, we need to find it.'

'I know. You're right.' Eddy sat down dejectedly but then raised her voice, 'House, you'd better not be hiding that book from us.'

House made a sound like it was blowing a giant raspberry.

'Can I help?' Lucy had been watching Eddy and George frantically thumb through books of all shapes and sizes for the last half an hour. Upon returning from Lady Elizabeth's, she had told her aunts all that she had seen and heard. When she got to the bit about Malys and one of the Mr Greens, the news had sent her aunts frantically scurrying off in different directions in the workshop, pulling out anything that remotely resembled a book, no matter how big or small.

'Of course you can. We've searched everywhere but it certainly wouldn't do any harm to have another set of eyes look again. You might spot something we didn't.'

'Okay. Why don't I start over here?' Lucy headed to a large dresser set back behind a long workbench on the opposite side of the room.

'You could do, although we have searched that area thoroughly and there's not much there anyway. It used to be your Grandmother Jo's work area but we've been using her books for years. There's definitely no Book of Ascension amongst them.'

'Alright, I'll look somewhere else,' Lucy replied as she trailed her hands across the dresser, pausing to look at the odd collection of jars and bottles that were still there. She picked up a purple bottle and opened the lid. A strange smell wafted out and she quickly closed it, screwing up her nose. She selected a jar that was filled with some sort of gloopy green substance and gingerly lifted the lid to sniff before smiling. This one smelt like butterscotch. She put it back and was just picking up a small blue bottle when a metal grinding sound made her freeze mid motion. The floor beneath her feet shuddered and Lucy barely had enough time to grab the dresser with both hands before it pivoted wildly, swinging her out of the workshop and into pitch darkness.

Lucy heard screaming but then realised it was coming from herself. Her aunts frantically called her name from the other side of the wall.

'I'm alright,' Lucy called back, 'although I can't see where I am.'

The room filled with a gloomy light.

'Thanks House, that's better!'

House grunted.

'I can see now,' Lucy called again. 'I guess I'm in some sort of secret room behind the workshop.'

She took a hesitant step away from the dresser, her eyes starting to focus as they grew accustomed to the murky light.

'It looks like there's another workbench in here,' she hollered, 'and it's covered with jars and bowls and other stuff.'

Lucy gingerly picked up a long curved metal rod that had a giant ladling spoon on one end and three sharp needle-like points on the other. There was a little stove on the workbench with a small cauldron on top.

'I guess every self-respecting witch must have a cauldron,' Lucy muttered.

She stepped behind the workbench and stopped abruptly. There, in the corner was a carved, wooden book stand. Lying open on the stand was a very large and very old book.

'I think I've found something!' She cautiously lifted the pages, being careful not to move too quickly because they felt brittle and fragile to her touch. She tried to make out what was written but the light was too poor and the writing too unfamiliar to make any sense of.

Very slowly, she reached for the cover and gently folded the book closed. There on the front, embossed into the dark leather in gold leaf were the words everyone had been looking for. *The Book of Ascension.*

'I've found it,' Lucy yelled. 'I've found the book. It's here!'

Lucy could hear her aunts screeching in delight on the other side of the wall.

'Alright, Lucy,' Eddy called back to her, 'Now we need to get you and the book out of there. Can you see anything that looks like a lever or a handle that might make the wall swivel again?'

Lucy went back to the dresser and searched the wall on either side of it. There were no levers and no handles to be seen. She started to feel a little panicky. She went back over to the workbench and felt all over for something that might trigger the dresser to pivot back.

'I can't find anything,' Lucy squeaked with alarm.

'Not to worry,' George called back, 'we'll get you out of there. House? Can you help?'

House responded with what sounded like a frustrated grunt.

'I guess that's a no then. Don't worry Lucy, we'll figure something out.'

On the other side of the wall, Eddy was feeling along the bare stones covered in decades of undisturbed cobwebs and dust, but to no avail. There was nothing that looked like a lever or a button that would trigger the wall to spin again.

'I've had an idea,' Eddy called out. 'You were picking up bottles when the dresser spun round. Do you remember what order you picked them up in?'

Lucy scratched her head. She hadn't really been paying attention. She started picking up bottles at random but nothing happened.

George sensed her panic.

'I think we need the Remembrance Dust, Eddy. I use it all the time when I'm trying to remember which of the concoctions I make for Jack seem to be working. That might help Lucy.'

George hurried over to her workbench and started gathering ingredients, putting them into a bowl. She mixed quickly and then grabbed a small bottle containing a cloudy, amber liquid and shoved it into her pocket before returning to the wall.

'Calm your mind, Lucy, and listen to my voice. I want you to stay still and close your eyes. Let your mind empty so that all you see is a floating white of nothingness.' George added a few drops of the amber liquid to her bowl and quickly mixed it together. Rather than forming a paste, the result was a small pile of tiny glistening shards. She poured them into her hand and, holding it out straight, blew the shards into the seam of the wall where the dresser had disappeared. The shards floated into the secret room beyond.

'Now, I want you to go back to the moment when you entered the workshop. Can you see yourself?'

'Yes!' Lucy exclaimed with relief, her eyes firmly shut. Inside her mind, it was as if someone was slowly revealing a picture, the floating white mist cleared and she had a perfect image of herself entering the room.

'Follow yourself in your mind Lucy. What do you do next?'

'After I offer to help, I walk over to Grandmother Jo's dresser and… I picked up the purple bottle,' Lucy cried with delight at having remembered.

'Then I pick up the jar of the green gloopy stuff. And finally the little blue bottle.'

'That's good, that's very good, Lucy. Now try picking those bottles up in that order.'

Lucy reached for the bottles on the dresser and hurriedly grabbed all three. Nothing happened.

'It didn't work!'

'Did you pick them up in the right order?' George asked.

'Yes, I definitely did… oh wait. I think I put each one down first before picking up the next. Let me try that.'

George and Eddy managed to step back just in time as Lucy reappeared with a whoosh.

She held out the *Book of Ascension* triumphantly in her hands. 'I have it. We're saved!'

CHAPTER 21

A VERY OLD CAT

'We are so not saved,' Eddy stared at the book dejectedly half an hour later.

'Are you quite sure it's not there, Eddy? Let me look.' George shoved Eddy aside and carefully started to turn each of the delicate pages, but it was no good, the Ascension Ceremony was not there. The missing pages had been clearly torn out of the book leaving a gap where they should have been.

'I don't understand. Why would mother have gone to all that effort to hide the book in a secret room if the pages weren't in it in the first place?' Eddy complained.

'Maybe she's not the one who tore out the pages? Maybe she didn't realise they were missing?'

'Perhaps, but it's clear she deliberately hid the book in the secret room and she somehow made certain that House couldn't reveal it to us otherwise House would have by now. House began changing when Aunt Harry disappeared which was over twenty-five years ago. House would have uncovered the room by now if she'd been able to.'

'That's right. House started to change about the same time as Jack was…um…became ill,' George corrected quickly.

'How ancient is that cat?' Lucy asked incredulously. 'I've never known such an old cat. He doesn't even look old. He just looks big.'

As if on cue, Jack prowled into the room, eyeing up George and Eddy suspiciously before making his way over to Lucy and beginning to wind himself around her legs.

'Stop that, Jack, that's no way to behave around a lady,' George admonished

Jack hissed at George but carried on rubbing himself against Lucy's ankle.

'I don't mind. You're a curious old cat but I like you.' Lucy scratched Jack behind his ears and was rewarded with the sound of loud purring. Jack looked over at George with an air of defiance.

George heaved a heavy sigh, 'Lucy, there's something I need to tell you. Something you need to know about Jack.'

Jack arched his back, his hair standing on end and spat violently at George.

'I'm sorry, Jack but it's time Lucy knew the truth.'

Jack hissed again and leapt onto George's worktable, seeming to deliberately knock over as many pots and jars as he could. He finally sat down and fixed George with his unblinking green eyes.

'Jack is my friend,' George admitted quietly.

'Oh George, of course he is,' Lucy almost laughed. 'Pets are often their owner's best friend. That's completely normal.'

'No, you don't understand. Jack is actually my friend. He's the friend I had when I was fourteen years old.'

'Wow, so he *really* is a very old cat.'

George shook her head. 'What I'm trying to say, Lucy, is that Jack was my friend when I was fourteen. And he was also fourteen at the time. A fourteen year old boy.'

'What?' Lucy laughed incredulously. 'Are you trying to tell me that Jack is not a cat but really a boy? That's nuts.'

'Actually, yes, that's exactly what I'm trying to say.'

Jack was now stalking up and down George's workbench, purposefully pushing whatever he could off the worktop and onto the floor.

'Stop that Jack, it was well time Lucy knew the truth. We couldn't have kept it a secret much longer.'

Jack hissed and jumped up onto the top of a high dresser. He backed himself into the corner. Only his eyes and twitching ears peaked out as he watched them below.

'I don't understand. How did Jack turn into a cat?'

'Well, that's the thing, I still haven't worked it out. Jack moved to the village about four years before it happened. He stayed with these nasty foster parents but spent as much time out of their house as he could.'

Lucy gasped, 'He's the one everyone thinks was murdered or stolen by gypsies. Jack's the child that disappeared!'

'The very same. Back then, there was a village school but none of the other kids wanted to play with me as they thought I was too odd. Jack was considered odd too as he was an outsider without real parents. He used to spend all his spare time in the woods and so did I, so we became friends. After a while, I knew I could trust him with the family secret and I told him about our gifts. That was when Jack and I started making potions together. At first, they were silly potions just for fun. We once made the vicar burp uncontrollably. It was a different vicar back then and he wasn't very nice. Another time we made all the dogs in the village start to meow and all the cats bark. That was funny.'

The sound of a strange meowing laugh came from the top of the dresser.

'We gave the whole class sneezing fits once and made the teacher bray like a donkey. This was when mother realised what we were up to and put a stop to it. She sat us both down and lectured us about the dangers of potions and how we could end up hurting ourselves or others.

For a while, we stopped but then we noticed some mysterious goings on in the village. People we'd never seen before started popping up everywhere. I realise now that it must have been the WI. They seemed to be everywhere we were. Jack and I got it into our minds that we were being followed. So we decided we wanted to follow them instead. I found a potion in one of Aunt Harry's books that made you change into a cat but the effect was only supposed to last for twenty minutes. We decided we would both change into cats and then follow these mysterious visitors without being detected. Cats are so agile and stealthy. We thought it was a perfect plan.

It took a few days to make the potion. I had to keep it secret from mother and Aunt Harry as I knew they would put a stop to it, so I worked on it whenever I could. The ingredients were hard to come by and we only had enough for one go each. We had agreed to meet in the woods. I brought the potion bottles with me, they were identical. Jack took his first and immediately changed. I remember how funny it was to watch. He first started to twitch all over. Then it was like his body turned into a human tornado. There was a final popping sound and then this large black cat stood where Jack had been. It was my turn next. I swallowed the remaining potion and waited but nothing happened. After a few minutes, it became clear that something had gone wrong and the potion either didn't have the same effect on me or, somehow, they weren't the same. But the bottles were with me the whole time except for a brief moment when I left them on my workbench. For some silly reason, I decided I wanted to look nice for Jack and had gone to my room to fetch a ribbon for my hair. I was only gone for a moment and the potion bottles were exactly where I'd left them when I returned so I just couldn't figure out what could have changed.

Anyway, rather than Jack go off and follow the mysterious people on his own, we decided it would be safer if we waited for him to return to normal and try again another time. At least, this is what I said but he obviously couldn't talk back so he just sat down next to me. We waited and waited. Twenty minutes came and went and still he remained a cat. After an hour, I was starting to get concerned. After two hours, I knew something was seriously wrong.

I went back to the house to find Aunty Harry's potion book to look up the antidote but neither her book nor Aunt Harry were anywhere to be found. That was the day she disappeared. We've not seen her since.

Jack has remained a cat from that day forward. He's also stayed the same age. I've been trying to find a cure ever since. I've tried to replicate the potion so many times because then I'll be able to figure out an antidote. But even though I've used the exact same ingredients, I've not been able to reproduce it. Sometime between me finishing the original potion and going to my room, the bottles must have been tampered with. The only person who could have done that was our ditzy Aunt Harry. But as loopy as she was, I can't believe she would deliberately do such a horrible thing and then just disappear. Something must have happened.

All I can do is keep trying to find the cure. I've had some mild success over the years. I can now turn Jack into a boy for short periods of time, but it never lasts long. In fact, I suspect you met Jack when he's been a boy, but he introduced himself as Jake.'

Lucy gasped. 'You!' she pointed an accusing finger at the cat who slunk further into the corner.

'Don't be cross with him, Lucy, he's been so lonely. All these years on his own, stuck forever as a fourteen year old boy. He was so excited when you arrived; finally someone closer to his age. Eddy and I have just been getting older and he's been stuck in time. It's not been easy for him.'

'I suppose you're right,' Lucy agreed. 'I don't blame you Jack. Come back down and I'll scratch your ears.'

Jack let out a plaintive meow but stayed put.

'I think he's feeling a little embarrassed now the truth is out. Give him time, he'll come around. Now, let's get back to our search.'

George turned each page of the Book of Ascension carefully. The pages were filled with writing and hand drawn diagrams. Some writing looked familiar but others looked strange. It was clear that many different people had added to the book over the years. George eventually came to the end.

'Well, the Ascension Ceremony is definitely missing but there's a lot of good stuff in here that we can get started with. There are charms to aid protection and disguise. There are potions to increase strength and agility and lots more. We can start by further arming House against uninvited visitors in case the WI try to come sniffing around. Then we can begin planning what we need for the day of the ceremony itself, like cloaking charms and protection balms.'

'But that doesn't help us if we can't actually perform the ceremony,' Eddy said despondently.

'No it doesn't, Eddy, but at least it's something constructive we can be getting on with. It's only a few days before your birthday so the Ascension Ceremony might need to take place at any moment and, from what Harris told us, you can bet the WI will already be preparing. They will be doing all they can to disrupt or prevent it from happening.'

Eddy grunted in response but dutifully walked over to her workbench and started to take stock of her ingredients and what she was running low on while George began to earmark potions and charms that might be useful.

Lucy watched for a moment and then an idea came to her. 'Did you search my mum's room?'

'Not properly. That's the only room we haven't been in. The door's locked and House won't open it no matter what we try but I used probes to search the room remotely,' Eddy responded.

'How can you search a room remotely? And what's a probe anyway?'

Reaching into the folds of her skirt, Eddy retrieved a clear glass jar with a lid punched through with breathing holes. Inside was a collection of garden beetles, including a couple of ladybugs and a dung beetle.

'These are my little friends. They often do jobs for me in places I can't reach. It's normally in the garden but today I used them to go through the crack beneath Sam's bedroom door. I use a recipe for Probing Potion which I sprinkle onto their backs. If what you desire to seek can be found, the potion glows green. I sent them into Sam's room but they all returned the same colour. So I'm pretty sure the missing pages are not in there. Besides, House would definitely have opened the door if they were, right House?' Eddy raised her voice to make sure House was listening.

House snorted.

'Do you think I could try anyway?' Lucy asked.

'Try what, dear?' George replied, distractedly thumbing through yet another old book. 'Oh, this one's got some good defence and protection charms in it.'

'I would like to try to get into my mum's old bedroom,' Lucy pressed.

George looked up over her half-moon reading glasses. 'I suppose it won't hurt to try. I just don't want you getting your hopes up. Sam's door has not opened in more than a decade. Not since she last visited here with your father just before she... just before... well, you know.'

'My hopes aren't up,' Lucy promised, her fingers crossed behind her back.

CHAPTER 22

A ROOM FILLED WITH NOTHING

Lucy raced up the stairs which, for once, were back in their usual place and reached her mother's bedroom in a matter of minutes. She paused, panting, before she reached out and slowly turned the handle. Nothing. She tried again. Nothing. She pushed and shoved the door but it didn't budge. Leaning against it, Lucy slowly slid to the floor, pulling her knees up to her chest. She didn't know why today of all days she felt it would be different and the door would open for her, even though it had been shut fast every other time she had tried, which had been every day since she'd arrived. It was just that so much had happened in the last few days and everything felt different. She didn't feel like the old sceptical Lucy anymore. She felt like a new Lucy, filled with optimism and, well, magic. She felt like anything was possible, even opening her mother's old bedroom door.

House appeared to notice her sitting dejectedly on the floor and made a low rumbling sound, like a hundred bricks knocking gently together.

'House, please open the door,' Lucy pleaded. 'I'm stronger now than when I arrived and I need to help protect George and Eddy just as much as they need to protect me. We are a family. All of us. George, Eddy, me and you. But we can't do this without you.'

House grunted.

'Did you make my mother a promise, House? Did you promise not to let anyone into her room?'

A strong gust of air blew through the corridors as House sighed.

'I don't think she would want you to keep that promise if she knew her family was in danger and what's inside her room could possibly help protect them, do you?' Lucy continued.

House creaked loudly in protest.

Lucy smacked her hands against the floorboards in frustration. Both Lucy and House were quiet for a moment, as if each was waiting for the other to make the first move.

Then Lucy felt a cold draft blow past her followed by the sound of a soft click. Moments later, she fell backwards and hit her head on the floor with a crack as the door to her mother's room suddenly flew open.

She jumped to her feet, whooping with joy. 'House, I could kiss you but you could have given me a bit of a warning. That hurt!' Lucy rubbed her head where it had connected with the floor.

The shutters on the house banged back and forth in reply.

Lucy stood still for a moment in awe. She was standing inside her mother's bedroom. This was the closest she had ever got to anything of her mum's. A small lump formed in the back of her throat and her eyes started to prick as she struggled to control her emotions. The room was decorated in pale blue and white and shimmered in the light of a thousand tiny crystals and glass decorations. Everything seemed to sparkle as if it was somehow alive. Lucy stepped further into the room. There wasn't much to it really. There was a bed covered in a soft white throw. A painted white wardrobe stood against a wall, which Lucy was disappointed to find completely empty.

The same was true of a chest of drawers. Lucy felt carefully inside each drawer to see if there was a secret compartment or something hidden underneath. She even pulled the drawers out completely and craned her neck inside the openings, but there was nothing. Finally, she sat down at the dressing table. The first two drawers were also empty but, when she got to the last one, it actually had something in it. She carefully pulled out a white leather bound book and placed it on top of the empty dressing table. Lucy took a deep calming breath. She felt nervous. Finally, she had something of her mothers, something that looked like a diary. She couldn't wait to see what she would discover; perhaps her mother's deepest, darkest secret; perhaps just boring details of her everyday life. Lucy didn't care. She just wanted to know something, anything about her mother.

She turned the first page, holding her breath in anticipation.

The page was blank.

She quickly turned over the next page. And the next. And the next.

They were all blank.

'Argh!' Lucy shouted in frustration and slammed the drawer shut. As she did, she heard something rattle. Quickly opening the drawer again, she felt along the back and pulled out a stubby, round, pale blue jar.

Perhaps it was an old beauty product. She opened the lid and sniffed, screwing up her nose in disgust. It smelt like rotten eggs. It must have gone bad sitting here all these years. She tentatively pushed her finger into the powder and rubbed some onto her skin. Instead of dissolving, it just stayed on top like a little brown blob of dust.

Just then, something furry wrapped itself around Lucy's right ankle. She screamed and fell backwards off the stool, knocking the jar over and spilling it all over her mother's diary.

'Oh Jack, it's just you. You scared the life out of me.'

Lucy bent down to scratch Jack behind the ear and was rewarded with a thunderous purr. It seemed that he was now feeling a little less embarrassed about his big secret being revealed.

Lucy straightened up. 'I'd better clear up this mess you've helped me make, Jack.'

Picking up the diary covered in powder, she brought it up to her mouth to blow off the dust and froze.

The page was no longer blank. Wherever the powder had landed, words appeared on the page.

'This isn't a beauty product after all,' Lucy exclaimed.

Jack padded over to the book, gave it a sniff and sneezed.

'I know, it smells disgusting but it's worth it.'

Lucy sat back down and turned to the first page. She lifted the jar over the diary and began to sprinkle it back and forth. As soon as the powder landed, careful, neat handwriting appeared. Lucy read feverishly, sprinkling more powder every few lines.

My darling Lucy,

I knew your name before you were born. In fact, I knew your name before I even met your father. You have been in my dreams ever since I was a little girl. Your father is downstairs this very minute talking with your aunts. This will be our last trip to Wicker House.

You are in my tummy but nobody knows yet, not even your father. But I know. I can feel our connection already. I don't know if I can change the future but, to protect you, I am going to try. Keeping you as far away from the Keepers and magic is the one thing I can do that might keep you safe. The WI will be tracking the Keepers closely. If I keep you away from them, it might just save you.

But, if you are reading this, it means that I failed and the future I tried to change has come to pass.

It also means I couldn't find the strength to stay with you. I am truly sorry. I have been preparing for your birth my whole life, but my mind and body are not as strong as I would like them to be. Knowing the future, knowing what is going to happen is sometimes a burden I just cannot bear. My aunt Harry had this gift too and it drove her mad.

Even though I am no longer with you, I know that George and Eddy will take good care of you. Trust them but know that they need you as much as you need them. Together, you are more powerful than you are apart. There is power in three.

Danger is approaching and you must be ready. I am sorry I can't be there to protect you. It is what a mother should do and I have failed.

But even though I can't be with you, I can still help. My dreams have told me what you must do.

First, you need to ~

Lucy tapped the jar of powder but nothing came out. It was empty.

'No!'

Grabbing the diary and the empty jar, she ran as fast as she could back to the workshop and screeched to a halt. Panting heavily, she leaned against George's workbench, brandishing the diary and jar in front of her aunts like a maniac, too out of breath to speak.

'Diary. Mother. Powder. Empty,' she eventually wheezed.

George gently prized the diary and empty jar out of her hands.

'Ah, you've found your mother's secret diary but there's not enough powder for you to finish reading everything she wrote,' George deduced.

'That's it,' Lucy gasped. 'Can you believe it? My mother wrote this diary especially for me. She knew I would find it one day. She knew I would be here with you. And she knew that we would be in danger. She's written exactly what we need to do to prepare for what's to come, except I didn't get to that part; the powder ran out. Do you have any more?'

Eddy took the jar from George and smelt it.

'Ew! This isn't something I've made before but we must have a recipe for it somewhere.'

George chimed in, 'Do you know, I'm sure I've seen the recipe not that long ago. It was in one of the books I've looked at recently. Now where is it?'

George walked over to the pile of books that had accumulated on the spare workbench. She waved her hand slowly back and forth in front of them as if trying to feel which one was right.

Pausing, she placed her hand on a small, thick, battered book and pulled it out of the pile. She laid it on the table and rested both hands on top. Satisfied, she opened the book to just over half way.

'Here you are,' she declared triumphantly.

Eddy turned the book around until it faced her and studied the recipe for Revealing Powder.

'I've got most of the ingredients on my shelf but I'm out of Hawkweed and Wormseed but there's more growing in the greenhouse. Fresh might be better than dried anyway.'

'Why don't I collect them for you?' George offered. 'You can start preparing the rest of the ingredients in the meantime.'

'Good idea, although be careful you don't kill my plants by accident. You can't even keep weeds alive.'

'I think I can be trusted to snip a few herbs. Even I can't get that wrong.'

Eddy and Lucy had barely begun to measure out ingredients when the sound of George shouting made them drop everything and race after her.

They found George in the greenhouse, red faced, hands on hips standing across from Mr Merchant who stood mirroring her stance, equally red faced. They were staring at each other so ferociously, Lucy worried they might combust.

'What's going on?' Eddy took a tentative step between them.

'He's killed them,' George pointed an accusing finger at Mr Merchant.

'Who has he killed?' Eddy looked around with alarm, trying to find the bodies.

'Them!' George pointed to the far side of the greenhouse. Following her finger, Eddy turned and gasped with dismay.

'No, not the Silver Nightweed!' Eddy ran over and inspected the damage. The rare herb lay drooping and shrivelled. She picked up a wilted frond and sniffed.

'Poison! Who would do such a thing?'

'Him!' George pointed at Mr Merchant.

'If you don't stop pointing your finger at me, woman, I will break it off. And remember, I'm a surgeon, so I know just how to break bones so they can never be repaired,' Mr Merchant growled.

George gasped and withdrew her accusing finger, hugging it protectively to her chest.

Mr Merchant turned to Eddy. 'I didn't poison the Nightweed. I had only just discovered it myself when this woman came in and went all ballistic. She's a raging nutcase, that one, needs her head read.'

George snorted and muttered something rather unladylike.

'So, Mr Merchant, what do you think might have happened here?' Eddy asked.

'There's only one explanation in my mind. It must have been that lunatic.'

'If you insult me one more time, you horrible man, I will sew your mouth shut,' George snapped.

'Hush, woman, you're not the lunatic I'm referring to, although you're clearly barking. I'm talking about the mad one with all the bells.'

'Dolores Moonbeam you mean?' Lucy offered.

'That's the one. I keep finding her in here. She's always got some excuse or other for why she's here but she was definitely up to something, I could tell. I just didn't realise what it was until it was too late. I should have kept a closer eye on her.'

Eddy placed a reassuring hand on his arm. 'It's not your fault, Mr Merchant.'

'Perhaps not but it is my responsibility to care for each and every one of these plants according to this book my uncle left me.' He retrieved a battered well-thumbed book from his coat pocket. 'It's all part of the agreement I'm bound to under the contract and you know what happens if I do anything to violate it.'

This time it was George's turn to reassure him, 'Mr Merchant, whether you believe us or not, my sister and I really do not know anything about a curse or an agreement but, this I do know. When Eddy and I have dealt with the rather big thing that needs dealing with right now that I can't go into detail about but it's very, very big. Well, then, after that, we will turn our attention to how we can free you from this agreement.

It's quite clear that you despise us and I'd rather have someone working in our garden that wants to be here, not one that so obviously doesn't.'

Mr Merchant stared at George for a long time. 'Do you know, I think I actually believe you? I'll clear this mess up. Fortunately, there are a few Nightweed seeds left in the store cupboard so all is not lost.'

'Thank you, Mr Merchant.'

George looked like she wanted to say more but Eddy took her arm and steered her back towards the house. 'Do you think Dolores could be connected with the WI?'

'She may have done this terrible thing to our plants, Eddy, but I just can't believe Dolores is one of them. If anything, she tries to do everything she can to be one of us.'

Lucy watched Eddy and George return to the house and then turned to Mr Merchant who was consulting his book.

'Does that book really tell you everything you need to do for every plant in this garden?'

Mr Merchant, who seemed to have softened somewhat since George's announcement, held the book up for Lucy to see.

'Yes. Look, every page is dedicated to one plant. There's also a complete calendar of what needs to be done on every single day of the year. So, each day, I simply consult the book and follow its exact instructions. Which is a good thing, really, as I don't know anything about gardening. Before this I couldn't even keep weeds alive.'

'You sound just like Aunty George.'

Mr Merchant snorted. 'Anyway, it's a good thing I have this book because, even if I had known about plants before now, I'm pretty certain that most of the plants in this garden do not exist anywhere else in the world.'

'Really?'

'Yes, I've never seen such strange shaped and coloured plants and flowers before. Have you?'

'No,' Lucy agreed. 'Why do you think that is?'

'I don't really know. I'm guessing this garden is hundreds of years old and your aunts and their family before them have been very good at preserving these plants which have died off in other parts of the world.'

'Maybe,' Lucy agreed, 'or maybe it could be magic.'

'Magic!' scoffed Mr Merchant. 'I know there is all kinds of weird stuff going on around here but there's no such thing as magic.'

'So you don't believe in magic then?'

'Of course not, I'm a man of medicine. There is always a logical explanation, even for the most illogical things, like this silly curse. One of the reasons I agreed to take my uncle's place was so that I could get to the bottom of the events that led to this so called curse being made in the first place. Once I have the evidence to prove it's just an elaborate hoax with a bit of trickery added in to fool my relatives, I'll be able to get my family to agree that there is no curse and it no longer has a hold on us. But until I have proof, I need to keep on going through the motions of being the gardener to your two batty aunts.'

'So you definitely don't believe in magic then?' Lucy confirmed.

'I already told you...'

But whatever Mr Merchant was going to say next was forgotten as he stared at the place where Lucy had been standing only a moment before but now was just thin air.

'I never used to believe in magic either,' the air told Mr Merchant, 'until I came here.'

CHAPTER 23

GUARDIAN CALLING CARD

Lucy had been helping her aunts mix potions, make up charms and assemble talismans for most of the afternoon. Between the potions, charms and talismans, they had covered everything from silencing feet to befuddling foe, from causing violent hiccups to rendering someone speechless. George was determined that, in the absence of exact instructions of what to do at the Ascension Ceremony, they should focus on how to avoid being ensnared by the WI. Eddy had also mixed up a new batch of Revealing Powder and Lucy was tapping the floor impatiently while it stewed. Unfortunately, the recipe said it needed to stew overnight and no amount of tapping was going to make it brew any faster.

Eddy finished the potion she was mixing and put it alongside the growing collection of containers. 'This is all very well but we need a plan on how and when we are going to use all of this stuff, not to mention on whom. Unless we know how the ceremony should take place, we won't even know how to start making this plan,' she said, wiping her hands on her apron.

'I might be able to help you there.'

'Argh,' Eddy screamed, dropping her mixing bowl with a clatter. 'You need to stop doing that, Harris. How is it that you can creep up on us without House sounding a warning?'

'I think it's because House knows I'm a friend,' Harris suggested.

House grunted in acknowledgement. 'And it's probably because I'm still carrying your mother's handkerchief. Anyway, I think we might have another avenue to explore that could give us more answers.'

'What do you mean?' George asked.

'Barry gave me this.' He showed them the card from Lady Elizabeth.

Eddy turned it over, studying the drawing. 'What does it mean?'

'That's the symbol of the Guardians. It's how we recognise each other. Typically Guardians don't know each other. It helps protect our identity if we are ever discovered by the WI. It's also part of the Guardian Code. We're supposed to keep our distance, both from the Keepers and from other Guardians. But, from time-to-time, it's necessary to break our cover. We then use this symbol to discretely indicate our identity. Everyone carries the symbol somewhere on their person, you just need to know to look for it. Here, look at the stitching on my jacket collar.'

The three crowded closer and, sure enough, now that they were looking for it, the symbol of the eye inside the triangle was clearly sewn in small stitches around the edge.

'Does this card mean Lady Elizabeth is also a Guardian or could it be a WI trap?'

'That's a very good question, Lucy. The truth is, I don't know. We know for sure that her maid, Malys, is definitely in the WI. What we don't know is if Lady Elizabeth is involved. There's only one way to find out. I have to make contact with her.'

'That sounds risky. What if it's a ploy? Besides, you have no legitimate reason to visit Lady Elizabeth. Won't it look suspicious if you just show up?' George asked.

'Actually, Barry and I have come up with a plan. Let's hope it works.'

* * *

Later that evening, in the bungalow at the bottom of Bottoms End Lane, Nigel and Barry were sitting down to supper.

Harris made an elaborate show of serving them their macaroni cheese, just how Nigel liked it. The silver plated serving dish was wheeled through on the rickety dinner trolley which had one of its legs held together by duct tape. Harris lifted the lid with a flourish and spooned generous portions of macaroni onto their plates, finishing them each off with a sprig of parsley picked from a neighbour's garden.

'So Master Barry,' Harris began as he carefully placed a plate in front of Barry, 'how was your day?'

Barry, spotting his cue, eagerly responded. 'Brilliant. We went to visit Lady Elizabeth at Snordom House.'

Nigel wasn't paying any attention. He was too busy guzzling macaroni and trying not to be obvious about the fact he was watching the TV out of the corner of his eye.

'And is Lady Elizabeth nice?' Harris continued.

'Oh yes, she's lovely, although I didn't care much for her maid. Now what was her name? Malet? Missit? Ah, now I remember, Malys. Malys is her name.'

At hearing Malys's name, Nigel started choking on his food and Harris quickly poured him a glass of water. It was a few moments before Nigel had recovered enough to speak.

'Sorry, what was that you were saying, young Barry? You know I love hearing about what you and your friends get up to.'

'I was telling Harris about Lady Elizabeth and her maid, Malys. We went to visit Lady Elizabeth today who was very nice but I didn't like Malys. She acted suspiciously. I think she's up to something.'

'Wha-what makes you say that?' Nigel took a large gulp of

water nervously.

'It's just a hunch. She was always sneaking around and having secret conversations. We caught her talking to Mr Green, not once but twice and each time they quickly stopped speaking when they spotted us. I just don't trust her. I think Malys is planning on robbing Lady Elizabeth or worse!' Barry finished dramatically.

'Well, now, I'm sure it was all perfectly innocent. You say she was talking to Mr Green?'

Barry nodded enthusiastically. 'Twice,' he held up two fingers for emphasis.

'She wouldn't be making plans without me, would she?' Nigel muttered to himself anxiously.

'What was that you said, Uncle?' Barry asked cheerily.

'Oh nothing, I was just pondering whether I might call on Lady Elizabeth myself.'

'Why's that?' Barry asked innocently.

'I, er, well, I was thinking of, um, hosting a charity event. Yes, that's it. A magic show to raise money for charity and you mentioned earlier that Lady Elizabeth had lovely gardens which would make the perfect location for the event.'

Barry smiled widely and nodded in agreement, deciding not to correct his uncle about the fact that he had never mentioned Lady Elizabeth's gardens.

'Might I accompany you, sir?' Harris enquired.

'Whatever for, Harris?' Nigel looked bewildered by the suggestion.

'Well, I just thought that, in order to convince Lady Elizabeth of your serious intentions and your upright character, she might be encouraged to see that you are a man of upstanding that has his very own man servant.'

'Ah yes, very good Harris, very good indeed. I think that would do very well. Shall we go?'

'Now sir? It's perhaps a little late and we wouldn't want to inconvenience Lady Elizabeth. Might I suggest we go first thing tomorrow morning, when the lady is well rested?'

'Ah yes, very good, Harris, very good indeed. Be ready to

leave promptly after breakfast.'

'Yes, sir, excellent suggestion.' With a little smile in Barry's direction, Harris cleared away the plates and wheeled the battered dinner trolley back into the kitchen.

* * *

The next morning dawned bright and clear. It was going to be another hot day and Nigel was already starting to feel the sweat break out on his forehead as he fiddled with his tight collar whilst waiting for the door to be answered at Snordom House.

Malys finally opened the door with a scowl which immediately deepened when she saw who was standing on the threshold.

'What is the meaning of this?' she barked just as she spotted Harris behind Nigel's shoulder.

'Good day ma'am, my name is Nigel Jones. I was wondering if I might have a word with Lady Elizabeth. Here is my card.' Nigel reached into his pocket and brought out a silver embossed card.

'And what do you want to talk to milady about?' Malys asked suspiciously, not making any attempt to take the card from Nigel.

Before Nigel could respond, a voice called out from within the house. 'Who's at the door Malys?'

'Nothing to worry yourself about, milady. It's just some travelling salesman. I'll get rid of him.'

Lady Elizabeth wheeled herself closer to the door.

'Nonsense Malys,' she scolded gently, 'I recognise this gentleman from the village. You're Barry's uncle aren't you?'

Feeling incredibly pleased that he'd been recognised, Nigel drew himself up to his full height and bowed deeply, 'Nigel Jones at your service, ma'am.'

Lady Elizabeth smiled sweetly at Nigel, 'What can I do for you Mr Jones?'

Nigel briefly outlined his plans for a magic charity event in her gardens.

Lady Elizabeth listened intently. 'What charity did you say

this was in aid of Mr Jones?'

'It's for the, um, for the, er, Retired Magicians Benevolent Fund.'

'Well that sounds like an excellent cause, Mr Jones. I'd be more than happy to offer my garden as the venue for this event. Why don't you come in and talk through the details with Malys. She can help you with the arrangements. I would like some fresh air before the day gets too hot. May I borrow your man to take me around the gardens?'

Nigel couldn't believe his good fortune. He could now talk to Malys openly without having to find a reason to speak with her. If she was planning something, he wanted to make sure he wasn't left out. Again.

Malys opened her mouth to object but before she could, Lady Elizabeth interjected. 'Malys, could you kindly fetch my walking stick for me?'

'Your walking stick? What on earth for? You haven't used it in years.'

'I know that, Malys, but there's something about today. It makes me feel like anything is possible, so I might give it another try.'

'I really don't think that's a good idea.'

'Noted Malys, but please go and fetch it all the same.'

Malys's scowl deepened further, if that was at all possible, but she sullenly did as she was told. 'Here you are,' she grumbled upon her return.

'Thank you, Malys. Hang it off the back of the chair. We'll take it from here.'

She smiled at Harris who quickly positioned himself behind the chair and started to push her gently down the ramp towards the gardens.

When they were out of ear shot, Harris introduced himself.

'I know exactly who are you, Harris. I see you got my message from young Barry then?'

'I did indeed.'

'Wheel me over to the walled garden. Once we're inside, no one will be able to see us from the house and the sound of the fountain will ensure no one can overhear.'

'Very good, ma'am.'

Once they were safely inside, Harris stopped the wheel chair next to the fountain.

'Hand me my walking stick please.'

Harris picked up the stick and handed it to her. It was made from elaborately carved ebony wood and had a large golden handle on the end.

'Do you want a hand getting out of the chair, ma'am?'

Lady Elizabeth looked up with surprise and then laughed sadly.

'Unfortunately, my days of getting out of this chair are long behind me. No, Malys was right, I have no more use for this walking stick except for one purpose.'

She twisted the handle until it had unscrewed entirely.

'I've been looking after this for years but now it's time that I pass it on.'

She upended the stick and tapped gently. A small tube of tightly rolled paper fell into her lap. She handed the sheaf to Harris who cradled it in his hand, feeling the delicate brittleness of the ancient papers.

'These are the missing pages from the Book of Ascension. May I ask how you came by these?'

'I was Jo's Guardian after they reassigned you. Jo had been extremely anxious in the weeks leading up to George's ascension. She could sense danger was close by but didn't know from where it would come. I was more able to get around those days, only needing this stick to support me. As you know, Jo could sense things and she sensed that I was her new Guardian. She sought me out and made me promise to keep these pages hidden until it was time for the ceremony.' Lady Elizabeth turned her head towards the fountain, a shimmer of tears wet her eyelashes.

'On that fateful day I had been getting ready to meet her when my stepson arrived unannounced. It took me some time before I could find a reasonable excuse to leave him without raising suspicion. We knew the time was close for the ceremony. You probably know it doesn't always happen on the Keeper's actual birthday. Sometimes it may be a few days before, sometimes a few days after. It all depends on the alignment of the moon and the forces of the elements. You will know when the ceremony is drawing near. Strange weather phenomena will happen. The day before George's twenty-first birthday, all the leaves turned brown overnight even though it was mid-summer. That's when we knew the ceremony needed to take place that very night. I had promised to help Jo perform the ceremony. It needs to be conducted by at least one fully fledged Keeper, more if possible. This helps bind the magic more strongly to the witchling. While I'm not a Keeper, I had studied the ceremony and knew what had to be done and when. I was going to help with the non-magical parts, like the blessing of the stones and carving the element symbols into the ground.'

Lady Elizabeth paused, her voice catching in her throat.

'But I was too late. By the time I arrived at her house, Jo was already dead. I found her lying in the middle of a scorch patch with my old housekeeper lying dead beside her. It broke my heart but I had to leave her where she lay on the ground. I couldn't break my cover and risk being exposed. That might have put others at risk. It was then that I decided to give up being a Guardian. I had failed Jo. I was not physically strong enough to protect her and I had known for some time that our friendship was preventing me from doing the right thing which would have been to step down and let someone more able take my place. If I had done that, maybe she would still be alive.'

Harris, who had taken a seat on the bench next to the fountain, put his hand on her shoulder.

'You can't blame yourself, I should know. I too have blamed myself all these years. If I hadn't got too close to Jo, I could have remained her Guardian and been there to protect her. I've finally come to realise that it was no one's fault but the WI. They were more organised, more devious and more informed back then than we realised. None of us knew just how much danger Jo was in until it was too late. But what matters now is protecting her daughters and granddaughter, and making sure Eddy has her Ascension Ceremony. The balance of nature is depending on it.'

'Thank you, Harris. You are right, there's no time to waste. Eddy's birthday is only three days away. The ceremony might need to take place any moment now.'

Harris returned Lady Elizabeth to the main house just in time to see Nigel exiting swiftly like a scalded cat. Clearly his meeting had not gone to plan.

Malys was watching Nigel's rapid departure with her habitual scowl.

Lady Elizabeth handed her walking stick to Malys.

'Here you go, Malys, you can do what you like with this. I have no further use of it.'

CHAPTER 24

ALL IS REVEALED

First, you need to summon your Guardians. I know this is unusual but these are unusual times. By now, Harris will have made himself known to you. Harris can help contact the other Guardians.

On the night of the ceremony, there will be many who will try to harm you all. Be careful who you trust. Friends may be enemies. Enemies may be friends. You need as many people as possible to help defend against those who wish to hurt you. The Guardians can help with this.

My visions show that someone will be harmed. I see pain and loss. My fear that it may be you, my darling girl, prevents me from seeing the vision clearly. This is one of the problems with having the gift of sight. The more the vision affects my emotions, the harder it is for me to see it plainly. So any vision that involves you is never clear. I can only get a sense of what might happen, but no true picture of what will actually occur.

George and Eddy will already be preparing potions and charms to help fend off the impending danger. But these will only cause temporary distractions. What you all need to do is work on your special gifts. As Keepers, we are all connected to one of the elements. Fire for George, Earth for Eddy and, for you, Wind. You need to connect with your element. You need to feel it. Once you do, you'll be able to make it do your will. There is no book or guide to show you how to do this, but you all need to master it.

This is something that your grandmother Jo started to teach George and I before she died, but George was always too distracted to pay it much attention.

George – I know you'll be reading this with Lucy. You need to remember.

Eddy – help George remember.

If you are to defeat those that wish you harm, you need to master your element.

Lucy, my darling girl, there is so much more I want to tell you but it's time for me to go.

My greatest regret is that I'm not there with you now, where I should be. I wish I could have been stronger and stayed in this world with you.

I will always love you.

Your mother

Lucy slowly closed the diary. She had read it so many times she could recite it by heart. The Revealing Powder was starting to wear off and the words were beginning to fade but Lucy didn't care. She had something of her mother's and it had been written especially to her.

Harris had returned from his successful visit with Lady Elizabeth only a few hours earlier and had immediately left again on his mission to notify the Guardians.

Eddy had spent the afternoon concocting a potion to help jog George's memory while George had paced up and down muttering, 'Remember, remember, I must remember'.

Eddy finally wiped her hands on her apron.

'Here, drink this Memoria Serum,' she instructed and handed George a beaker filled with a bright yellow liquid that was bubbling violently.

'Will it work?' George sniffed the potion apprehensively.

'I have no idea; I've not made one before but now's a great time to find out. Come on, drink up, all in one go.'

George gulped back the serum and burped loudly. Her face turned bright red and then deathly pale.

'I think I need to sit down.' She lowered herself heavily onto the nearest available seat which happened to be an upturned bucket.

Her face suddenly went an alarming shade of green.

'I don't feel so good.' She quickly stood up, grabbed the bucket and heaved violently into it. Straightening up, she wiped her mouth on her sleeve. 'That's better.'

George had regained her normal colour and there was even a sparkle in her eye.

'My goodness, this is incredible, so many memories whirling around my brain. Do you know, I can remember every ingredient and every combination I've ever used to try to cure Jack? Oh this is brilliant, it's much better than Remembrance Powder. If I can sift through all these memories about which concoction achieved which result, I just know I can figure out what combination is needed to give Jack a permanent fix!'

'Focus, George, that can wait. Your first priority is to help us connect with our element.'

'Yes, yes of course. I know just what to do for that too. Come with me, we need to do this outside. We need a large space to work in.' George grabbed their hands and marched them purposefully into the back garden.

'It makes so much sense now,' George began. 'It explains why I seem to accidentally set things on fire without trying. Why you, Eddy, are so extraordinarily good at growing plants and why we've had so many little gusts of wind blow up and out ever since you arrived, Lucy, particularly when you're upset. Now, I want you to each find a spot a little way apart from each other. Then close your eyes and focus on feeling your element. Imagine what it would feel like to hold it in your hands. Imagine what it would feel like to push it back and forwards.'

Lucy went and stood a few feet away from her aunts. She closed her eyes and tried to think about air. It was a strange thing to think of. You couldn't see it, you couldn't touch it or hold it, you could only feel it. She really didn't know how she was supposed to connect with it. She cracked one eye open to peep at her aunts. Both were standing still, their eyes closed and arms raised, with serene looks on their faces. They clearly were having more luck connecting with their element than she was.

Lucy sighed. She closed her eyes even tighter and tried as hard as she could. She even held her hands out in front of her and moved them back and forth, as if she was pushing the air, but she still didn't feel anything. There was no connection. Not with air or anything else.

She heard an exclamation and opened her eyes to see George holding a small ball of fire in her hands as the ground in front of Eddy rippled backwards and forwards like a giant centipede wriggling just beneath the surface.

Frustrated, Lucy walked further away, turning her back to her aunts. She closed her eyes and tried to think of air. But instead, she found herself thinking of her dad and just how much she missed him. And then she started thinking about how crazy all this was and how part of her wished she'd never come here and never found out who she really was. She felt tears of both anger and sadness well up inside her.

'You can calm it down a bit, Lucy,' Eddy called over to her laughing.

Lucy opened her eyes to see both her aunts trying to hold down their skirts as a strong wind blew all around them.

Lucy whooped with joy and the wind immediately stopped.

George ran over and hugged her. 'That was brilliant, well done, Lucy. I think that's enough practice for now. How about a cup of tea and a slice of my raspberry ripple cheesecake?'

George walked arm in arm with Lucy back to the house. Holding up a hand, she clicked her fingers and a small flame appeared at the end of her index finger.

'I think this is going to be quite handy,' she laughed.

Neither Lucy nor George noticed Mr Merchant staring open mouthed from the top of a ladder, where he had been pruning the hedge.

CHAPTER 25

STINK BOMBS AND BOOBY TRAPS

It had been two days since George had taught them how to connect with their inner element and all three of them had been practicing at regular intervals ever since.

George was able to create balls of fire in her hands and was now attempting to throw them. Mr Merchant was getting extremely cross with all the scorch marks she was leaving behind on the lawn.

Eddy was able to make the ground move beneath their feet like a tiny earthquake. She had also successfully created a few sinkholes but was less successful in closing them back up again. Mr Merchant was equally unimpressed when he fell into one of Eddy's recent creations.

And Lucy was now able to conjure up gusts of wind at a moment's thought. She lifted a pile of leaves into the air, which Mr Merchant had spent all morning raking up, and turned them into a mini tornado. Unfortunately, when she released the tornado, the leaves went flying all over the garden. Mr Merchant, having just returned from his lunch break, yelled with frustration, threw down his gardening tools and stomped off, muttering about living in a nut house.

Eddy looked up from where she'd been trying to encourage the earth to fill in a sink hole, and said 'Your friends are here, Lucy.'

Moments later, the doorbell rang.

'How do you do that?' Lucy marvelled as she leapt to her feet and ran back into the house to let them in.

It had been a couple of days since Lucy had last seen her friends. She and her aunts had been so focused on preparing for the ceremony that each hour had been filled with either potion making, charm building or strengthening their control of their elements.

Beatrice, Ben and Barry entered the house in a flurry of excitement and made their way to the kitchen with Lucy.

'We're prepared for the attack,' Beatrice announced animatedly.

'What are you lot up to?' Eddy enquired as she entered the kitchen, her hands covered in dirt.

'Well,' Beatrice explained, 'we know you've been preparing your magical ways to thwart the WI but we mere mortals have got a few tricks up our sleeves too.'

George, who had followed Eddy into the kitchen, began rummaging around in her big pot by the sink.

'Ah, I thought I'd left it in here. Cake anyone?'

She held aloft a large Victorian sponge smothered in cream and strawberry jam.

'All this preparation has given me quite an appetite. How many slices am I cutting?' She looked up as all the children raised their hands eagerly in the air.

'So what tricks do you have up your sleeve?' George asked as she handed around plates of generously sliced cake.

Ben took a large mouthful and proceeded to explain, crumbs flying from his mouth.

'Weeb got 'inck 'ombs an' 'oobie 'aps,' he began.

'What he's trying to say is, we've got stink bombs and booby traps,' Barry interpreted as Ben nodded his head vigorously, his mouth still full of cake.

'We've also got some trip wires all ready to go,' Beatrice continued. 'The three of us have rigged up a large net that Ben got his hands on, don't ask us how. We've covered it with branches and leaves so when someone steps onto it, it will trip a wire and they will be hoisted up into the air. Isn't that brilliant?'

George looked at each of the three eager faces.

'That all sounds wonderful but I'm just not sure it will be safe for you to be there when the ceremony takes place.'

All three protested at once.

'That's not fair, I want to see the action,' Ben cried.

'We really think we can help,' Barry exclaimed.

'You can't stop us,' Beatrice declared, a look of steely determination in her eyes.

George heaved a sigh, 'Look, I know you want to help but it could be dangerous and I can't take that kind of responsibility. Someone could be hurt, or worse.'

The children started complaining again when a small voice was heard above their protests.

'What if I give my permission?'

Everyone looked around to see Dolores Moonbeam standing just outside the back door.

'Dolores, what are you doing here?' Eddy's voice was less than welcoming. Dolores was still the prime suspect in the greenhouse poising incident and she'd been noticeably absent ever since.

'May I come in?' Dolores asked hesitantly.

'Um, well...yes, of course, Dolores. Cake?' George proffered a plate.

Dolores waved away the offer as she stepped meekly into the room.

Lucy was trying to figure out what was different about her and then she realised. There were no bells. In fact, Dolores was dressed rather conservatively. Gone were the bellowing skirts, the tie-dyed clothes and the multitude of scarves. In their place was a pale blue buttoned down shirt and a pair of jeans.

'Firstly, I've come to apologise.' Dolores looked sheepishly at the ground.

'And what are you apologising for?' demanded Eddy testily, although she had a pretty good idea.

Dolores replied, 'I did it. I poisoned the Nightweed.'

Dolores's confession seemed to take the heat out of Eddy's anger. 'Why did you do it?'

'I'm not sure I fully understand my own motivation, but I think it comes down to jealousy. For the last few years, I've tried to be something I'm not. I've tried to find a purpose for myself other than just being a mother and carer. So when I started getting interested in natural remedies, I thought I'd found it. I thought I could be a healer. But no matter what I did, I never seemed to have the same success as you. Nobody who asked for my help ever came back twice. But everyone always comes back to you. I guess I couldn't accept that I was no good at it because then I thought I wouldn't have anything to be proud of. But I've realised how wrong I've been. I am proud of being a mother to my two wonderful children.'

Beatrice and Ben looked both embarrassed and pleased at the same time.

'I overheard Ben and Beatrice talking when they thought I couldn't hear them. I discovered they weren't sure if they could trust me, their own mother. That's when I realised I'd been such a fool. I'd been so obsessed with my twisted little plot to undermine your business that I didn't see how out of hand my behaviour had become, so much so that my own children were suspicious of me. It made me take a long look at what I had been doing. I'm ashamed of how I behaved. I'm ashamed of what I have done but I can promise you this, I am not your enemy.'

Beatrice stepped forward and took her mother's arm, tugging her further into the room.

'I know you said we weren't to tell anyone but Ben and I knew we could really trust our mother, no matter how weird she'd been acting recently and we were right. She's not a member of the WI. She wants to help, don't you Mum?'

'Yes. I've got a lot to make up for so it's the least I can do. The kids and I have been making all kinds of crazy concoctions. We've got stink bombs, crazy goo, green sludge and fire crackers.'

'Yeah, Mum is crazy good at making really yucky stuff.' Ben looked at his mother with surprised admiration.

'I don't know,' George still looked concerned. 'We have no way of knowing just how dangerous it will be on the night.'

'I agree, George,' Dolores responded. 'That's why I've explained to the kids that we'll only lay traps around the perimeter and keep watch from a distance. Ben and Beatrice have agreed that they won't get involved, haven't you kids?'

Her children mumbled their promise but didn't quite meet their mother's eye.

Dolores clapped her hands together in satisfaction. 'Well, now that's taken care of, why don't you kids get yourself over to the fair, it will be starting soon.'

'What fair?' Lucy asked

'It's the High Summer Festival, a long standing village tradition. It's an evening fair and everyone goes.'

'I can't go. There's still too much to do and we have no idea when the ceremony will be,' Lucy said despondently.

'You go ahead, Lucy, we've done plenty already. There's nothing else to do now but wait. I'll know how to find you if we need to.' Eddy smiled encouragingly at Lucy.

'Here,' George rummaged in a drawer and handed a small bottle to Beatrice. 'Take this just in case you need it.'

Beatrice read the label and smiled. 'I hope I get to use this. That would be fun.'

CHAPTER 26

HIGH SUMMER FESTIVAL

Lucy was in high spirits. It had only been a matter of days since she found out she was a Keeper of the Elements but it already seemed like a lifetime. She'd grown up a lot in the last few days, what with finding out about her gifts and how to use them, and the duty her family had to keep nature in balance. It was a big responsibility and quite a heavy burden to bear. But this evening felt different. She felt happy and filled with anticipation for the fun they would have at the festival. It would just be good to hang out with her friends and feel normal again.

Beatrice, Ben and Barry were in a similar mood and by the time they arrived at the village, they were laughing and messing around as if they had not a care in the world.

Lucy paused at the edge of the square to take in the sight before her.

'Wow, I had no idea it would be this big.'

'It's pretty cool, right?' Ben agreed. 'This festival attracts people from far and wide.'

'There are even rides.' Barry pointed to the opposite side of the square where they could see lights and hear music from the fairground.

'Let's get some candy floss first, I'm starving.' Ben rubbed his tummy in anticipation. 'Then I fancy a go at the coconut shy.'

The children paid for their candy floss and made their way over to the coconut shy stand.

'I definitely want to win that gigantic teddy bear.' Beatrice pointed to the large fearsome looking yellow bear with wonky eyes and a crooked smile.

'You have to knock over three coconuts with three throws,' the small, weasel faced man at the stall told them.

'No problem,' Beatrice replied confidently.

She took up position, drew her arm back and hurled the first ball. It was a direct hit. Beatrice's whoop of delight soon turned to outrage as the coconut she had so squarely hit remained firmly in place.

'Hey, that coconut should have been knocked over. This game is rigged. I bet you've nailed those coconuts onto their posts.'

'Now miss, you shouldn't go around accusing good hard working folk of trickery. You simply didn't hit it straight on.'

Beatrice was unconvinced. 'Fine, I'll try again.'

She took careful aim and this time threw the ball with even more force than before. Once again it was a direct hit. Everyone heard the resounding smack the ball made when it connected hard but the coconut didn't budge.

'Unlucky,' weasel face said as he shifted uneasily from foot to foot.

'You crook,' Ben shouted.

'If you children can't behave properly and accept that you simply haven't hit the coconut straight on, then I'm going to have to insist you leave.'

Lucy stepped up to Beatrice and whispered in her ear, 'Give it one more shot.'

'What's the point?' Beatrice replied gloomily. 'I'm clearly

never going to win anything from this crooked little man.'

Lucy smiled back at her. 'Just give it one more shot.'

Beatrice sighed and shrugged. 'Fine.'

She lined up once more to take aim but this time didn't put any effort into her throw. What was the point if the stall owner was a cheat?

As Beatrice's ball flew through the air, Lucy forced her hands together and then out towards the coconuts. A violent gust of wind tore each and every coconut from its post and threw them to the ground just as Beatrice's ball hit.

Weasel face's mouth hung open in shock.

'Gosh, if the teddy bear is worth three coconuts, what's the prize for knocking them all down?' Ben crowed.

Weasel face didn't respond, simply muttering "not possible" over and over as he bent down to investigate how each of his carefully nailed down coconuts could have been ripped from their posts so violently.

'I tell you what, why don't we just settle for the teddy bear,' Beatrice said as she plucked the bear out of its central position amongst the other prizes and the four friends scampered off as quickly as they could before weasel face decided to come after them.

Their laughter had barely died down when they rounded a bend and bumped straight into Tom Winkle-Smith, the postmistress's nephew.

'Lucy,' Tom declared, 'how lovely to see you and your friends out and about. I haven't seen you for a few days now. Is your charming aunt with you?'

Tom looked around as if hoping to catch sight of Eddy.

'No, aunt George had things to do at home,' Lucy replied, deliberately misunderstanding him.

'Oh yes, of course, George is a very charming lady but I was referring to your aunt Eddy. I haven't seen her in a while and I was hoping I might be able to spend some time in her scintillating company.'

Lucy shrugged in response. She didn't like Tom Winkle-Smith. It wasn't just the overly formal way he spoke. There was something about him that was more than just a little bit creepy.

'Do you know the history of this festival?' Tom continued.

Lucy shrugged again, hoping her lack of response might encourage him to leave her alone.

'According to village folklore, hundreds of years ago this village was teeming with witches. And this festival was the witches' annual celebration of themselves, can you imagine? Of course there's no such thing as witches, is there Lucy?' Tom sneered.

Lucy simply shrugged again.

'Good talking to you, Lucy. Enjoy the festival. I'm sure I'll see you later.'

'Blugh, that guy gives me the serious creeps,' Beatrice said licking the final bits of candy floss off of her fingers. 'I think it's time for the Helter Skelter, don't you?'

They made their way over to the rides where they bumped into Reverend Pickles.

He smiled at them warmly. 'It's so nice to see you young folk out and about in the village. We've missed having children around.'

'There are lots of children here tonight.' Barry indicated towards the rides where families from neighbouring villages were squealing with delight as they spun round in cups or rode the carousel.

Reverend Pickles looked at them wistfully. 'Indeed, this is a great family event. I so wish that more families would return to Wickham.'

'Is it true this festival used to be a celebration for witches?' Ben asked through a mouthful of candy floss he had stolen from Lucy, having long since finished his own.

'Witches, you say? I don't know anything about witches. But it is true that this festival has its roots in celebration. A celebration for a bountiful harvest; a celebration to Mother Nature, if you will, for giving enough sunshine, a fertile soil and plentiful rain to make the crops grow tall and strong. So if we were being true to the real purpose of this festival, we probably shouldn't be having it today because we haven't had a drop of rain in nearly six months. The water reserves are running dry. I hear the farmers say that if it doesn't rain soon their crops will be ruined.'

The children all looked a bit glum at this and Lucy couldn't help feeling guilty, like it was somehow her job to make it rain, even though she knew she couldn't. Making it rain had been her mother's gift apparently. But, when they had the Ascension Ceremony, that should put the balance back in nature and the rain would come anyway.

Reverend Pickles picked up on the children's mood. 'Oh don't listen to an old man's ramblings. This is meant to be an evening of fun so go off and enjoy yourselves.'

The children said goodbye and paid for their Helter Skelter rides.

They had each had two goes when something remarkable happened.

'Barry, why do your shoulders have white blobs on them?' Ben peered at Barry in the growing dark.

Barry looked down at his shoulders and then over at Ben.

'Hey, you have them too.'

'Guys, it's snowing!' Beatrice exclaimed looking up at the sky.

'How can it be snowing, it's summer?' said Ben incredulously.

'This is it, this is the sign. It's time!' Lucy felt a mixture of fear and excitement.

'Oh my goodness, of course it is,' squealed Beatrice. 'We need to get you out of here, Lucy.'

'Not so fast.' A heavy hand came down on Beatrice and Lucy's shoulders.

Mrs Smite glowered at the children. 'I've had enough of you lot causing mischief. Where are your parents?'

Mrs Smite looked around but couldn't see any sign of a responsible adult.

'Right, you lot are coming with me. Perhaps some quiet time shut up in the library might make you reconsider whatever misdeeds you are plotting.'

She gripped Lucy and Beatrice painfully by their shoulders and started marching them across the village square.

'Hey, let them go. You can't do this.' Barry and Ben ran protesting after her, trying to grab Lucy and Beatrice out of Mrs Smite's vice like grip.

'I can and I will. I'm fed up with you children thinking you can do what you want, when you want, making fools out of people and getting away with it. Well, no more. If your parents can't keep you in control, I will!'

'Ah children, there you are. Are you ready to do me that favour I asked?' Reverend Pickles stepped in front of Mrs Smite.

Mrs Smite stopped dead in her tracks but kept her grip firmly on the girls.

'What are you talking about, Reverend? I've just found these four plotting mischief so I've apprehended them before they could do anything about it.'

'Oh dear Mrs Smite, you must have been mistaken. These children are preparing to do me a big favour.'

'A big favour, you say, Reverend. What sort of favour?'

'Yes, well, they are, um, going to sing for the elderly,' Reverend Pickles said having just spotted the mini-bus from the retirement home pull up next to the square.

'Sing, you say?' Mrs Smite looked unconvinced.

The children immediately broke out into song. Unfortunately, none of them chose the same one with Beatrice belting out "When the saints come marching in" at the same time as Barry broke into "Bah bah black sheep" and Ben tunelessly began to sing the national anthem.

'Ah yes, very good, children. I think a little more practice is in order before you perform. Why don't you run through your songs a few more times and I'll come and find you when it's time.'

He winked at the children before physically turning Mrs Smite around and starting to walk with her in the opposite direction. 'Now Mrs Smite, I've been meaning to ask you, how do you get your scones so light and fluffy? My wife can never seem to get it right. What's your secret?'

Mrs Smite practically swelled with pride as she proceeded to explain the finer points of scone baking.

By now, the few specks of snow had started to come down harder and everywhere people had stopped and were pointing up at the sky.

'There's no time to waste. We need to get Lucy back to her aunts but we can't risk being waylaid again. I have an idea.' Beatrice pulled out the little bottle George had given to her and ushered the friends behind a stall where no one could see.

'Ow,' Lucy exclaimed as Beatrice yanked a piece of her hair out. 'What did you do that for?'

'You'll see.' Beatrice placed the hair inside the bottle, gave it a shake and then drank the lot.

'Now what?' Ben asked.

'Now we split up. Here Lucy, you take my army cap and put your hair up in it. Barry, you go with Lucy and Ben, you can come with me. Hopefully, if someone is looking for you, Lucy, they'll think I'm you and you're me.'

'Why on earth will they think that? You look nothing like Lu...' Ben trailed off as he stared open mouthed at his sister.

They said their goodbyes and headed out in opposite directions.

Barry and Lucy made their way furtively behind the stalls, trying to stay out of sight.

Beatrice and Ben strolled boldly down the centre of the square where festivities had ground to a halt as everyone stared up in amazement at the falling snow.

They hadn't even made it a few feet when a hand grabbed at Lucy's silver blonde hair and pulled it hard.

'Why wait for later when you're right here in front of me now,' a voice snarled.

'Ow, let go!' Beatrice yelled as she turned to face her attacker.

Tom Winkle-Smith dropped his hand immediately and stared open mouthed. 'You're not Lucy! But your hair! How come your hair... how come... how?' he stuttered looking from Beatrice to her hair and back again as Beatrice stroked the long silvery locks that were identical to Lucy's.

'Oh this?' she picked up a bunch of her hair and waved it in Tom's direction. 'I just felt like being blonde for a change.'

They left Tom staring speechless after them, his mouth moving soundlessly up and down, as they made their way quickly to the opposite side of the square where they could see their mother waving at them.

Meanwhile, Lucy was starting to feel anxious as she and Barry made slow progress, keeping to the shadows and stumbling over the tent ropes.

'Ah, there you are Lucy,' Eddy appeared in front of her.

'How did you know where I was?' Lucy asked but quickly continued. 'Never mind, you always know how to find me when I need you.'

'Exactly. As soon as it started snowing, I knew I needed to find you. Come with me you two, I know a short cut.'

She hurried them away from the square and towards the stores of the Messrs Green.

'Quick, in here before Mr Green sees us.' Eddy hurried them into the darkened butcher shop.

'There's a secret passage at the back of this shop that's a shortcut to the forest,' Eddy explained as she ushered the children quickly through the darkened store.

Eddy had just opened the door at the back of the shop and was herding Barry and Lucy through it when a light came on, momentarily blinding them.

Mr Green stood in front of them, a stern expression on his face.

Barry didn't hesitate and threw himself around Mr Green's legs, knocking him backwards, as he yelled, 'Quick, get away while I keep him busy.'

Rather than grab Lucy by the hand and run, Eddy came over and helped Mr Green to his feet.

'What are you doing? He's one of them,' shouted Lucy as Barry still held firmly to Mr Green's legs.

'Not this Mr Green. Look.' She pointed to Mr Green's

waistcoat that was visible under his butcher's jacket. The children peered closer and noticed it was cleverly covered in an interweaving pattern of the Guardian symbol.

'Come, you must be quick, I was keeping an eye on my brother and he disappeared about twenty minutes ago. The WI will have noticed the strange weather and they will be gathering in the forest as we speak,' Mr Green said.

'So your brother is one of the WI then, which one?' Barry asked, reluctantly releasing Mr Green's legs.

'I'm not one hundred percent sure yet but I have a good idea,' Mr Green replied as he helped Barry to his feet.

'Now go. Barry and I can't follow you as the passage is charmed. It will only let Keepers enter. We'll make our way to the forest as soon as you're safely through.'

Lucy and Eddy hurried through the damp, slippery passage that was lit with an eerie green light.

'How did you know the butcher was a Guardian?' panted Lucy as she hurried to keep up with Eddy.

'I didn't. He came to us while you were at the fair. Harris had sent out his message to gather the Guardians, just as your mother instructed. But the message made it clear not to reveal themselves to us until there was a clear sign. Well, snow in the middle of August is clear enough don't you think?'

'But are we sure we can trust him? What if he's the wrong Mr Green? He could just be pretending. He could be wearing someone else's waistcoat. What if he's the one that's part of WI and wants to stop us, not help us?'

'I had thought of that, but Harris gave the Guardian code words that only they would know and only we would recognise.'

'What is it?'

Eddy chuckled, 'It's very simple really and it's something the WI would never say.'

'What's that?'

'The code that Mr Green gave us was "I love magic".' Eddy giggled again. 'I can't imagine old beak face Malys ever muttering those words, can you? She'd probably choke on

3333

them. Ah look, we're here. Mind the steps, they're slippery and steep.'

CHAPTER 27

NO TIME TO WASTE

Lucy and Eddy emerged into the forest on the edge of the clearing. Lucy looked back at the hatch they had just come through and struggled to find it. All she could see now was a smooth mossy bank.

'There's no time to waste, everyone is here already.' Eddy hurried Lucy towards the people huddled together inside the whispering stones. The stones were lit by flame torches positioned in a large circle around them.

'I lit those torches myself. No matches,' George exclaimed proudly as she greeted Lucy with a hug.

'Lucy, my darling one, let me have a look at you!' Lucy found herself wrenched out of George's arms and enveloped in a flowery kaftan, her face smothered inside its voluminous folds.

Pulling back, she looked up at her assailant. 'Mrs Kahn! What are you doing here?'

'Well, Mr Harris summoned the Guardians so here I am of course.'

'What? You're my Guardian? You've been my Guardian all this time?'

'Not exactly, little one, you see, I've been your temporary Guardian while your Guardian-in-Waiting was being trained for the job. Unfortunately I am too old and too, how should we say, cumbersome,' she gestured at her large girth, 'to be the active type of Guardian a young Keeper like yourself needs.'

'Oh,' Lucy couldn't help but feel disappointed. Mrs Kahn had been the only mother figure in her life until she met her aunts, and she was very fond of her.

'I have, however, been helping things along to get to this point,' Mrs Kahn continued with a twinkle in her eye.

'What do you mean?'

'Well, child, do you think it was a miraculous happenstance that your father's old professor contacted him out of the blue? Do you think it was mere coincidence that your aunt's phone number happened to appear in the top drawer?' Mrs Kahn wasn't waiting for Lucy to answer. 'And do you think I really couldn't have looked after you this summer while your father was away? It broke my heart to lie to you like that but it had to be done. It was time you were united with your aunts. Your father is so loyal to the promise he made your dear mother, even though she never explained why and she's not here today,' Mrs Kahn paused to draw the symbol of the cross on her chest. 'He wasn't going to break that promise without a really big nudge. So that's what I did, I gave him a nudge.'

'More like a great big push,' a voice said from behind Lucy.

Recognising the voice, Lucy spun round.

'Ali!' she cried as she flung herself into his arms.

'How you doing, kid?' Ali squeezed her back.

'I can't believe you're here too.'

'Well, it turns out that my no-good, good-for-nothing son is actually good at something,' Mrs Kahn said with her hands on her hips but affection in her voice.

'What's that?' Lucy asked.

'He's a pretty good Guardian.'

'You're my Guardian?' Lucy said with astonishment,

realising for the first time that Ali was not wearing his usual gold chains, leather jacket and baseball cap but was instead dressed in jeans and a plain t-shirt.

Noticing Lucy take in his changed appearance, Ali shrugged, 'It's hard to blend in wearing my usual getup when you're in the countryside.'

Despite the seriousness of the night, Lucy felt happy. She had Mrs Kahn and Ali back in her life, two of the people who meant the most to her. The only person missing was her dad.

Final preparations were by now well underway. The clearing was buzzing with activity. Mr Green had re-joined them having come the long way from the village and he and Harris were helping George and Eddy with the final setup for the ceremony.

'So whose Guardian is Mr Green?' Lucy asked as she helped Eddy tie a series of intricate amulets at the four corners of the clearing as an extra deterrent against the WI.

'He's mine. He was very reluctant to tell me at first but I needed to make sure we could trust him.'

Lucy looked around the clearing. Other than her aunts, Mrs Kahn, Mr Green, Ali and Harris, there was no one else there. Her friends were probably somewhere in the forest making certain their booby traps were set up and then hopefully getting well out of the way of any danger. Lucy trusted Dolores would make sure her children and Barry came to no harm.

'So if Harris is no longer anyone's Guardian. Mr Green is your Guardian and Ali and Mrs Kahn are here for me, who's George's Guardian.'

Eddy paused and sighed, 'It turns out that the Guardian Council haven't assigned a Guardian to George. She used to have one when she was younger but, because she never had her Ascension Ceremony and has hardly left the house since Jack's accident, the Council decided she didn't need one as there wasn't anything to really guard. George has only just found this out.' Eddy looked over to where George was keeping herself busy, her shoulders were a bit more hunched than usual. 'She feels terrible. I think she's finally realised what

I've been trying to tell her for years. That she's wasted her life obsessing over a cure for Jack. For her life not to be considered something worth guarding has really shocked her.'

Harris walked over to them. 'It's time to begin. We haven't seen any sign of the WI but we know they will be gathering somewhere close by so the sooner we start the ceremony the better. Please take your places.'

Eddy, George, and Lucy positioned themselves in front of the stone carved with the symbol of their element. Harris positioned himself in front of the one representing water, where Lucy's mother would have stood had she been there. Immediately the three stones that Eddy, George and Lucy stood next to began to make a noise as if they were chattering quietly to each other. It almost sounded as if the stones were excited for what was about to happen, like how an audience whispers eagerly before the theatre curtain rises.

But the stone beside Harris remained still.

'It's time for us to take up our positions too,' Mr Green announced as he picked up his large butchers cleaver which made Mrs Kahn gasp in alarm.

'I don't plan to use it,' Mr Green explained. 'I'm just hoping that the sight of an angry cleaver wielding butcher will be enough to send the WI running for the hills.'

Mrs Kahn picked up her sturdy hand bag, 'I've never found anyone I couldn't talk sense into after a firm whack from my bag.' She patted it affectionately.

Ali had a cricket bat which he thumped rhythmically against his hand, 'And if that doesn't do the trick, I'll send them packing with a few well-placed smacks from my trusty bat.'

The Guardians made their way out of the clearing and melted into the trees, each taking up positions at different vantage points.

'Let's get started,' said Harris, smoothing out the pages of the Ascension Ceremony.

Lucy, Eddy and George glanced at each other nervously. This was it.

CHAPTER 28

THE MN327

Two figures dressed in stretchy night camouflage suits made their way carefully to the fringe of the clearing, taking care to stay well hidden behind the wall of trees. One was tall and thin, the other short and squat. They both carried what looked like futuristic space guns, except they weren't guns. They were the MN327s, otherwise known as the Magic Neutraliser version 327, because that's how many versions were made before getting it right. And while "magic neutraliser" didn't sound too deadly, it belied its true nature. The weapon looked like a ray gun from a bad science fiction movie. It had a heavy silver handle and a blue conical shaped barrel.

'These MN327s are heavier than they look,' Nigel observed as his hand started to ache from clutching it so hard.

'I can't wait to use this baby on one of those stinking witches.' Malys, seemingly unaffected by the heavy weapon, caressed it lovingly. 'Finally HQ have developed the weapon we need to bring down these hags once and for all. Remember Nigel, the trick is to make sure you always wear these protective gloves.' She waggled her fingers at him through her thick black rubber gloves. 'They will protect us from the ricochet when we shoot the confounded creatures. These gloves change everything. We can finally do what we want to those wretched excuses for human beings without worrying about what will happen to us.'

'We're not going to k-k-kill them are we?' Nigel stuttered in alarm.

'Unfortunately not,' Malys replied glumly. 'HQ wants to transport them to the London lock-up where they can be studied so we are only allowed to stun them.'

Malys flipped a large switch on the side of the gun from the 'KILL' to the 'STUN' position.

'Mind you, I wouldn't want to be stunned by these babies either.' She stroked her gun fondly once more. 'They will send a bolt of electricity through you that's so fierce it will completely fry the brain of a normal human. You might as well be dead. You won't remember who you are if you're on the receiving end of one of these. So make sure you have your gloves on at all times otherwise you won't be protected.' Malys reluctantly gave this last piece of advice, her euphoria about what was about to unfold making her feel unusually charitable towards Nigel.

The Witchfinder General and Malys had decided that the best time to capture the witches was at the ceremony. That way they could get them all at once without the risk of one or more slipping through their nets and making an escape.

In planning their attack, Malys had decided that the best place for Nigel was right next to her where she could keep an eye on him and make sure he didn't do anything stupid and ruin the plan like last time. As much as she loathed the man, he had been useful in getting the WI to this momentous occasion although the fact that he had somehow inherited Josephine's powers made Malys's skin crawl. In fact, once this mission was over and the hags were safely neutralised, Malys had a special plan for Nigel that involved a nice little lock-up all of his own.

'Right, get into position, Nigel, just as discussed. The others should be circling round the clearing and surrounding those vermin as we speak. They will be watching for my signal. Before long those four cages in London will be fully occupied.'

'Why four cages? There are only three of them.'

'Did I say four? Silly me, I meant three of course,' Malys quickly corrected. 'Now hurry man, get into position before you give us away.'

They turned off their torches and took their places. All was eerily quiet. The only noise was the sound of the soft falling snow as it hit a leaf or branch.

'I can't see anything,' Nigel whispered as he peered out from behind the tree trunk he was trying to hide behind, despite the fact he had chosen a sapling whose trunk was much thinner than he was.

'Here, try these.' Malys shoved a pair of strange looking binoculars at him. They fitted over the head like goggles but had slightly elongated eye sockets with bright red lenses at the end.

'These were made especially for us by HQ,' Malys continued. 'They are not just night vision goggles. They also have special filters that help us see beyond the magic.'

'What do you mean?' Nigel pulled the goggles over his head and spent a good bit of time fiddling with them so they would fit more comfortably.

Malys tutted, 'Obviously, those wicked women are going to attempt to use their evil charms and spells to try to confuse us or hide themselves or worse. But we've been studying their ways for centuries. We have used that knowledge, combined with the wonders of modern science, to outwit those revolting crones. These Demagifier Binoculars are the outcome of all that research. Look around you Nigel. Anytime you see something that looks like a puff of green smoke it means there is magic about, like a charm or a potion that's been released, and then we know to avoid it.'

Nigel looked around him. At first he couldn't see anything but then he noticed a tinge of green at the edge of his vision. He looked up into the branches above them just as he heard a voice cry, 'Bombs away!'

Before Malys and Nigel could react, a small package hit the ground by Maly's feet and a cloud of dust rose into the air.

Malys screamed in rage as she started scratching frantically. 'Itching powder!' she roared. 'Who dares do such a thing to me?'

In the branches above their heads, they could hear muffled giggling even though no one could be seen, the perpetrator clearly shrouded in magic to hide his presence.

'Oh you think that's funny do you? Well try this for funny.'

Malys raised the MN327 and aimed it at the branches above her head, pulling the trigger. The deafening boom of the gun blast was followed by a body falling slowly out of the trees and landing with a thud at their feet.

Nigel gasped and crouched down beside the motionless body.

'Barry!' he cried as he recognised his lifeless nephew. He turned his head towards Malys who was nonchalantly checking her gun. 'What have you done?' he croaked.

'Pah!' she responded. 'It's nothing more than he deserved. Running around with that revolting witchling and playing with magic. It's despicable.'

'He was just a child,' Nigel cradled Barry's limp head in his lap, stroking the hair off of Barry's forehead.

'Oh tish. You didn't even like the boy. You were just using him to get what we wanted and now his usefulness is over. So there's no point pretending to care.' Malys started fiddling with her gun.

'Hmm, the trigger appears to be jammed.' She took off one of her rubber gloves to get a better grip as she tried to release the trigger.

'I do care for him,' Nigel muttered.

'What's that? Speak up, man, I can't understand you when you mumble.'

'I said, I do care!' Nigel thundered with fury as he jumped to his feet. He stretched out his hands and a small dark cloud appeared, floating above Malys's head, sprinkling her with raindrops.

Malys threw back her head and laughed cruelly as she realised Nigel was making it drizzle over her.

'Is that the best you can do? Shower me with a bit of water? Oh dear, that's told me, hasn't it? I'm so sorry for what I did to little Barrykins,' she cackled. 'Now stop this nonsense and get back to work, Nigel, I'm not finished with you yet.'

'Maybe not,' Nigel replied, 'but I'm definitely finished with you.'

He thrust his hands out once more and the soft rain turned into a torrent, with rolling thunder and lightning streaking around Malys's ears.

'Right, that's enough.' Malys raised the MN327 and pointed it at Nigel. 'No point in wasting precious space with you in the London lock-up. You're just as disgusting as the rest of those mucky hags,' she said as she flipped the switch from 'STUN' to 'KILL'.

She pulled the trigger but it was still jammed.

Nigel realised his chance and ran towards her. He knocked Malys to the ground and rolled away just as she pulled the trigger once more. This time, there was a deafening boom as the blast hit the small pool of water in which Malys had fallen. When the smoke cleared, Malys lay prone in the puddle, her hair sticking up on end. The smell of singed flesh hung in the air.

Malys slowly pushed herself up as Nigel lifted Barry's still form into his arms.

'Ooh pretty,' Malys said in a sing song voice as she lifted her arms and tried to catch snowflakes in her open hands.

A look of confusion crossed her face.

'Why am I itchy?' she scratched herself like a monkey.

Malys noticed Nigel carrying Barry in his arms.

'Hello there,' she said in her sing song voice. 'Who are you? My name is… my name is…oh, how strange, I don't seem to know my name,' Malys giggled like it was the funniest thing she'd ever heard. 'Do you know who I am?'

Nigel looked at her in disgust. He couldn't believe that this was the person he had tried so hard to impress, the person he had tried to imitate. He could now see her for what she really is – a truly despicable human being who could take the life of a mere child with no hesitation. Nigel shifted Barry's body more firmly in his grip and stepped straight over Malys, his long legs striding away.

'I don't know who you are and I don't care,' he said without turning back.

* * *

Meanwhile chaos reigned in the clearing. The rest of the WI had barely got into their allocated positions when they heard the first blast of the Magic Neutraliser that knocked Barry out of the tree. Thinking they must have missed Malys's signal, they abandoned their positions and rushed haphazardly into the clearing.

Harris, Lucy and her aunts turned just in time to see masked figures in black tight fitting outfits, holding weird looking space guns, charging at them.

'Quick, this is what we've been training for,' George yelled as she swung towards a masked figure baring down on her, her hands ablaze with two large fire balls. She hurled them at her assailant whose camouflage suit burst into flames in at least three places. The assailant dropped his gun as he frantically tried to extinguish the fire.

'Behind you!' Harris yelled. Eddy whirled around and leapt out of the way as she commanded the earth before her to split open, swallowing up another attacker.

'Push them back, Lucy,' George called as more masked figures rushed at them. Lucy planted her feet firmly into the ground and shoved her hands forward. A gale force wind blew three masked attackers off their feet and they tumbled head over heels towards the edge of the clearing.

'I've got you now,' snarled a voice behind Lucy. She barely had time to register the barrel of the gun pointing right at her when a large hissing ball of black fur and claws hurled itself onto the man, knocking the MN327 out of his hands as he pulled the trigger. The blast narrowly missed Harris as it ricocheted off the stones. 'Thanks Jack,' Lucy called as the cat chased his foe into the woods.

George, Eddy and Lucy stood shoulder to shoulder as they repelled the remaining masked figures back into the woods through an onslaught of fire balls, rolling waves of earth and raging wind. Soon, each one of the assailants turned on their heels and ran for cover.

'Let the Guardians take it from here,' Harris advised. 'We need to get back to the ceremony. We're running out of time.'

CHAPTER 29

THE CEREMONY

'They're leaving,' Ben exclaimed a short while later as he ran into the clearing, stopping to put his hands on his knees, panting heavily.

Beatrice followed, a little less out of breath. 'Yes, they've gone. We've scared them away.' Her face shone with pride.

'You should have seen it, it was carnage,' Ben joined in. 'We used up almost everything in our arsenal. It was a bit scary at first. These guys in black masks started rushing through the woods. There were so many of them and they were all carrying a strange sort of gun. Look, I captured one.' Ben held up the MN327 triumphantly.

Mr Green, Mrs Kahn, Ali and Dolores Moonbeam had by now also joined the children in the clearing.

'I admit, at first I was a little frozen in fear by the sight of the WI. They looked pretty menacing dressed head to toe in black,' Beatrice confessed. 'But then Mrs Kahn went mental. She charged out from behind the tree and hit two with her handbag before they even knew what was happening. Then we started throwing stink bombs and laughing juice, while Ali took them out at the knees with his cricket bat and Mr Green charged around like a lunatic with his big cleaver raised above his head. I think half of them ran away in fright at that point.'

'One fell down the pit we had camouflaged and that annoying Tom Winkle-Smith is currently hanging in the rope net. I think he's crying,' Ben crowed.

'I heard one guy yelling about being attacked by a demonic black cat before he ran away. So Jack must be somewhere around here too.'

Ben and Beatrice had been so caught up in their retelling of events that they hadn't noticed what was happening in the middle of the clearing. Beatrice finally paused and realised that Lucy, Harris and the aunts were standing dejectedly in the centre of the stones.

'What's the matter? What's going on?'

'It's not working,' Lucy replied miserably. 'We've performed the ceremony three times and it's not working.'

'It's all my fault,' George wailed. 'My magic is not strong enough to complete the ceremony. Lucy is still a fledgling and Eddy's magic is no stronger than mine. And of course, Harris has no magic. If I hadn't had my head in the clouds when it was my turn to ascend, we wouldn't be in this mess.'

'Perhaps I can help?'

Everyone turned as a masked figure stepped into the clearing.

'You get back, I'm not afraid to use this.' Mrs Kahn stepped forward, brandishing her handbag quickly followed by Ali and Mr Green, their weapons raised.

'Wait!' Lucy cried. 'He's got Barry.'

They all noticed the lifeless figure of Barry cradled gently in Nigel's arms.

Nigel moved towards them and tenderly placed Barry on the ground. Pulling his mask off his head, tears streamed down his face as he lightly stroked Barry's hair.

'I've been such a fool,' he sobbed. 'I was so desperate to be accepted, to feel like I belonged, that I didn't see what I had right in front of me. Barry. He's my family. That's where I belong.'

Nobody moved or spoke as they watched Nigel stroking Barry's face, consumed by his grief. Slowly the children came forward and knelt next to Barry's limp body.

'This is what my mother predicted,' Lucy whispered.

'How did it happen?' Beatrice looked accusingly at Nigel.

'I did it,' Nigel moaned.

'You killed him!' Ben howled as he jumped to his feet, fists raised.

'Well no, I didn't actually kill him, Malys did that. But I'm the one who got involved in all of this. I'm the one who brought him here. So it may just as well have been me that did it.' Nigel sniffled and wiped his nose on his sleeve. 'I've been such a fool.'

'How did he die?' Lucy couldn't stop staring at Barry as she spoke. His face was so pale but he looked peaceful.

'She had this gun, it's called an MN327. It's supposed to be only used on, um, on witches,' Nigel said apologetically. 'But Malys turned it on Barry after he threw an itching bomb at her. She shouldn't have done that. It's against the WI code. The WI is supposed to protect all mankind from witches, but she deliberately hurt one. She hurt my one. So I had to hurt her back.'

'What did you do?' George rested a reassuring hand on Nigel's arm which made him flinch. 'It's all right. I'm not going to hurt you.'

Nigel nodded, but he still looked fearful. 'Sorry, it's just that, for so many years I've been told how evil and bad witches are. But now, as far as I'm concerned, there's no one more evil than Malys. And if she could be so evil, maybe the rest of the WI are too.'

George smiled encouragingly at him. 'Can you tell us what happened to Malys? Is she still out there? Can she still harm us?'

'Malys will never hurt anyone again.'

'You killed her?' Ben's voice sounded both thrilled and

horrified.

'No, not exactly, but let's just say that Malys is having a hard time remembering who she is right now, let alone anything to do with the WI or witches. The MN327 did that, with a little help from the rain.'

'What rain?' Beatrice asked. 'It hasn't been raining, it's been snowing,'

'I made it rain,' Nigel confessed, 'but just over Malys.'

Nigel looked at Eddy and George and then down at the ground. 'There's something you need to know. Something that happened the night your mother d- d- died,' Nigel stuttered, still looking intently at the ground.

'It's alright, we know.' Harris stepped forward.

Nigel looked at Harris in shock, noticing him for the first time.

'You knew? But how? And why are you here?'

'I'll explain later but right now, we have a ceremony to perform and we're running out of time. Are you serious about wanting to help?'

Nigel straightened up and smoothed back his hair.

'Yes, I'll help anyway I can. I owe that much to you all. I owe it to Barry.'

Nigel was about to step into the stone circle when a low moan made him stop and spin round.

Barry was groaning and holding his head as he tried to sit up.

Nigel leapt to his side, putting his arms around Barry and taking his weight as he gently helped him. 'My boy, my darling boy, you're alive!' Nigel cried softly as he cradled Barry in his arms like a precious cargo.

'What happened?' Barry tentatively felt the sticky lump on his head where the blood was starting to dry.

'Do you know who you are? Do you know where you are?' Nigel asked worriedly.

'My name's Barry and I'm in the woods. But who on earth are you?' Barry asked weakly as he pointed a shaky finger at Nigel.

'Oh no, oh no, my poor boy, that horrible woman has wiped your memory. That can be the side-effect you see,' Nigel explained to the group. 'That's what happened to Malys. The MN327 wiped her memory and it looks like it's done the same to my Barry.'

'There's nothing wrong with my memory,' Barry said sitting up a little straighter and looking quizzically at his uncle, 'it's just you I don't recognise. What happened to my grumpy uncle who's not interested in me? This is a new and much nicer uncle. I really must have hit my head hard.'

Nigel roared with laughter and hugged Barry hard to his chest, making Barry wince with pain but he smiled nevertheless.

'I hate to hurry you Nigel, but it's almost midnight. The ceremony must take place before the stroke of twelve. I'll take care of Barry for the moment.' Harris eased Barry out of Nigel's embrace. Nigel didn't seem to notice that his butler was now giving him the orders as he dutifully let Barry go.

Lucy, George, Eddy and Nigel took up their places in front of the stones that reflected their element; Lucy for air, George for fire, Eddy for earth and Nigel for water. Then as one they began to slowly walk between the stones, calling to the elements and anointing the pillars with the offering of their own element. They dipped their fingers into the containers placed on each of the stones and smeared it along their forehead while they repeated, 'Terra, ventus, aqua et igni fiere unum.'

Once they had completed a full circle, each had a smudge of ash, dirt, water and air on their forehead. The water was a special concoction that looked like a drop of liquid was permanently falling down the forehead but never dripping to the ground. For air they each had a silvery swirl on their brow that was rotating in perpetual motion.

'Ignis,' cried George and two small balls of fire appeared in her hands. She pushed her arms forward and fire shot out of her hands. As it hit the centre of the circle, it twisted and went straight up in the air.

'It worked,' George whispered incredulously. 'This time it worked.'

'Aqua,' Nigel said following George's lead and a flume of water appeared in his hand. He too pushed it out and the water shot forward and joined the streak of fire reaching up to the sky.

'Ventus.' Lucy felt rather than saw the force of the air in her hands as it spun round like a mini hurricane. She pushed her hands forward and the wind whipped the water and fire into a spiralling tornado reaching up to the heavens.

'Terra.' Eddy was the last to speak. As her sphere of earth hit the centre and went swirling skywards together with fire, air and water, a blue lightning bolt split the sky above them. For a moment, Eddy was surrounded in a green glow and then everything went deathly still. The snow stopped and the skies cleared, but only for an instant, as a second bolt of lightning split the sky again and storm clouds rapidly formed overhead.

'Quick, run for the house,' George cried as the heavy rain began to fall, drenching everyone to the bone within seconds.

'I guess the drought is over,' Eddy cried happily as she helped George gather their equipment.

CHAPTER 30

THE CORPORATION

It had been a week since the Ascension Ceremony. Lucy wasn't sure what she had expected to happen afterwards but she hadn't imagined everything to go back to normal quite so quickly.

It had rained torrentially for three days and three nights, which had the farmers rejoicing but the children grumbling as they were forced to stay indoors. Mr Merchant was also in a bad mood as he muttered about not being able to stick to the schedule because of all the rain. In fact, he was so grumpy that, after just one day of constant downpour, George and Eddy combined their powers to divert the rain so it didn't continue to fall over the garden. If Mr Merchant noticed that his garden was the only one not drowning in water, he didn't mention it and silently went about his work, occasionally frowning at the sky and then at the rain that he could see falling on the other side of the garden wall.

No one saw Malys again although it was rumoured she was last seen being bundled up and carted away in the back of an ambulance by men in white coats. Mr Green from the hardware store packed his bags overnight and declared he was going on a round the world trip and would be gone a long time. This confirmed Mr Green the butcher's suspicion that this was the brother who, although appearing to be easily confused and muddled, was really the one on the inner circle of Malys's WI.

Tom Winkle-Smith was seen hurriedly leaving the village, still crying, having not even stopped long enough to pack his things.

After a few days, once it appeared that the local WI was no longer an immediate threat, Ali and Mrs Khan had also reluctantly returned to London. Lucy was sad to see them leave but was comforted to know that she'd be seeing them soon enough when school started and she was back in London herself.

The villagers had been out celebrating in the downpour. Not only was the drought well and truly over but news had spread that a young village couple were expecting a baby. No baby had been born in Wickham for such a long time that, at the local meeting of the real WI, knitting needles were flying as they happily prepared baby clothes for the new arrival under the watchful eye of Mrs Smite.

As for Barry, he had phoned his mother on her boat cruise and informed her that he wanted to stay with his Uncle Nigel for a while and go to the local school in Snordom with Beatrice and Ben. If his mother had been upset by this announcement, she didn't show it as she simply replied, 'That's lovely, dear, but now I must be off. The salsa dance class is about to start.'

But Barry was not upset by his mother's reaction, or lack thereof, because Nigel was throwing himself fully into the role of loving uncle. While Lucy missed spending as much time with Barry, she was delighted to wave to him as she saw the pair of them happily eating ice-creams by the duck pond or Nigel worriedly running after a wobbly Barry who was learning to ride a bicycle for the first time.

Ben and Beatrice had also been absent as their dad had

decided to take a break from work and whisked the Naran family off to the seaside for a few days.

Everything had almost returned to the quiet and calm that prevailed in Wicker House before Lucy's arrival. As had been their custom, George and Eddy were taking a break in the sitting room, enjoying a cup of tea while Lucy sipped a glass of lemonade. Eddy had spent the morning in the greenhouse planting out more Nightweed seedlings while George and Lucy had finished cleaning out Jo's old workbench making it ready for Lucy to take over as her own. They had all agreed that, from now onwards, Lucy would be spending lots of school holidays at Wicker House.

Having settled down over the last week, House was back to simply redecorating rooms rather than moving them. Today, one of the sitting room walls was covered in purple and yellow striped wallpaper, two were painted pink and the fourth one royal blue. George was once more reunited with her favourite overstuffed armchair which was newly upholstered in red polka dot fabric. Eddy sat in a matching chair, her feet propped up on a new footrest, and Lucy was reclining on a large squidgy bean bag, stroking the extra-large black cat that was pretending not to enjoy it.

Suddenly, a shrill ringing sound pierced the quiet morning air.

'WAH!' George screeched, leaping six inches into the air, knocking a pile of papers flying and, more importantly, a cup of hot tea all over Eddy.

'Ahhhh!' Eddy yelped in pain. 'Do you have to do that every time the phone rings?'

'I don't know,' George replied as she helped to mop up the spilt tea, 'this is only the second time it has ever rung. It will be for you, Lucy.'

Lucy had stopped questioning how her aunts knew these things and walked to the hallway to answer the phone.

Opening the cupboard door beneath the stairs, she suddenly had a strong sense of who was calling.

'Hello Dad,' she said after picking up the receiver.

'Lucy! It's so good to hear your voice. How did you know it was me?'

'Just a lucky guess, it's good to hear your voice too. How are you?'

'I'm fine, Lucy. In fact, I'm more than fine. We've finished our research. The professor is really pleased with my work and has offered me a permanent position as his assistant at the university. This means a new start for us. We can even afford to move and get a bigger flat with what he's offering to pay me. Isn't that great?'

'That is great, Dad, but let's not move straight away. I like living above Mrs Khan's shop.'

'Of course, darling, we don't need to rush anything. But things are definitely looking up for us. The boat is heading back to London now. I should dock in a day or two and then I'll be straight on the train to come and get you and bring you home without a moment to waste.'

'As soon as that?' Lucy tried to muster her enthusiasm. While she had missed her dad terribly, she realised she wasn't yet ready to leave her aunts and her new found friends.

'How has your stay with your aunts been? It hasn't been too dull, has it?'

Lucy twisted to face the hallway just in time to see a hat stand appear by the front door which turned bright yellow before her eyes and was instantly bedecked with multi-coloured hats sporting feathers and plumes. House was clearly making a start on redecorating the entrance.

'"Dull" is definitely not the word I'd use to describe my visit,' Lucy told her dad.

* * *

At about the same time Lucy was telling her aunts she would soon be leaving, a hundred miles away on a rundown road in the rundown part of town, a large sedan pulled up outside a shop with grubby windows, peeling paint and a fizzing neon sign that should read "Al's Dry Cleaners & Repairs". But more letters had broken so the sign currently said "D e s pair".

Sir Walter Witherbottom climbed clumsily out from the back seat, his enlarged belly making his exit less than gracious as he hoisted himself out of the car. Sir Walter looked up and down the street to check that no one was watching and then entered the shop to the sound of "The Wheels on the Bus".

Phyllis Farley was yet again installed behind the counter, eyes glued to the TV, another bag of sloppy, greasy fries in front of her, looking as if she hadn't moved since Sir Walter's last visit.

'I've come to pick up the red sequined dress,' Sir Walter wasted no time in informing her.

Phyllis looked up from the TV for a moment and then returned her eyes to the screen.

'Oh it's you,' she declared unimpressed. 'I think you'll find that the red sequined dress has already been picked up.'

'What are you talking about?' Sir Walter demanded.

'See for yourself. Door's open.' Phyllis waved her hand towards the back of the shop.

'What's the meaning of this?' Sir Walter spluttered.

'Don't ask me. I only work here. Although I'm not sure you do anymore,' Phyllis chortled as she stuffed her mouth with fries.

Alarmed and unnerved, Sir Walter made his way to the back of the shop and became increasingly anxious as he saw the rack of garments pulled back and the elevator door on display for anyone to see.

He was just retrieving his Pooches & Poodles Grooming Salon Loyalty Card, when a tall man wearing a dark suit and even darker sunglasses stepped out from behind a rack and stood in front of him, hand raised.

'Put the card away. It no longer works here.'

'But, but –' Sir Walter spluttered.

'They've been expecting you, Sir Walter. I will escort you down and let them know you have finally arrived.'

'Who are "they"?' Sir Walter asked worriedly but the man in the dark suit did not reply as they silently descended into the belly of the basement.

When the elevator doors opened, Sir Walter was shocked to behold the scene in front of him. There were men in dark suits everywhere, most of them wearing dark glasses despite the fact that there was no sunshine or bright light. Some of the dark suits were boxing up papers and files while others were dismantling equipment.

'Stay here and don't move,' the dark suit told Sir Walter.

Sir Walter couldn't have moved if he wanted to. He looked on at the scene in front of him with growing panic and the sinking feeling that something bad was about to happen but not quite sure what that something was.

Steven Smittle spotted Sir Walter and hurried over to him.

'Smethers!' Sir Walter proclaimed in relief. 'What in darnation is going on here?'

'It's Smittle, sir,' Smittle said through gritted teeth. 'Where have you been? Didn't you get my message that it was urgent?'

'Yes, yes, Smathers, but you know I can't just drop everything when you call. I had to make arrangements for that idiot, Malys. And then I've had a five day diplomatic meeting with the under-secretary to the under-secretary of the Republic of Djibouti.' Sir Walter puffed out his chest with importance.

'Well, you should have dropped everything. You were a fool not to, what with everything that occurred in Wickham. Something big happened while you were swanning about at your diplomatic meeting.'

Sir Walter was stunned that Smittle no longer appeared to be treating him with the respect and borderline fear he had on all his previous visits. Something big must have happened indeed.

'What happened, Smittle?'

If Smittle noticed that Sir Walter had finally got his name right, he didn't mention it.

'The witch escaped.'

'What?' Sir Walter screeched. 'Why didn't you inform me?'

'I tried but you were in your meeting and left specific instructions with your assistant that you were not to be disturbed under any circumstances, so she told me. Not even if world war three broke out, apparently.'

'But how? How could she have escaped? She was in the strongest lock room that modern technology could provide.'

'The night of Malys's botched attempt to capture the witches, there was a power surge stronger than any we have ever experienced. It fried all our circuits and this centre was plunged into darkness. Then there was a high pitch noise that was so piercing, we had to go up to the top floor to escape it. We switched on the emergency generators and immediately came back down. When we returned, the noise had stopped and her cell was empty. We searched everywhere but she was gone.'

'This is unacceptable, Smittle. Losing that hag will put us back years. I'll have your job for this.'

'Actually, that's no longer your decision.'

'What on earth are you talking about? Of course it's my decision. You're fired!'

'Actually Mr Smittle is right, Walter.' Three men, all slim in smart buttoned down suits and slightly greying hair had entered the room while Walter and Smittle had been talking.

'Who are you? What's the meaning of this?' Walter sputtered.

'Our names are not important. You can simply refer to us as "The Corporation".'

'What's going on?' Walter squeaked, beads of nervous sweat breaking out on his brow.

'Well, for one, Mr Smittle is not fired. In fact, he's getting a promotion and a pay rise. You see, Mr Smittle figured out a way to harness the power from the hag. When she escaped, under your watch I might add, the power surge she created was harvested by the clever machine Mr Smittle has been working on. There was so much power created in that one surge, it can provide electricity to the whole city of London for an entire year.'

'Is that good?' Walter asked feebly.

All of the three corporation suits laughed. 'Is that good? That's more than good. That's world changing.'

'We've spoken to the prime minister,' another of the three suits interjected, 'and he agreed that we'll be taking over your pet project from now onwards. You see, what's the point in trying to rid the world of these witches and their power when we should be capturing them and harvesting their power instead? If we capture enough of these hags, we could be providing electricity to the whole country, even the world. We've naturally promised to pay the British government a healthy percentage of our profits. In fact, the prime minster wasn't too happy to hear that you'd been sitting on this gold mine all along and had failed to mention it. I believe he wants a meeting with you first thing in the morning.'

Walter gulped.

'So we're no longer trying to kill witches,' he asked timidly.

The three suits laughed again. 'Oh no, although, after what we'll do to them in order to harvest their power, they'll probably wish they were dead.'

* * *

Over on the other side of town, an ambulance pulled up outside a two storey grey concrete medical institution for long-term care.

The doors opened and Malys was rolled out, strapped into a wheel chair.

'I'm the high commander of the WI,' she sing-songed in a shrill little voice as she was wheeled inside.

'We've got a new one here,' the ambulance attendant said as he greeted the nurse at the front desk. 'Thinks she can see witches. That's all she's been muttering about since I picked her up.'

'Poor lamb,' the nurse stroked Malys's arm as she unstrapped her. 'Don't you worry about a thing, pet, we'll look after you.'

One floor above, nobody noticed as the door to one of the bedrooms quietly opened and a small, slight woman with wild grey hair slipped inside. Within the room, a woman lay sleeping, her silver blonde hair fanning out around her head. She had been asleep for over ten years but none of the medical experts could explain why she wouldn't wake up. They had tried every medicine and every treatment, but still she slept on. The experts had concluded that her brain had simply decided to stay asleep and all they could do was keep her comfortable and wait for her to wake up on her own.

The visitor moved silently over to the bed. She started muttering under her breath. Her voice got louder and louder until finally she clapped her hands together and a faint green puff of smoke escaped through her fingers.

'It's time to wake up, Sam, your daughter needs you.'

Downstairs, the nurse was busy entering Malys's details into the computer. Malys was singing softly to herself as she played with the edges of the blanket covering her knees. She looked up just in time to see two women running out of the door. One with wild grey and the other with silvery blonde hair.

'Witches!' Malys screeched pointing. 'Witches!'

'There, there, dear,' the nurse crouched next to her, looking at the empty doorway Malys was pointing to. 'You see, there's nothing there. After all, there's no such thing as witches.'

ACKNOWLEDGMENTS

I first need to thank my children. If they hadn't said "tell me a story, Mummy" all those years ago, there would never have been a puff of green smoke escaping the exhaust of a rickety old car as it came to a juddering stop alongside a never seen before train platform. That puff of green smoke was the spark to my imagination that led to the creation of The Power of Three. My boys were also my first test audience – I read the story out loud to them before I let anyone else see it and they gave me some brutally honest feedback as only children can. My thanks also go to my early reviewers. Firstly to my husband who read the first ever draft, even though children's chapter books is really not his genre. To Jo and Ally for their proof reading skills and ability to spot my stupid mistakes. To Nigel for his twenty plus pages of detailed feedback – it was only fair that I named a character after him. To Debbie, an experienced primary school teacher, who generously gave of her time to validate that this book hit the mark of the target audience. And to Hannah and Milly, avid readers from the target audience, who gave me confidence that children (of all ages) will love this story.

Finally, thanks to Mark and his team at Technique Print for donating their time and expertise to create this amazing book cover. They took my words and painted a picture.

ABOUT THE AUTHOR

L. L. Wiggins was born and bred in South Africa but moved to the UK fifteen years ago after a brief stint in New York. She lives with her husband, two boys and a female dog (to help even the odds) in the English countryside.